Robert Charles Hope

The Legendary Lore of the Holy Wells of England

Robert Charles Hope

The Legendary Lore of the Holy Wells of England

ISBN/EAN: 9783337374976

Printed in Europe, USA, Canada, Australia, Japan

Cover: Foto ©Andreas Hilbeck / pixelio.de

More available books at **www.hansebooks.com**

THE LEGENDARY LORE

OF THE

HOLY WELLS OF ENGLAND:

INCLUDING

Rivers, Lakes, Fountains, and Springs.

COPIOUSLY ILLUSTRATED BY CURIOUS ORIGINAL WOODCUTS.

BY

ROBERT CHARLES HOPE, F.S.A., F.R.S.L.,

PETERHOUSE, CAMBRIDGE; LINCOLN'S INN;
MEMBER OF THE COUNCIL OF THE EAST RIDING OF YORKSHIRE ANTIQUARIAN SOCIETY,
AUTHOR OF "A GLOSSARY OF DIALECTAL PLACE-NOMENCLATURE," "AN INVENTORY
OF THE CHURCH PLATE IN RUTLAND," "ENGLISH GOLDSMITHS," "THE
LEPER IN ENGLAND AND ENGLISH LAZAR-HOUSES;"
EDITOR OF BARNABE GOOGE'S "POPISH KINGDOME."

LONDON:
ELLIOT STOCK, 62, PATERNOSTER ROW, E.C.
1893.

PREFACE.

THIS collection of traditionary lore connected with the Holy Wells, Rivers, Springs, and Lakes of England is the first systematic attempt made. It has been said there is no book in any language which treats of Holy Wells, except in a most fragmentary and discursive manner. It is hoped, therefore, that this may prove the foundation of an exhaustive work, at some future date, by a more competent hand.

The subject is almost inexhaustible, and, at the same time, a most interesting one. There is probably no superstition of bygone days that has held the minds of men more tenaciously than that of well-worship in its broadest sense, "a worship simple and more dignified than a senseless crouching before idols."

An honest endeavour has been made to render the work as accurate as possible, and to give the source of each account, where such could be ascertained. That sins of omission and of commission may herein be found it is not denied, but they are, it is hoped, few and far between.

No attempt has been made at scientific classification or arrangement other than the placing of the wells under their respective counties. Until those of Scotland, Wales, and Ireland have been collected, such a course would seem premature.

Should this work be favourably received, it is proposed to issue at no distant date similar collections of the Holy Wells, etc., in Scotland, Wales, and Ireland. The writer will be very grateful for any traditions or superstitions connected therewith, also any photographs or sketches illustrating the same for use and incorporation in the collections.

A portion of the legends appeared from time to time in the pages of the *Antiquary;* these have been revised and largely added to. A considerable number of them, however, and all the illustrations, are new.

For the kind and willing loan of blocks, etc., for illustrating the book, the best thanks are due, and here given, to Messrs. Netherton and Worth, Printers, 6 and 7, Lemon Street, Truro, who have generously supplied no less than eighteen; Messrs. W. Bemrose and Sons, Derby, for fifteen; Derby and Derbyshire Archæological and Natural History Society, for those of St. Thomas à Becket's Well; Mr. J. P. Birtwhistle, Halifax, for that of Stainland, York shire; Newcastle Society of Antiquaries, for those of Coventina and nymphs; Miss Cooper of Scarborough, for the well at Carrawburg; Messrs. Hall, for Bretton and Heath; and to Mr. John Owen for that of Oswestry.

For much valuable information respecting, and legends of, wells, my best thanks are given to Miss C. S. Burne, for so kindly placing her magnificent volume of Shropshire Folk-lore at the disposal of the writer; to Mr. G. T. Lawley, for Staffordshire Wells; to Mr. C. T. Phillips, Hon. Lib. Sussex Archæological Society, for those of Sussex; the Rev. J. Wilson, Chaplain to her Majesty's Prison, Carlisle, for those of Cumberland; Mr. A. C. G. Cameron, H.M. Geological Survey, for those of Bedfordshire; Rev. Dr. Cox., F.S.A., Editor of the *Antiquary*, for many of Derbyshire, etc., etc.; and also to the writers of various articles on the subject in the numerous archæological and other publications.

CONTENTS.

INTRODUCTION.

W ELL-WORSHIP, embracing that of Rivers, Lakes, Fountains, and Springs generally, is of great antiquity. From
all parts of the globe a vast accumulation of legendary
lore connected with this cult has from time to time been brought
to light, taking us back to ages far anterior to Christianity, through
days of darkness, when all traces of the one and only true religion,
revealed to man by God, as recorded in Holy Scripture, had been
forgotten, or had died out. The tower of Babel had caused the
dispersion of nations, and the farther they receded from the
common centre, which was also the seat of the religion, the more
corrupted became the forms of worship adopted, and gradually,
in course of time, retained little, if any, of the truth at all.

These legends and traditions have, in the main, a twofold
origin or source, sacred and pagan. The sacred are derived from
the accounts of the Deluge, the miraculous passages of the Red
Sea and of Jordan—the Jordan is still a sanctified stream, to
which thousands make pilgrimages to perform ablutions in it ; the
members of the Royal Family are baptized with water brought
specially from this river—the pools of Bethesda and of Siloah—
the latter the precursor of eye wells—and other similar miracles
recorded.

Those of a purely pagan source are the growth of a primitive
belief in what has been termed Naturalism, or the worship of
Nature. In countries, in early times, where all trace of the true
religion had disappeared, the heathen, ever prone to obey a
natural instinct to worship something, looked upon every object
around him from which he derived personal benefits, as a physical
iota like himself—the sun, which gave him warmth and light,
hence fire-worship ; the trees, that sheltered him, hence tree-

worship ; and, in an especial manner, the waters from above that moistened his soil, and those below which provided him with a very necessity of life. The upheaval of the waves, the rise and fall of the tides and floods, would greatly intensify his belief in the vitality and reality of their powers. As he advanced in this "Natural Religion" his mind would, at a later stage, associate a specific deity with attendants, as presiding over these physical objects of adoration. The water gods were aided by nymphs or naiads, one or more of whom had the care of, and watched or presided over, particular wells, rivers, lakes, etc. The Indians, Egyptians, Persians, and Greeks all had deities of fountains and streams. In Roumania each spring was supposed to be presided over by a spirit called *Wodna zena* or *zona*. The river Seine was under the protection of the goddess Sequana. In our own country we find the river Wharfe under the guardianship of Verbeia, the Tees of Peg Powler, who has an insatiable desire for human life, as also has the Jenny Greenteeth of Lancashire streams, the Ribble of Peg o'Nell, Blackwater of Easter, the Severn of Sabrina and of Nodens, the Skerne, etc. At Proclitia, *i.e.*, Carrawburg, on the Roman wall in Northumberland, was a well under the care of a British water goddess, Coventina. The river Dee was worshipped as the image of a deified patriarch and his supposed consort.

Among the rustics only, now, does the nymph or mermaid, as at Rostherne, Cheshire, Chapel-en-le-Frith and Hayfield, Derbyshire, in the Shropshire meres, etc., find belief and inspire awe. The rapacity for human life has been traditionally attributed to several of our rivers as the old rhymes relate :

THE RIVER DART.

" River of Dart, river of Dart !
Every year thou claims't a heart."

THE RIVERS TWEED AND TILL.

" Tweed said to Till,
  ' What gars ye rin sae still ?'
Till said to Tweed,
  ' Though ye rin wi' speed,
And I rin slaw,
  Yet where ye drown ae man,
I drown twa.' "

Or,

" Div ye no ken
Where ye drown ae man
I drown ten."

THE DELUGE.

The following is a small selection of legends from a large number, scattered all over the globe, which preserve to some extent the account given to us in Genesis :
" In the Eddic, the flood is caused by the blood which sprang up to heaven from the body of the giant *Ymer*, whom Odin, Vilj, and Ve, the sons of Bor, slew, and not by rain as in the Bible."

INDIA.

The Indian " Mahâbhârata " gives us the following version :
" King Manus one day standing on the bank of a river, doing penance, suddenly heard the voice of a small fish imploring him to save it. He caught it in his hand, and laid it in a vessel ; but the fish began to grow, and demanded wider quarters. Manus threw it into a large lake, but the fish grew on, and wished to be taken to Gangâ, the bride of the sea. Before long he had not room to stir even there, and Manus was obliged to carry it to the sea ; but when launched in the sea, it foretold the coming of a fearful flood. Manus was to build a ship, and go on board with the seven sages, and preserve the seeds of all things, then it would show itself to them horned. Manus did as he was commanded, and sailed in the ship ; the monster fish appeared in fulfilment of his promise, had the ship fastened to its horn by a rope, and towed it through the sea for many years, till it reached the summit of the *Himavân*. There it bade him moor the ship, and the spot to which it was tied still bears the name of *Naubandhanam* (ship-binding). Then spake the fish : ' I am Brahmâ, lord of created things ; a higher than I there is not. In the shape of a fish have I delivered you. Now shall Manus make all creatures, gods, asuris, and men, and all the world's things moveable and immoveable.' And as he had spoken, so it was done. The first part of the Indian poem, where Brahmâ as a fish is caught by Manus, and then reveals to him the future, lingers to this day in our nursery tale of the small all-powerful turbot or pike, who gradually elevates a fisherman from the meanest condition to the highest

rank ; and only plunges him back into his pristine poverty when,
urged by the counsels of a too-ambitious wife, he desires at last
to be equal with God."—*Grimm's Teutonic Mythology*, ii. 578.

PERSIA.

In the ancient Persian account, Taschcter—the spirit ruling the
waters—found water for thirty days and thirty nights upon the
earth.   Every water-drop was as big as a bowl! (*sic*).   The earth
was covered with water the height of a man.   All idolaters died
through the rain ; it penetrated all openings.   Afterwards a wind
from heaven divided the water, and carried it away in clouds, as
souls bear bodies ; then Ormuzd collected all the water together,
and placed it as a boundary to the earth, and thus was the great
ocean formed.

GREECE.

Ovid, Metam. 1, 240 *et seq.*, represents the world "as con-
federate in crime," and doomed therefore to just punishment.
Jupiter sends down rain from heaven, and rivers and seas gushing
forth from their caves, gather over the earth's surface, and sweep
mankind away.   Deucalion and his wife alone, borne in a little
skiff, are stranded on the top of Parnassus.   By degrees the
waters subside ; the only surviving pair inquire of the gods how
they may again people the desert earth.   They are ordered, with
veiled heads, to throw behind them the bones of their great
mother.   Half doubtful as to the meaning of the oracle, they
throw behind them stones, which are immediately changed into
men and women, and the earth spontaneously produces the rest
of the animal creation.—*Bundehesch*, 7.   *Quoted in the Old Test.
Leg. by the Rev. S. Baring-Gould.*

CHINA.

A Chinese tradition from the writings of the disciples of Tao-tse
is that Kong-Kong, an evil spirit, enraged at having been overcome in war, gave such a blow against one of the pillars of the
sky with his head that he broke it (the pillar) ; the vault of heaven
fell in, and a tremendous flood overwhelmed the earth.   But
Niu-Noa overcame the water with wood, and made a boat to save
himself, which could go far ; and he polished a stone of five
colours (the rainbow), and therewith he fastened the heavens,

and lifted them up on a tortoise-shell. Then he killed the black dragon, Kong-Kong, and choked the holes in heaven with the ashes of a pumpkin.—*Mém. concernant les Chinois*, ix., p. 383.

Among the Dog-rib Indians, America, Sir John Franklin found the story as follows: They say that Tschäpiwih, their great ancestor, lived on a track between two seas. He built a weir, and caught fish in such abundance that they choked the water-course, and the sea overflowed the earth. Tschäpiwih, with his family, entered the canoe, and took with him all kinds of beasts and birds. The land was covered for many days; at last Tschäpiwih could bear it no longer, so he sent out the beaver to look for the earth, but the beaver was drowned. Then he sent out the musk-rat, which had some difficulty in returning, but it had mud on its paws. Tschäpiwih was glad to see the earth, and moulded it between his fingers till it became an island on the surface of the water, on which he could land.—*Lutke, Voyage autour du Monde*, i., p. 189.

The various accounts of the Deluge, as given by non-Christian peoples, are, it seems, but distortions of the Biblical story, which is not only the most ancient one, but a record of truth.

The flood recorded in Genesis is now pretty generally under-stood not to have been absolutely universal, being limited over the countries known to the Hebrews, and which made their world, neither were all living things literally destroyed that were not in the ark. A negligent reading of chapters vi.-ix. of Genesis, without reference to the texts of other chapters of the same book, has led to the literal view. After the death of Abel, God banished Cain from the *earth*, which had received his brother's blood, and laid a curse on him—" A fugitive and a vagabond shalt thou be in the *earth* "; using another word, one which means earth in general (éréç), in opposition to *the* earth (adâmâh), or fruitful land to the east of Eden. Cain went forth still further east, and dwelt in the land of Nod, *i.e.*, "wandering" or "exile." Chapter iv. tells of Cain, his crime, his exile, and immediate posterity. The descendants of Sheth or Seth are enumerated in chapter v., and the list ends with Noah. These are parallel races : the accursed and the blest.

Chapters vi.-viii. describe the covenant with Noah, and re-peopling of the earth by his posterity (chapter ix.). Chapter x. gives the generations of Noah's three sons, Shem, Ham, and Japheth ; "of these were the nations divided in the earth after the flood." Each name in this list is that of a race, a people, a tribe, not that of a man. St. Augustine says the names represent "nations, not men." The authors of this chapter consistently ignore all those divisions of mankind which do not belong to one of the three great *white* races. Neither the Black nor the Yellow races are mentioned at all, being left outside the pale of the Hebrew brotherhood of nations.   .

What became of Cain's posterity, of the descendants of those three sons of Lamech, whom the writer of Genesis iv. 19-22 clearly places before us as heads of nations, specifying their occupations? Nothing more is said of this entire half of humanity, severed in the beginning from the other half—the lineage of the accursed son from that of the blest and favoured one. They were necessarily out of the pale of the Hebrew world. The writer tells us they lived in the "land of exile" and multi-plied, and then dismisses them. They did not count, being ex-cluded from all other narratives ; why should they, then, be included in that of the flood ? The antiquity of the yellow race —the Turanians—which everywhere preceded their white brethren, who invariably supplanted them, tallies well with the Biblical account ; for of the two Biblical brothers, Cain was the eldest. And the doom laid on the race, "a fugitive and a vagabond shalt thou be on the earth," continues, for wherever pure Turanians are they are nomads.—*See " Chaldea," by Zénaïde A. Ragozin*, 128-143.

In Great Britain, as at Gormire and Semerwater in Yorkshire, Mockerkin Tarn in Cumberland, Llyn Llion in Brecknockshire, Lough Neagh and Fior Usga in Ireland, we have instances of other partial floods.

The extraordinary Chaldean account of the Deluge, the most ancient recorded one as opposed to traditional ones, closely fol-lowing the Biblical story in its general details, will be found in the volume "Chaldea," pp. 314-17, in the "Story of the Nations" series quoted above, and should be read by all interested in the truth of the Holy Scriptures.

Among the Dravidian tribes of Assan, all chief deities are merely the rivers of the country.—*Journal of the Asiatic Society of Bengal,* 1849, p. 723. In the Vedas, rivers are constantly invoked for aid : see Lassen, *Indische Alterthümer,* i. 766. Amongst all the Slavonic tribes, rivers received distinguished homage and adoration. The ancient German addressed his prayers to the Rhine, *Herodotus,* iv. 59. The Alamanns and Franks worshipped rivers and fountains, prayed on the river's banks ; at the fountain's edge they lighted candles and laid down sacrificial gifts. The Franks on crossing a river sacrificed women and children. Bulls were sacrificed to the god Mourie, who had his well on an island in Loch Maree, Scotland, as late as 1678. Horses were sacrificed at St. George's Well, near Abergeleu, in Wales. In Germany and Sweden the nymphs required the sacrifice of a black sheep or cat. The Persian magi sacrificed horses to the rivers crossed by Xerxes. In the first instance, adoration was not made to an Anthropomorphic deity (*i.e.,* a god in human form), who, like the kelpies, lived in the waterfalls and made his residence in the stream, but to the visible stream itself, considered as possessing soul and will, rising and falling at its pleasure, capable of human affections and aversions. Hesiod, in his *Works and Days,* i. 735, gives us sufficient proof of this statement, where he warns his hearers not to cross a stream before washing their hands and praying, looking earnestly at the stream. It must have struck all readers of Homer that so many of his heroes were children of the river gods, who appeared in human form, showing to what degree Anthropomorphism had arrived at in his day. In the contest of Achilles with the outraged river Scamander, recorded in the 21st book of the Iliad, the former, not content with choking the stream with dead bodies, dares even to address insulting words to the deity, first deriding his lack of power to the Trojans who had honoured him with numerous sacrifices, striking down Asteropæus, taunting him with the lowness of his origin, he being the son of a small river, while Pelides was descended from Zeus himself, the founder of the Æacid race. Scamander rises from his waves in human form to reproach the too daring hero, and to demand him to carry on his murderous warfare elsewhere than amid the sacred waves of a river-descended stream. With taunts only does Achilles reply, when, in bitter wrath, calling upon Apollo in vain, Scamander in fierce fury hurls himself upon Achilles in the form of the river, in waves and waterspouts, trying to overthrow him, and mingle his body with those of his many victims. Achilles, flying to the shore, is pursued by the river, until the timely intervention of Hephæstus, who comes down in fire, burning the trees on the banks of the river, slaying his fish, striking his waters, until he submits and sues for peace. It will here be observed Scamander addresses the hero in human form, but attacks him as a river— his voice is a man's, his hands as rivers. Other instances might be given. See *Greek River Worship*, Percy Gardner, Trans. R.S.L., xi. 173, and also legend under "Tweed," p. 103, in the following collection, where the spirit of the Tweed visits the lady of Drummelziel in human form.

We are told (St. John v. 2-4) that "in Jerusalem, by the sheep-market, was a pool, which in Hebrew was called Bethesda, having five porches. In these lay a great number of impotent folk, of blind, halt, withered, waiting for the moving of the water. For an angel went down at a certain season into the pool, and troubled the water : whosoever then first after the troubling of the water stepped in was made whole of whatsoever disease he had."

In the Antiquities of Rome, Fontinalia was a religious feast, celebrated on October 13th, in honour of the nymphs of wells and fountains. The ceremony consisted in throwing flowers into the fountains, and placing crowns of flowers upon the wells.

ODE OF HORACE TO THE FOUNTAIN OF BLANDUSIA.

"O fons Blandusiæ, splendidior vitro,
Dulci digne mero, non sine floribus,
     Cras donaberis hædo,
     Cui frons turgida cornibus
Primis et Venerem et prœlia destinat ;
Frustra : nam gelidos inficiet tibi
     Rubro sanguine rivos
     Lascivi suboles gregis."
                    Ode xiii., 3rd Book of Horace's Odes.

In the first stanza he addresses the fountain as brighter than glass, and worthy of offerings of sweet wine and flowers.

The custom of well-dressing with flowers, common to Derbyshire, Staffordshire, Shropshire, Westmoreland, and North Lancashire, is most probably but a survival of making floral offerings to the spirit of the waters or to the waters themselves.

To certain mineral, sulphurous, or warm wells or springs, mystic powers are ascribed, other than the peculiar characteristics which give to them sometimes their curative properties. The ancient Greek, when consulting the oracle of Amphiaraüs, threw money into the well sacred to the hero. When a Roumanian or Wetterau draws water she spills a few drops to do homage to the spirit of the well. This is also done in England, in Derbyshire to wit. Some wells possessed virtues of a restricted nature in regard to divination. Pausanias (vii. 21-5) tells us of a well sacred to Demeter, to which resorted those afflicted with a disease, wishful to learn whether they would recover or die. The mode of consultation was quaint. A mirror, suspended by a cord, was lowered to the surface of the water. After prayer and sacrifice, the inquirer gazed at the mirror, and from its reflected appearance inferred a favourable or unfavourable answer. See Colan, "Our Lady of Nantswell," p. 31. At the spring of Inus, Laconia, was a small but deep lake, through which the water rose. Into this lake suppliants threw small cakes, judging whether these gifts were acceptable or not, and auguring accordingly, by their sinking into the depths, or by their rejection by the bubbling waters.—*Pausanias*, iii. 23-25.

Before the introduction of Christianity or Christian baptism, the heathen Norsemen had a hallowing of new-born infants by means of water; they called this *vatni ausa*, sprinkling with water. Very likely the same ceremony was practised by all the Teutons, and they may have ascribed a special virtue to the water used in it, as the Christians do to baptismal water.—*Grimm, Teut. Myth.*, ii. 592.

There is a "Woden's" Well at Wanswell, in Gloucestershire, and at Burnsall, Yorkshire, we have "Thorskill, or Thor's Well," signifying the well of the god of thunder. The latter was, undoubtedly, dedicated by the pagans, and after them, according to the custom of the Christians of the early Church, rededicated in honour of her saints; hence the two here dedicated in honour of St. Margaret and St. Helena. Up to the middle of last century, young people used to visit these wells every Sunday evening, and drink the waters, with sugar added. A similar custom obtains in Cumberland, Derbyshire, Shropshire, and Yorkshire.

b

There is an interesting Swedish superstition, that the old pagan
gods, when worsted by Christianity, took refuge in the rivers,
where they still dwell.— *Welcker, Griech. Götterlehre,* i. 269.

The best known prophetic wells were the springs called Palici,.
in Sicily, now rising into a small lake.   Diodorus, xi. 89, says in
his day were two deep basins of water agitated by volcanic
springs, in the temple of Palici.   They were regarded especially as
the deities who watched over our oaths.   The most solemn oaths
were taken in their presence; and so present was the force of
these deities, that perjurers departed from their presence blinded.
Seneca, in Epistle iv., says: "We worship the head of great
rivers, and we raise altars to their first springs. . . . . Every river
had its nymph presiding over it."   The sites of many Roman villas
and dwelling-houses have been discovered near the springhead of
streams.   A well occurs at the west end of the Romano-British
church which has just been laid bare at Silchester.   Roman pave-
ments have been found at East Dean, Throxton, Cundall, Brun-
dean, etc.   We find also in Britain traces of the connection
of water with divination — for there exist, or did until quite
recently, numerous wells—as at Gulval, Roche, and Nantswell
in Cornwall; Langley in Kent; Boughton and Oundle in
Northamptonshire; Uttoxeter in Staffordshire, etc., sought for by
those in difficulty or anxiety, and sometimes by throwing in a pin,
needle, coin, or other small object, would judge by the nature
of the bubbles which arose, the issue of the consultation.
A discovery of Roman coins and fictile vessels, in a meadow
at the village of Horton, Dorsetshire, was made in June, 1875,
by some boys playing about the streamlet which rises on the
north side of the meadow, who found in its bed a small vase
and some coins lying in the gravel.   The spring was eventually
searched, and one hundred and forty coins, the earliest being
one of Augustus, and the latest a coin of Valens, A.D. 364, and
seven perfect vases were found.   At Chester a large altar inscribed
on two sides NYMPHIS ET FONTIBUS, was found not far from the
Abbot's Well, which probably, even in Roman times, supplied
water to the city.   Close to the latter site, vases and coins in
some quantity have from time to time been turned up, no doubt
offerings.—*Journal of Brit. Arch. Assoc.,* vol. xxxii., part i., p. 64.
See p. 112 in this volume.

Some years ago by London Bridge, were found in the river-bed

a heap of various coins, dating in an unbroken line from the days
of the Roman republic, probably thrown into the water as a
tribute to the tutelary deity of the Thames.

The late Canon Rock, referring to ancient spoons, said : "They
almost always occur in pairs, and are occasionally found in springs
of water, or in rivers."

Running water is said to have been held sacred by the Druids.
It will have been noted that healing only took place at the Pool
of Bethesda *after* the water had been moved by an angel. In
Germany running spring-water gathered on holy Christmas night,
while the clock struck twelve, and named *heilwag*, was considered
good for pain at the navel. In this heilawâc we discover a very
early mingling of heathen customs with Christian. The common
people believe to this very day that at twelve, or between eleven
and twelve on Christmas or Easter nights, spring water changes
into wine ; and this belief rests on the supposition that the first
manifestation of the Saviour's divinity took place at the marriage
in Cana, where He turned water into wine. Now, at Christmas,
they celebrate both His birth and His baptism ; and combined with
these, the memory of that miracle, to which was given a special
name, Bethphania. Durandus, Ration. Div. Offic., 6-16, says the
first manifestation of Christ was His birth, the second His baptism
(Candlemas), the third the marriage in Cana : " Tertia apparitio
fuit postea similiter eodem die anno revoluto, cum esset 39
annorum et 13 dierum, sive quando manifestavit se esse Deum
permutationem aquæ in vinum, quod fuit primum miraculum
apertum, quod Dominus fecit in Cana in Galilaeæ vel simpliciter
primum quod fecit. Et heac apparitio dictur bethphanie a βητοω
quod est domus, et φανειν, quod est apparitis, quia ista apparitio
facta fuit in domo in nuptiis. De his tribus apparitionibus fit
solemnitas in hac die :" The Church consolidated the three mani-
festations into one festival. As far back as 387, St. Chrysostom,
preaching an Epiphany sermon at Antioch, said people at that
festival drew running water at midnight, and kept it a whole year,
and often two or three, and it remained fresh and uncorrupted.
Superstitious Christians then believed two things : (1) a hallowing
of the water at midnight of the day of baptism, and (2) a turning
of it into wine at the time of Bethphania : such water the Germans
called heilawâc, and ascribed to it a wonderful power of healing
diseases and wounds, and of never spoiling. Magic water for

unchristian divination is to be collected before sunrise on a Sunday, in one glass, from three flowing springs; and a taper is lighted before the glass, as before a Divine being.

On Easter Monday the Hessian youths and maidens walked to the Hollow Rock in the mountains, drew water from the cool spring in jugs to carry home, and threw flowers in as an offering ; none would venture to go down without flowers. This water-worship was Celtic likewise ; the water of the rock-spring Karnant makes a broken sword whole again, but—

> " Du most des urs pringes hàn
> Underm velse, ê in heschin dertae (ere day bestrive it)."

Curious customs show us in what manner young girls in the Pyrenees country tell their own fortunes in spring waters on May-day morning.

Many places in Germany are called *Heil*brunn, *Heil*born, *Heil*igenbrunn, from the renewing effect of their springs, or the wonderful cures that have taken place at them. A Danish folk-song tells of a *Maribokilde*, by whose clear waters a body hewn in pieces is put together again. Not only medicinal but salt wells were esteemed holy.

Wishing wells are a curious survival. Their origin must be looked for in remote antiquity. Bright bubbling springs, as has been shown, were sacred objects long before the Christian Church consecrated them to the honour of God and of His saints. Abraham set aside seven ewe lambs as a testimony that he had digged a well (Gen. xxi. 30) ; and one of the special marks of the Divine favour to the chosen people was that they should come into possession of wells which they had not digged (Deut. vi. 11). The Jews had great faith in the healing properties of their sacred wells, which were frequented by the diseased and infirm, Siloam and Bethesda being much in request. The belief was not condemned by our blessed Lord. Mohammed speaks of the abandonment of wells as a sign of extreme desolation. " How many cities which had acted wickedly have we destroyed ? and they are laid low in ruin on their own foundations, and wells abandoned and lofty castles " (Korân, Sura xxii., Rodwell's Trans.). Homer supplies evidence :

It seems but yesterday . . . . .
. . . . . that when the ships
Woe-fraught for Priam, and the race of Troy,
At Aulis met, and we beside the fount
With perfect hecatombs the gods adored
Beneath the plane-tree, from whose root a stream
Ran crystal-clear, there we beheld a sign
Wonderful in all eyes.
(*Iliad*, iii. ll. 364-372, Cowper's Trans.)—E. Peacock.

Gildas, who is supposed to have lived in the sixth century, says :
" Neque nominatim inclamitans montes ipsos, aut fontes vel
colles, aut fluvios olim exitiabiles, nunc vero humanis usibus
utiles, quibus divinus honor a cæco tunc populo cumulabatur."—
Par. 4.   "Nor will I call out the mountains, fountains, or hills, or
upon the rivers, which are now subservient to the use of men,
but once were an abomination and destruction to them, and to
which the blind people paid divine honour."

This species of idolatry was interdicted by the Council of Tours,
A.D. 567, and by other laws, but such commands are seldom
obeyed.

So deeply rooted was this feeling of veneration for the Holy
Wells, that efforts were made from time to time to suppress the
custom of worshipping at them, but without effect.   King Egbert's
" Poenitentiale " prescribes adoration, offering libations, and sacrifices to fountains : "if any man vow or bring his offering to any
well."

"If any keep his wake at any wells, or at any other created
things except at God's church, let him fast three years, the first
on bread and water, and the other two, on Wednesdays and
Fridays, on bread and water ; and on the other days let him eat
his meat, but without flesh."

(A.) The " Penitentiale of St. Cummin," who died 669, has this
canon : " Si quis ad arbores, vel ad fontes, vel ad angulos, vel
ubicunque, nisi ad Ecclesiam Dei vota voverit, aut solverit, tres
annos pœnitiat, unum in pane et aquâ ; et qui ibidem comederit
aut biberit unum annum."

(B.) The " Bobbio Penitentiale," which is Irish, repeats St.
Cummin's canon.   In an Irish homily, in MS. of the eighth
century, preserved at the Vatican Library, is the following sentence : "Cum ergo duplica bona possitis in Ecclesia invenire quare
per cantatores, et fontes, et arbores, et diabolica filacteria pre-

catorios aurispices et divinos, vel sortilegos multiplicia sibi mala
miseri homines connantur inferre."

A Saxon homily against witchcraft and magic says: "Some
men are so blind that they bring their offerings to immovable
rocks, and also to trees, and to wells, as witches teach." One of
the most curious ceremonies relating to wells was the watching or
waking of them at night. Waking the well continued all through
the Middle Ages. The prevalent custom appears to have been
the following: The well was visited on the eve of the patron
saint's day, some of the water was drunk, and the offering was
made. The visitor lay all night on the ground near the well,
drank the water again in the morning, and carried some away in a
bottle. But the practice of waking, that is, keeping the vigil of
the saint's day, led to such immorality that it was discontinued.

The 16th of the canons of the reign of Edgar, A.D. 963,
enjoins the clergy to be diligent to advance Christianity, and
extinguish heathenism in withdrawing the people from the worship
of trees, stones, and fountains, and other heathenish practices
therein specified; and the laws of Knut, 1018, prohibit the worship of heathen gods, the sun, moon, fire, rivers, fountains, rocks,
or trees, some of which had probably been venerated by the
preceding Romano-British and ancient British inhabitants from
time immemorial.

The 26th canon of St. Anselm, A.D. 1102, directs: "Let
no one attribute reverence or sanctity to a dead body or a fountain,
without the Bishop's authority."

Dr. Mitchell "never knew a case in which the saint was in any
way recognised or prayed to, and there was reason to believe that
these wells were the objects of adoration before the country was
Christianized, and it was a survival of the earlier practice to which
Seneca and Pliny referred."

Mr. G. L. Gomme remarks: "A worship that was formerly and
officially prohibited in the tenth and eleventh centuries, and has
been formally accepted in modern times could not, under any
circumstances, have been brought over by, and become prevalent
through the medium of, the Christian Church."—See *Ethnology
in Folk-lore*, p. 80.

The adorning of fountains and springs with a lion's head,
through which the water flows, is supposed to have been introduced
from the Egyptians, "who practised the same under a symbolized

illation. For, because its sun being in Leo, the flood of Nilus was at the full, and water became conveyed into every part, they made the spouts of their aqueducts through the head of a lion."— Brown's *Vulgar Errors*, London, 1686, book v., xxii.

The custom of affixing ladles of iron, etc., by a chain, to wells, is of great antiquity. Strutt, in his *Anglo-Saxon Æra*, tells us that Edwine caused ladles or cups of brass to be fastened to the clear springs and wells, for the refreshment of the passengers.— Ven. Bede in his *Eccl. Hist.*, ii. 16.

A spring of pure water was absolutely essential to the early missionary for the regeneration of the newly-made converts, hence it is so large a number of holy wells and springs are found close to the churches which were afterwards built. Many of such wells had been rededicated in honour of the saints, others were founded by the early missionaries. Chapels were frequently erected over them, and a priest provided. Occasionally, as at York Minster, Carlisle Cathedral, Glastonbury, St. Michael's, Tenbury, and elsewhere, they are found within the walls of the buildings. At the present time in some places, the water for the font is still drawn from the well dedicated in honour of some saint, if not of the patron saint, near at hand, in preference to that of any other well.

The wells in England, as elsewhere, had not all the same virtues attributed to them. Some were blessed and used for baptisms, to others were attributed curative properties, especially for sore or weak eyes, and for leprosy, while others possessed mystical and prophetic powers, at which offerings of cakes, pins, needles, and small coins were made, and sugar and water drunken. Wells are frequently found on the boundaries of counties.—See Berkshire Wells. The positions of the Holy Wells may also have marked the route pursued by pilgrims to certain shrines.

Tradition often ascribes the rising up of a well on the spot where a saint was martyred, rested, or buried; instances occur at Rome, near a church where St. Paul was beheaded, and at

St. Alban's	St. Alban.
St. Winifred's	St. Winifred.
Exeter	St. Sidwell.
Wareham	St. Edward the Martyr.
St. Osyth	St. Osyth.

East Dereham	St. Withburga.
Stoke, St. Milborough	St. Milburga, cf. Ov. Met., 5, 257 *seq.*, Grimm, ii. 585.
Morwenstow	St. Moorin.
Winchcombe	St. Kenelym.
Oswestry	St. Oswald.
Clent	St. Kenylm.
Coverdale	St. Simon.
Marden	St. Ethelbert.

Or where a staff has been planted, or the ground struck by or at the command of some saint or notable personage, as at Stoke St. Milburga's, Cerne, St. Augustine, Carshalton, Anne Boleyn.

The hanging of rags and scraps of clothing on the branches of trees, and on bushes about the Holy Wells, is probably a remnant of the old tree-worship; it obtains all over the globe; it is very common in Great Britain. In the church-prohibitions this tree-worship is variously mentioned as "vota ad *arbores* facere; *arborum* colere; votum ad *arborem* persolvere; etc.

The tree most usually found at these wells is the ash, formerly held to be sacred, "a world-tree which links heaven, earth, and hell together; of all trees the greatest and holiest."—Grimm's *Teutonic Mythology*, ii. 796 (Stallybrass's ed.).

The particular times, when it was considered most propitious to visit the wells, appear anciently to have been at daybreak or sun-rise in May and at the summer solstice; later, Easter and Ascension-tide were the favoured seasons.

Mermaids appear to have a preference for appearing on Easter Day and at daybreak.

Two general sort of rules will be noticed with regard to the wells, when any benefit or divination was sought: 1. The observation of a particular day and time was necessary; and 2. The making of an offering.

The legend of St. Milburga, given on page 137, has a counter-part in that of our blessed Lord, St. Mary and St. Joseph in their flight into Egypt, coming to a field where a man was sowing, and, as they feared pursuit from Herod, they desired him to tell any-one that followed that Jesus had passed by while he was sowing his seed. The Holy Family went on, incontinently the corn sprang up, and the husbandman began to reap and carry. Soon some soldiers appeared, to whose inquiries the man answered as instructed; further pursuit being accounted useless, the soldiers returned from whence they came.

The connection between bells and hidden treasure with some of the pools is not quite clear. Their presence is generally ascribed to the wicked act of someone having attempted to steal them.

The Red Sea is the reputed resting-place of exorcised spirits.

WORKS CONSULTED.

Antiquary.
Archæologia Æliana.
Aubrey's Gentilisme and Judaisme.
Baines' Lancashire and Cheshire, Past and Present.
Berkeley Manuscripts.
Book of Humorous Poetry.
Brand's History of Newcastle-upon-Tyne.
Brand's Popular Antiquities, 3 vols., Bohn's Edition.
British Archæological Association's Journals.
Britton's History of Northamptonshire.
Camden's Britannica.
Chambers' Book of Days, 2 vols.
Clavis Calendaria, 2 vols.
Cox's Notes on Churches of Derbyshire, 4 vols.
Denham Tracts.
Derbyshire Archæological Society's Journal.
Duncan's History of Lewes and Brighthelmstone.
Dyer's Popular Customs.
East Anglian Handbook.
Excursions into the County of Norfolk.
Exeter Diocesan Architectural Society's Transactions.
Folk-Lore Society's Publications.
Gentleman's Magazine Library (Gomme).
Glover's History of Derbyshire, 2 vols.
Gomme's Ethnology of Folk-Lore.
Gomme's Primitive Folk-moots.
Grimm's Teutonic Mythology, Stallybrass, 4 vols.
Hampshire Field Club.
Hasted's History of Kent.
Hawkins' History of Music, 2 vols., Novello's Edition.
Henderson's Folk-Lore of the Northern Counties.
Hone's Every Day Book, 2 vols.
Hone's Year Book.
Horsfield's History of Sussex.
Howard's History and Antiquities of Horsham.
Hunt's Drolleries of the West of England, 2 vols.
Hutchins' History of Dorsetshire.

Leeds Mercury Supplement.
Leland's Itinerary.
Loudon's Magazine of Natural History.
Morton's History of Northamptonshire.
Murray's Guides, various.
Natural History and Antiquities of Surrey.
Nibb's and Lower's Churches of Sussex.
Nichols' History of Leicestershire.
Nicholson's Folk-Lore of East Yorkshire.
Norfolk and Norwich Archæological Society's Journals.
North Devonshire Herald.
Notes and Queries.
Old English Customs and Charities.
Oliver's Beverley.
Palatine Note Book, 4 vols.
Parkinson's Legends and Traditions of Yorkshire, 2 vols.
Parochial History of Cornwall.
Penrith Observer.
Rambles in Northumberland.
Records of Buckinghamshire.
Reliquary.
Royal Archæological Institute Journal.
Royal Society of Literature Transactions.
Rye's History of Norfolk.
Scott's Lay of the Last Minstrel.
Shrophire Archæological Society's Journals.
Shropshire Folk-Lore (C. S. Burne).
Strutt's Sports and Pastimes.
Surtees' Society's Publications.
Surrey Archæological Society's Transactions.
Sussex Archæological Society's Collections.
Tomkin's History of the Isle of Wight.
Transactions, various.
Western Antiquary.
Whittaker's Richmondshire.
Wood's Survey of the Antiquities of the City of Oxford, by Andrew Clark.
Yorkshire Folk-Lore.
Yorkshire Notes and Queries.
                 And others.

LIST OF ILLUSTRATIONS.

xxviii   *LIST OF ILLUSTRATIONS.*

SUMMARY OF WELLS.

HOLY WELLS, SPRINGS, RIVERS, AND POOLS
OF ENGLAND.

BEDFORDSHIRE.

HOLYWELL: HOLY WELL.

THERE was a holy well or spring in the village of Holwell,
on the borders of Bedford and Hertfordshire; unfortunately both history and site have been forgotten by the
villagers at Holywell.—A. C. G. Cameron, H.M. Geological
Survey.

HAIL WESTON: HOLY WELLS.

At Hail Weston, on the borders of the counties of Bedfordshire
and Huntingdonshire, about two miles north-west of St. Neots,
there are some mineral springs, formerly looked on as holy wells.
They are situated on the alluvium of a small stream, but may
have their origin in the underlying Oxford clay. Michael Drayton
describes them as "the Holy Wells of Hail Weston."—*Ibid.*

TURVEY: ST. MARY'S WELL.

At Turvey, six miles from Bedford, there is a mineral well,
known as St. Mary's Well.—*Ibid.*

PERTENHALL: CHADWELL.

"The other day, in passing through Pertenhall, I noticed the
Chadwell Spring, at Chadwell End, to be a big one. At one

I

time it was proposed to have a drain to carry the water to Kim-
bolton, a distance of seven miles. Within the last few years much
water from this spring has been bottled, and used for sore eyes.
The parish church is dedicated to St. Peter, and formerly Pertenhall was Saint Peter's Hall, and there were seven churches altogether in the parish once on a time, so my informant, an old
inhabitant I chanced upon, asserted."—*Ibid.*, March 14, 1891.

CRANFIELD : HOLY WELL.

In Batchelor's *Agricultural Survey of Bedfordshire*, 1813, referring to this well, after describing mineral springs at Bromham,
Turvey, and Clapham, it says : "Several others, as at Holcot and
Cranfield, sometimes used for sore eyes, being impregnated with
iron, holy well implying that at one time it was held in high
estimation." The spring is probably the one at Hartwell Farm,
near Cranfield Rectory.—*Ibid.*

HOLY WELL-CUM-NEEDINGWORTH.

There is a spring or well that rises in the churchyard on the
north bank of the river Ouse, which there separates Cambridge-
shire from Huntingdonshire. This well was at one time much
frequented by religious devotees. The Rev. S. M. Beckwith, a
former rector of the parish, had the well arched over (Kelly's
Hunts Directory, 1885, p. 205).—*Ibid.*

STEVINGTON : HOLY WELL.

There is a well or spring at Stevington-on-Ouse, seven miles up
the valley from Bedford. On the ordnance six-inch map it is
engraved "Holy Well," in Old English lettering, a plan adopted
by them for distinguishing ancient buildings or relics from modern
institutions. Stevington holy well is arched over, and built into
the churchyard wall of St. Mary's Church, and abuts upon the
modern alluvium of the Ouse, which there forms a considerable
flat. The church stands on rising ground, formed of alternating
beds of limestone and clay, which holds up the water percolating
the limestone—hence, probably, the spring. The water was clear,
sparkling, and tasteless, although I was prepared to find it a
mineral water of some kind. At one time people visited this holy
well in considerable numbers, but, like many others, it appears
now to have lost its popularity.—*Ibid.*

BERKSHIRE.

SPEEN : ST. MARY'S WELL.

A WELL about 200 yards above the church, on the side of a steep hill, is remarkable for a fine and distinct echo. It is called " Our Lady's Well," most probably in reference to the church having been dedicated to the Blessed Virgin. At the present day, the water is deemed to possess some peculiar healing qualities, and the spot is not even now wholly divested of some remains or impressions of its once sacred character. The appearance of the well has of late years been spoilt by the addition of a wooden curb and cover.

YATTENDON : MIRACULOUS WELL.

By the roadside as you go from Yattendon to Pangbourne, and near the kiln, is a small well, called by the cottagers the "Miraculous Well," because it is always quite full and never runs over.

BRADFIELD : ST. ANDREW'S WELL.

There is also a well a few miles from Bradfield, Berks, in honour of St. Andrew, patron saint of the parish.

SUNNING WELL, NEAR ABINGDON.

It was customary to read the Gospel at the springs, and bless them in processions ; it was discontinued at this well in the year 1688. (Aubrey: *Remains of Gentilisme and Judaisme*, p. 34, Folk-lore Soc. ed.)

BUCKINGHAMSHIRE.

MARSTON : SIR JOHN SHORNE'S WELL.

THE holy well, which bore Sir John Shorne's name, and was supposed to have derived its medicinal qualities from his prayers and benedictions, is situated about 150 yards from the church. It is still known by the villagers as "Sir John Shorne's Well," but is commonly called "The Town Well." It consists of a cistern, 5 feet 4 inches square, and 6 feet 9 inches deep. This is walled round with stone, and has a flight of four stone steps descending into the water. The cistern is enclosed by a building, somewhat larger than the well itself, with walls composed of brick and stone, about 5 feet high, and covered with a roof of board. From the size and construction of the building, it was probably occasionally used as a bath, but the sick were, doubtless, chiefly benefited by drinking the water. It is slightly chalybeate, containing a large portion of calcareous earth. Formerly its properties must have been very powerful, for its supposed miraculous cures attracted such numbers of invalids to it that houses had to be built for their accommodation. Browne Willis says that "many aged persons then living remembered a post in a quinqueniam on Oving Hill (about a mile east of the well), which had hands pointing to the several roads, one of them directing to Sir John Shorne's Well." He likewise says ceremonies were practised here on account of this gentleman. But Lipscombe's transcripts from Willis are not to be trusted; for instance, he says the miracle of Shorne "was recorded on the wall which enclosed the holy well when it was visited by Browne Willis," whereas Willis's own words are, "At the south end of the town is a well, known by the name of Sir John Shorn's Well (perhaps so named from the tonsure), which tradition tells us had this inscription on the wall of it :

> "'Sir John Shorn,
> Gentleman born,
> Conjured the Devil into a Boot.'"

In the marriage register of North Marston occurs this entry : "It is said that the chancel of this church of North Marston, nearly four miles south from Winslow, was built with the offerings at the shrine of Sir John Schorne, a very devout man, who had been rector of the parish about the year 1290, and that this village became very populous and flourishing in consequence of the great resort of persons to a well of water here, which he had blessed, which ever after was called ' Holy Well,' but my parishioners now call it 'Town Well'; its water is chalybeate. The common people in this neighbourhood, and more particularly some ancient people of this my own parish, still keep up the memory of this circumstance by many traditionary stories." This entry is signed,

"William Pinnock, September 12, 1860." One legend is that Master Shorne, in a season of drought, was moved by the prayers of his congregation to take active measures to supply their need. He struck his staff upon the earth, and immediately there burst forth a perennial spring. The water was a specific for ague and gout ; it is now obtained by a pump. There is still a tradition that a box for the receipt of the offerings was affixed to the well, but this has not been the case within the memory of any person now living. The building which enclosed the well when Willis visited it has been removed, and a comparatively modern one has taken its place. A glass of the water drunk at night was said to cure any cold ere daybreak. For much information *re* Sir John Shorne, see *Records of Bucks*, vols. ii. and iii., from which the above account is taken. Representations of Sir John Shorne occur on the rood-screens of Cawston, *c.* 1450 ; Gateby, *c.* 1480 ; Suffield, *c.* 1450, in Norfolk, and Sudbury (in the possession of Gainsborough Dupont, Esq.), Suffolk, *c.* 1550.

AYLESBURY : HARTWELL SPRINGS.

There is a local tradition that when Julius Cæsar invaded Britain, he found a hart drinking at a well or spring ; hence the name. The water is supposed to cure weak eyes and several other complaints. I myself can testify to having been cured of rheumatism by using it.—M. A. Smethurst, Aylesbury.

CAMBRIDGESHIRE.

ELY : ST. PANDONIA'S WELL.

'AT Ellely was sumtyme a nunnery, where Pandonia, the Scottish virgin, was buried, and there is a well of her name yn the south side of quire."—*Leland*, i., p. 96.

CRATENDON : ST. AUDRY'S WELL.

St. Audry's Well is situated southward of Cratendon about a mile from the city of Ely.

BRERETON : BAG OR BLACK MERE.

"HERE is one thing exceeding strange, but attested in my hearing by many persons, and commonly believ'd. Before any heir of this [Brereton] family dies, there are seen in a lake adjoyning, the bodies of trees swimming upon the water for several days together."—Camden : *Brit.* (Gibson's ed.), i. 677.

> That black ominous mere,
> Accounted one of those that England's wonders make,
> Of neighbours Blackmere named, of strangers Brereton's lake,
> Whose property seems farre from reason's way to stand :
> She sends up stocks of trees that on the top doe floate,
> By which the world her first did for a wonder note.
>
> —Drayton : *Polyolb.*, xi. 90-96.

Mrs. Hemans wrote a poem on this lake, " The Vassal's Lament for the Fallen Tree."

DODLESTONE : MOOR WELL.

The boundaries of the parish were marked by a series of wells, which used to be cleaned out by the parishioners in their perambulations. A curious entry exists respecting the well on Dodleston Moor, 1642 :

> This year the Curate of Gresford with some of the parishioners, having come for divers yeares to Moor Well, some of them over the Moor, and some of them through Pulford parish in procession, saying that they were sent thither to claim that well to be in their parish, and now this yeare when they were in the Moor, they saw some soldiers standing by the well, which wanted to see their fashions, on which the said Curate and his company went back again, and never came again to the well.—Murray's *Guide to Cheshire*, 156.

CAPESTHORNE : REEDSMERE.

In the grounds of Capesthorne is a fine sheet of water called *Reedsmere*, containing a floating island about 1½ acres in size, which in strong winds is blown here and there. A country legend accounts for this floating island by a story that a certain knight was jealous of his lady-love, and vowed not to look upon her face until the island moved on the face of the mere. But he fell sick, and was nigh to death, when he was nursed back to health by the lady, to reward whose constancy a tremendous hurricane tore the island up by the roots.—*Ibid.*, 95.

NANTWICH : OLD BRINE.

On Ascension Day, the old inhabitants of Nantwich piously sang a hymn of thanksgiving for the blessing of the Brine. A very ancient pit, called the Old Brine, or Biat (Partridge's *History of Nantwich*, 1774, p. 59), was also held in great veneration, and till within these few years was annually on this festival decked with flowers and garlands, and was encircled by a jovial band of young people, celebrating the day with song and dance. Aubrey says : " In Cheshire, when they went in perambulation, they did blesse the springs, *i.e.*, they did read the Gospel at them, and did believe the water was the better." (*Gentilisme and Judaisme*, p. 58.)

ALDERLEY EDGE : HOLY WELL.

In the woods at Alderley Edge, at the foot of a rock, is a dropping well called " Holy Well."

ROSTHERNE MERE.

All kinds of legends are current about Rostherne, as is the case with most lakes which are reported to be deep. One is, that a mermaid comes up on Easter Day and rings a bell ; another, that it communicates with the Irish Channel by a subterranean passage ; another, that it once formed, with Tabley, Tatton, Mere, and other lakes, a vast sheet of water that covered the country between Alderley Edge and High Leigh.

FRODSHAM : THE SYNAGOGUE WELL.

The Synagogue Well, evidently one of great antiquity, and, before an attempt was made to improve it, of most picturesque appearance, is in the grounds of Park Place, Frodsham, late belonging to Joseph Stubs, Esq. The origin of the term " Synagogue Well," has occasioned much discussion, but the tradition respecting it may be considered as embodied in the following stanzas. Of Frodsham Castle, which was contiguous to the well, scarcely a vestige remains.

THE SYNAGOGUE WELL.

I.

The Roman, in his toilsome march,
Disdainful viewed this humble spot,
And thought not of Egeria's fount
And Numa's grot.

II.

No altar crowned the margin green,
  No dedication marked the stone ;
The warrior quaffed the living stream
  And hasten'd on.

III.

Then was upreared the Norman keep,
  Where from the vale the uplands swell ;
But, unobserved, in crystal jets
  The waters fell.

IV.

In conquering Edward's reign of pride,
  Gay streamed his flag from Frodsham's tower,
But saw no step approach the wild
  And sylvan bower ;

V.

Till once, when Mersey's silvery tides
  Were reddening with the beams of morn,
There stood beside the fountain clear
  A man forlorn :

VI.

And, as his weary limbs he lav'd
  In its cool waters, you might trace
That he was of the wand'ring tribe
  Of Israel's race.

VII.

With pious care, to guard the spring,
  A masonry compact he made,
And all around its glistening verge
  Fresh flowers he laid.

VIII.

" God of my fathers !" he exclaimed,
  " Beheld of old in Horeb's mount,
Who gav'st my sires Bethesda's pool
  And Siloa's fount,—

IX.

" Whose welcome streams, as erst of yore,
  To Judah's pilgrims never fail,
Tho' exil'd far from Jordan's banks
  And Kedron's Vale—

X.

"Grant that when yonder frowning walls,
   With tower and keep are crush'd and gone ;
The stones the Hebrew raised may last,
And from his Well the strengthening spring
   May still flow on !"
                    —*Palatine Note Book*, iv. 99, 100.

CORNWALL.

A CORRESPONDENT of the *Gentleman's Magazine*, writing on this interesting subject, says : "In Cornwall there are several wells which bear the name of some patron saint, who appears to have had a chapel consecrated to him or her on the spot. This appears by the name of Chapel Saint—attached by tradition to the spot. These chapels were most probably mere oratories ; but in the parish of Maddern there is a well called Maddern Well, which is inclosed in a complete baptistery, the walls, seats, doorway, and altar of which still remain. The socket which received the base of the crucifix or pedestal of the saint's image is perfect. The foundations of the outer walls are apparent. The whole ruin is very picturesque, and I wonder that it is passed over in so slight a manner by all Cornish historians, and particularly by Dr. Borlase, who speaks merely of the virtues superstitiously ascribed to the waters. This neglect in Borlase is the more to be wondered at, as the ruin is situated in his native parish. I was struck with being informed that the superstitious of the neighbour-hood attend on the first *Thursday* in May to consult this oracle by dropping pins, etc. Why on *Thursday?* May not this be some vestige of the day on which baptisteries were opened after their being kept shut and sealed during Lent, which was on Maundy *Thursday?* My informant told me that Thursday was the particular day of the week, though some came on the second and third Thursday. May was the first month after Easter, when the waters had been especially blessed ; for then was the great time of baptism. When I visited this well last week, I found in it a polyanthus and some article of an infant's dress, which showed that votaries had been there. After the sixth century, these baptisteries were removed into the church."

MADRON : ST. MADERN WELL.

To this well, about a mile to the north, in the parish of St. Madron, many extraordinary properties have been ascribed. Dr. Borlase says: "The soil round this well is black, boggy, and light; but the strata through which the spring rises is a gray moorstone gravel. Here people who labour under pains, aches, and stiffness of limbs, come and wash; and many cures are said to have been performed, although the water can only act by its cold and limpid nature, as it has no mineral impregnation." "Its fame in former ages was greater for the supposed virtue of healinge which St. Madderne had thereinto infused, and manie votaries made anuale pylgrimages unto it, as they

DOOM WELL OF ST. MADRON.

doe even at this day, unto the Well of St. Winnifrede beyond Chester in Denbighshire, whereunto thousands doe yearelye make resort: but of late St. Maderne hath denied his (or her I know not whether) pristine ayde; and he is coye of his cures, so now are men coy of comynge to his conjured well, yet soom a daye resort." Though this writer seems to despise the efficacy of these waters, the tradition of their virtues still remained amongst the Cornish, only a century ago. Borlase said: "To this miraculous fountain, the uneasy, the impatient, the fearful, the jealous, and the superstitious, resort to learn their future destiny from the unconscious water. By dropping pins or pebbles into the fountain, by shaking the ground around the spring, or by continuing to raise bubbles from the bottom, on certain lucky days, and when the moon is in a particular stage of increase or decrease, the secrets of the well are presumed to be extorted." This super-stition continued to prevail up to the beginning of the present century, and is still spoken of with respect by some, particularly the aged. In the year 1640, John Trelille, who had been an absolute cripple for sixteen years, and was obliged to crawl upon his hands by reason of the close contraction of the sinews of his legs, upon three several admonitions in his dreams, washing in St. Madern's Well and sleeping afterwards in what was called St. Madern's bed, was suddenly and perfectly cured. Of all writers, Bishop Hall, sometime Bishop of the diocese of these western parts, bears the most honourable testimony to the efficacy of this well. In his *Mystery of Godliness*, when speaking of the good office which angels do to God's servants, the Bishop says :

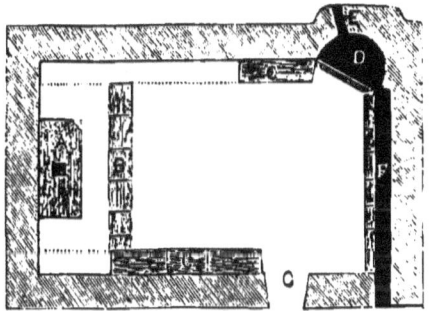

ST. MADRON.

" Of whiche kind was that noe less than miraculous cure whiche at Madern's Well, in Cornwall, was wrought on a poor cripple, whereof, besides the attestation of many hundreds of the neigh-bours, I saw him able to walk and get his own maintenance. I took strict and impartial examination in my last triennial visita-tion. I found neither art nor collusion, the cure done, the author an invisible God." At the side of Madron well, which lies on the moor, a mile or so from the church, is a stone seat, formerly known as St. Madron's bed (Madron is spelt Madden in some old manuscripts). It was upon this that impotent folk reclined when they came to try the cold-water cure. There was also a chapel, about 200 yards away. The chapel was 25 feet by 16 feet, and contained an altar ; a sketch of the ground-plan is given above. It was partially destroyed by Cromwell ; but the ruins remain, and still retain the old stone-altar—a rough slab of granite, with a small square hole in the centre, A. Those who were benefited gave alms to the poor and to the church. This was done down to the middle of the seventeenth century. The well of St. Madderne is still frequented at the parish feast, which takes place in July. On the top of the ruined wall is an old thorn-bush, covered with bits of rag fluttering in the wind, tied there as votive offerings.

LANEAST.

An illustration of this interesting old well is given below.

LANEAST.

POLPERRO : SAINT'S WELL.

The reputed virtues of this well have survived the entire destruction of the edifice which enclosed the spring, for it is still resorted to by those afflicted with inflamed eyes and other ailments, and if "ceremonies due" are done aright, with great benefit. It must be visited on three mornings before sunrise, fasting, a relic of a veritable ceremony, as witnesseth Chaucer's *Pardoner's Tale*, line 33.

> If the goode man that the beest oweth,
> Wol every wike er that the cok him croweth,
> Fastynge, drinke of this well a draught,
> As thilke holy Jew oure eldres taught,
> His beestes, and his stoor schal multiplie.

LINKENHORNE.

An engraving of this well with its curious covering is here given.

LINKENHORNE.

SANCRED: ST. EUNY'S, ST. EURINUS' OR UNY'S WELL.

St. Euny's Well, in the parish of Sancred, south-west of Madron, occupies a soil similar to the Madern Well. Its waters, and its various virtues, both real and imaginary, are similar. Contiguous are the ruins of an old chapel, among which are many stones curiously carved, which strongly indicate that there was a period when this place was in high estimation. Age and repute are the parents of veneration, and veneration, in process of time, frequently degenerates into superstition. Among the reputed excellences of this fountain, it is believed to have the property of drying humours, and healing wounds and sores, of various descriptions. But it is only at particular seasons of the year that the tide of its virtues can be caught. The last day in the year is generally supposed to be more fortunate than any other, and at this time many resort thither, to catch the holy impregnation. There is no doubt that many cures have been wrought by this fountain; but it is only superstition

that will attach these effects to any magical efficacy. Not only by
the water of this well, but by the water of others unknown to
fame, many wounds, sores, disordered eyes, and other complaints,
have been removed by their mere coldness and natural salubrity.
Cold braces the nerves and muscles, and, by strengthening the
glands, promotes secretion and circulation, the two grand ministers
of health. Dr. Borlase says : " I happened luckily to be at this
well upon the last day of the year, on which, according to vulgar
opinion, it exerts its principal and most salutary powers. Two
women were here, who came from a neighbouring parish, and
were busily employed in bathing a child. They both assured me
that people who had a mind to receive any benefit from St. Euny's
Well must come and wash upon the three first Wednesdays in
May." Children suffering from mesenteric disease should be
dipped three times in Chapel Uny "widderschynnes," and
" widderschynnes " dragged three times round the well.

ST. PIRIAN.

Beside a path leading to the oratory of St. Pirian's, in the sands,
there is a spot where thousands of pins may be found. It was the
custom to drop one or two pins at this place when a child was
baptized, and this custom was even retained within the recollec-
tion of some of the elder inhabitants of the parish. There are
other places in this county where pins may be collected by the
handful, particularly at the holy wells. The spring rises at the
foot of Carn Brea.

ST. KEYNE.

This well is half a mile east of the interesting Decorated and
Perpendicular Church of the same name, 2½ miles on the road
from West Looe. It is a spring of rare virtues in the belief of
the country people. It is covered in by masonry, upon the top of
which formerly grew five large trees—a Cornish elm, an oak, and
three antique ash-trees—on so narrow a space that it is difficult to
imagine how the roots could have been accommodated. There
now remain only two of these trees—the elm, which is large and
fine, and one of the ash-trees.

According to the legend, St. Keyne, a holy and beautiful virgin,
of British royal blood, daughter of Braganus, Prince of Brecknockshire, said to have been the aunt of St. David of Wales,
visited this country about 490. She was sought in marriage by

men of distinction. On a pilgrimage to St. Michael's Mount, and remaining sometime in Cornwall, she so endeared herself to the people, that she was hardly allowed to depart. Her nephew, St. Cadock, making a pilgrimage to the same place, in surprise found her, and tried to persuade her to return to Brecknockshire,

ST. KEYNE.

which eventually she did. Cadock stuck his stick in the earth, and originated the spring, which St. Keyne gave to the people in return for the church, which they had dedicated in her honour. One of her fancies was to reside in a wood at Keynsham. The chief of the country warned her of the venomous serpents which swarmed the wood. St. Keyne answered that she would by her prayers rid the country of snakes, and they were turned into the ammonites, frequently found in the lias rock in that district. The well is said to share with St. Michael's Chair at the Mount the marvellous property of confirming the ascendancy of either husband or wife who, the first after marriage, can obtain a draught of water from the spring, or be seated in the chair. This mystical well is the subject of the following lines by Southey :

> A well there is in the west country,
> And a clearer one never was seen ;
> There is not a wife in the west country
> But has heard of the well of St. Keyne.

> An oak and an elm-tree stand beside,
> And behind doth an ash-tree grow,
> And a willow from the bank above
> Droops to the water below.

> A traveller came to the well of St. Keyne,
> Joyfully he drew nigh,
> For from cock-crow he had been travelling,
> And there was not a cloud in the sky.

> He drank of the water so cool and clear,
> For thirsty and hot was he,
> And he sat down upon the bank
> Under the willow-tree.

> There came a man from the house hard by
> At the well to fill his pail ;
> On the well-side he rested it,
> And he bade the stranger hail.

> "Now, art thou a bachelor, stranger ?" quoth he,
> " For an' if thou hast a wife,
> The happiest draught thou hast drank this day,
> That ever thou didst in thy life.

> "Or hast thy good woman, if one thou hast,
> Ever here in Cornwall been ?
> For an' if she have, I'll venture my life
> She has drank of the well of St. Keyne."

> "I have left a good woman who never was here,"
> The stranger he made reply,
> " But that my draught should be the better for that,
> I pray you answer me why."

> "St. Keyne," quoth the Cornishman, "many a time
> Drank of this crystal well,
> And before the angels summon'd her,
> She laid on the water a spell.

" If the husband of this gifted well
　Shall drink before his wife,
A happy man henceforth is he,
　For he shall be master for life.

" But if the wife should drink of it first,
　God help the husband then !"
The stranger stoop'd to the well of St. Keyne,
　And drank of the water again.

" You drank of the well I warrant betimes ?"
　He to the Cornishman said :
But the Cornishman smiled as the stranger spake,
　And sheepishly shook his head.

" I hasten'd as soon as the wedding was done,
　And left my wife in the porch ;
But i' faith she had been wiser than me,
　For she took a bottle to church."

PELYNT : ST. NUN'S WELL.

On the western side of the beautiful valley through which flows
the Trelawny River, and near Hobb's Park, in the parish of Pelynt,
Cornwall, is St. Nunn's or St. Ninnie's Well. Its position was,
until very lately, to be discovered by the oak and bramble which
grew upon its roof. It is entered by a doorway with a stone lintel,
and overshadowed by an oak. The front of the well is of a
pointed form, and has a rude entrance about 4 feet high, and is
spanned above by a single flat stone, which leads into a grotto
with an arched roof. The walls on the interior are draped with
the luxuriant fronds of spleen-wort, hart's tongue, and a rich
undercovering of liverwort. At the farther end of the floor is a
round granite basin with a deeply moulded rim, and ornamented
with a series of rings, each enclosing a cross or a ball. The water
weeps into it from an opening at the back, and escapes again by a
hole in the bottom. This interesting piece of antiquity has been
protected by a tradition which we could almost wish to attach to
some of our cromlechs and circles in danger of spoliation.

An old farmer (so runs the legend) once set his eyes upon the
granite basin and coveted it, for it was no wrong in his eyes to
convert the holy font to the base uses of a pigsty, and accordingly
he drove his oxen and wain to the gateway above for the purpose
of removing it. Taking his beasts to the entrance of the well, he
essayed to drag the trough from its ancient bed. For a long time
it resisted the efforts of the oxen, but at length they succeeded in

2

starting it, and dragged it slowly up the hillside to where the wain was standing.   Here, however, it burst away from the chains which held it, and, rolling back again to the well, made a sharp turn and regained its old position, where it has remained ever since.   Nor will anyone again attempt its removal, seeing that the farmer, who was previously well-to-do in the world, never prospered from that day forward.   Some people say, indeed, that

PELYNT : ST. NUN'S WELL.

retribution overtook him on the spot, the oxen falling dead, and the owner being struck lame and speechless.

Though the superstitious hinds had spared the well, time and storms of winter had been slowly ruining it.   The oak which grew upon its roof had, by its roots, dislodged several stones of the arch, and, swaying about in the wind, had shaken down a large mass of masonry in the interior, and the greater part of the front.   On its ruinous condition being made known to the Trelawny family (on whose property it is situated), they ordered the restoration, and the walls were replaced after the original plan.

This well and a small chapel (the site of which is no longer to be traced, though still pointed out by the older tenantry) were dedicated, it is supposed, to St. Ninnie, or St. Nun, a female saint, who, according to William of Worcester, was the mother of St. David. The people of the neighbourhood knew the well by the names St. Ninnie's, St. Nun's, and Piskies' Well. It is probable that the latter is, after all, the older name, and that the guardianship of the spring was usurped at a later period by the saint whose name it occasionally bears. The water was doubtless used for sacramental purposes; yet its mystic properties, if they were ever supposed to be dispensed by the saint, have been again transferred, in the popular belief, to the Piskies.

In the basin of the well may be found a great number of pins, thrown in by those who have visited it out of curiosity, or to avail themselves of the virtues of its waters. A writer, anxious to know what meaning the peasantry attach to this strange custom, on asking a man at work near the spot, was told that it was done "to get the goodwill of the Piskies," who after the tribute of a pin not only ceased to mislead them, but rendered fortunate the operations of husbandry.

ALTARNUM : ST. NUN'S OR ST. NONNA'S WELL.

In the parish of Altarnum or Alternon, there is a well dedicated in honour of St. Nonna, who is said to have been the daughter of an Earl of Cornwall, and mother of St. David, whose waters were supposed to have the power of curing madness; and according to Carew and Borlase the process was as follows : The water running from this sacred well was conducted to a small square enclosure closely walled in on every side, and might be filled at any depth, as the case required. The frantic person was placed on the wall, with his back to the water; without being permitted to know what was going to be done, he was knocked backwards into the water, by a violent blow on the chest, when he was tumbled about in a most unmerciful manner, until fatigue had subdued the rage which unmerited violence had occasioned. Reduced by ill-usage to a degree of weakness which ignorance mistook for returning sanity, the patient was conveyed to church with much solemnity, where certain Masses were said for him. If after this treatment he recovered, St. Nun had all the praise; but in case he remained the same, the experiment was repeated so often as any hope of life or recovery was left. The mystic properties of this well have been transferred by the vulgar to the Pixies, whose goodwill is obtained by an offering of a pin.

ST. AGNES : HOLY WELL.

At the foot of the holy well in St. Agnes, a place formerly of great repute, Dr. Borlase says he thinks the remains of a similar well to the last are still discernible, though the sea has demolished the walls. The Cornish call this immersion " boussening," from *beuzi* or *budhizzi* in the Corno-British and Armoric, signifying to dip or to drown.

GULVAL : HOLY WELL.

This miraculous well, in the parish of Gulval or Gulfwell, was formerly in high repute. It was customary to resort thither at the feast time. Formerly it was famous for its prophetic properties. It is situated, like St. Madern Well, in a moor, called Forsis Moor, in the manor of Lanesly, which was the name of the parish in 1294. This name implies the existence of an ancient church upon the manor, and probably it stood near this well. The spirit of this fountain could not penetrate the recesses of futurity, but it could reveal secrets, and with the assistance of an old woman who was intimately acquainted with all its mysteries, could inform those who visited it whether their absent friends were alive or dead, in sickness or in health. On approaching this intelligent fountain, the question was proposed aloud to the old woman, when the following appearances·gave the reply: If the absent friend were in health, the water was instantly to bubble; if sick, it was to be suddenly discoloured; but if dead, it was to remain in its natural state. Probably this old woman could discern bubbles, or discoloured water, when no eyes but her own were competent to make the observation; and it was easy to regulate this by means which fortune-tellers usually know how to use.

This old priestess died about the year 1748. Her fame drew many to consult her, from various parts; some from motives of mere curiosity, and others to obtain intelligence of lost goods or cattle. Since her death, the well has suffered considerably in its character. Most of its ancient friends are dead; and many who secretly revere its power are silent in its praises. Multitudes totally disbelieve its miraculous efficacy, and suspicions of its magical virtues appear to be daily increasing.

ST. AUSTELL : MENACUDDLE WELL.

About half a mile from St. Austell there is an enclosed well of remarkably pure water, known as Menacuddle Well, *i.e., maen-a-*

WELL CHAPEL, MENACUDDLE, ST. AUSTELL.

coedl, the hawk's stone ; and also the remains of its little chapel or baptistry. The chapel is 11 feet long, 9 feet wide. There are north and south doorways, B B, 2 feet 9 inches wide, and 5 feet high. The spring rises on the east side, and the basin, A A, is divided by a stone bar. Its romantic situation moves us more than any idea of the virtue of the water. It is also a wishing well. It lies in a vale at the foot of Menacuddle Grove, surrounded with romantic scenery, and covered with an ancient Gothic chapel, overgrown with ivy. The virtues of these waters are very extraordinary, but the advantages to be derived from them are rather attributed to the sanctity of the fountain than to the natural excellence of its stream. Weak children have frequently been carried here to be bathed; ulcers have also been washed in its sacred water, and people in season of sickness have been recommended by the neighbouring matrons to drink of this salubrious fluid. In most of these cases, instances may be procured of benefits received from the application, but

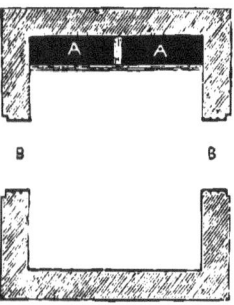

MENACUDDLE : GROUND PLAN.

the prevailing opinion is that the advantages enjoyed result rather from some mystical virtue attributed to the waters for ages past, than from the natural qualities. Within the memory of persons now living, this well was a place of general resort for the young and thoughtless. On approaching the margin, each visitor, if he hoped for good luck through life, was expected to throw a crooked pin into the water, and it was presumed that the other pins which had been deposited there by former devotees might be seen rising from their beds, to meet it before it reached the bottom, and though many have gazed with eager expectation, no one has yet been permitted to witness this extraordinary phenomenon.

GLONHILLY : LUGGER OF CROFT PASCO POOL.

In the midst of the dreary waste of Glonhilly, which occupies a large portion of the Lizard promontory, is a large piece of water known as the " Croft Pasco Pool," where it is said at night the form of a ghostly vessel may be seen floating with lug sails spread. A more dreary, weird spot could hardly be selected for a witches' meeting, and the Lizard folks were always—a fact—careful to be back before dark, preferring to suffer inconvenience to risking a sight of the ghostly lugger. Unbelieving people attributed the origin of the tradition to a white horse seen in a dim twilight, standing in the shallow water; but this was indignantly rejected by the mass of residents. (Hunt's *Popular Romances of the West of England,* 1st Series, p. 299.)

GWAVAS LAKE.

On the western side of Mount's Bay, between the fishing towns of Newlyn and Mousehole, is the well-known anchoring place known by the above name. It is not a little curious that any part of the ocean should have been called a lake. Tradition, however, helps us to an explanation. Between the land on the western side of the bay and St. Michael's Mount on the eastern side, there at one time extended a forest of beech-trees. Within this forest on the western side was a large lake, and on its banks a hermitage. The saint of the lake was celebrated far and near for his holiness, and his small oratory was constantly resorted to by the diseased in body and the afflicted in mind. None ever came in the true spirit who failed to find relief. The prayers of the saint, and the waters of the lake, removed the pains from the limbs and the deepest sorrows from the mind. The young were strengthened, and the old revived, by their influences. The great flood, how-ever, which separated the islands of Scilly from England sub-merged the forest, and destroyed the land enclosing this lovely and almost holy lake, burying beneath the waters churches and houses, and destroying alike both the people and the priest. Those who survived this sad catastrophe built a church on the hill, and dedicated it to the saint of the lake, or, in Cornish, St. Pol, modernised into St. Paul. In support of this tradition, we may see on a fine summer day, when the tide is low and the waters clear, the remains of a forest, in the line passing from St. Michael's Mount to Gwavas. At neap tides the people have gathered beech-nuts from the sands below Chyandour, and cut the wood from the trees imbedded in the sand.—*Ibid.,* 218.

ST. CLEATHER : BASIL'S WELL.

In the parish of St. Cleather, Cornwall, and on the granite-sprinkled banks of the Innay, lie the ruins of a well chapel. The

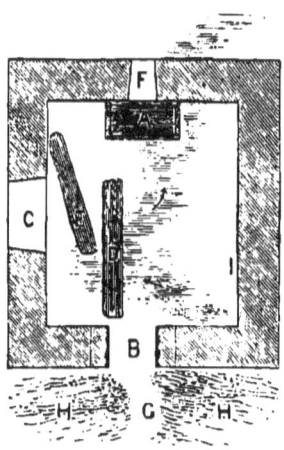

ST. BASIL GROUND-PLAN.

spring of water flows from under the altar, A, which is marked with four crosses.   The chapel is known by the name of Basil's Well.

BODMIN: SCARLET WELL.

Many extraordinary virtues have been ascribed to this well, which is situated one mile west of Bodmin ; but of late years its reputation has so much declined that its situation is scarcely known.   Its imaginary properties resembled those of the Madern Well, but the cures which it wrought were too scanty to secure its reputation.

TRELEVEAN : BRASS WELL.

In Trelevean, in the neighbourhood of Mevagissey, there was · in former years an extraordinary well, called the Brass Well, from the peculiar colour of the scum which floated on its surface.   Its efficacy was, however, insufficient to perpetuate its name, and to the present incredulous age its many virtues seem to be totally unknown.

ROCHE : ST. GUNDRED'S.

Roche, north of St. Austell, famous for the Roche rocks, with St. Michael's Chapel built amongst them.   Once tenanted by a hermit ; then by a leper, whose daughter waited on him, and drew water from a well, said to ebb and flow, called after her.   To St. Gundred's, near a group of cottages called Hollywell village,

ST. ROCHE : WISHING WELL.

maidens would repair on Holy Thursday, to throw in pins and pebbles, and predict coming events by the sparkling of the bubbles which rise up. Lunatics were also immersed in it.

LISKEARD : ST. CLEER.

The well of St. Cleer, the baptistery or chapel by which it was enclosed, and an ancient cross about 9 feet high, form a group by the roadside 100 yards eastward below the church, north of Liskeard. The chapel was destroyed by fanatics in the Civil War, but appears to have been similar in size and construction to that which now stands by Dupath Well, near Callington. It was restored in 1864 as a memorial to the Rev. John Jope, sixty-seven years Vicar of St. Cleer. The well is said to have been once used as a boussening or ducking pool, for the cure of mad people. Attempts have from time to time been made to cart away some of the stones of the chapel, but mysterious power has always

returned them at night.   The entrance is under two low round
arches, the roof covered with ivy and brushwood.   The water
flowing out of the well fills a pool or basin, supposed to have
been used as a boussening pool for curing mad people.

St. Clare was born about 1200, in Italy, and died 1252.   She

ST. CLEER.

became the abbess of a monastery of Benedictine nuns, and was
foundress of the order of the Poor Clares.—E. Ashworth, Esq.

CALLINGTON: DUPATH WELL.

Dupath Well is a pellucid spring, once the resort of pilgrims and
still held in esteem.   It overflows a trough, and entering the open
archway of a small chapel, spreads itself over the floor and passes
out below a window at the opposite end.   The little chapel, 12 feet
long by 11½ wide, is a complete specimen of the baptisteries
anciently so common in Cornwall.   It has a most venerable
appearance, and is built of granite, which is gray and worn by

age. The roof is constructed of enormously long blocks of granite, hung with fern, and supported in the interior by an arch, dividing the nave and chancel. The doorway faces west ; at the east end is a square-headed window of two lights, and two openings in the sides. The building is crowned by an ornamental bell-cote. The well is famed for the combat between Sir Colam and Gotlieb for

DUPATH WELL.

the love of a lady; Gotlieb was killed, and Sir Colam died of his wounds.

ST. LEVAN.

Near the edge of the cliff, on the right bank of the stream, close to the church, is the ruin of the ancient baptistery or Well of St. Levan, who, according to the legend, supported himself by fishing. He caught only one fish a day. But once, when his sister and his child came to visit him, after catching a chad, which he thought not dainty enough to entertain them, he threw it again into the sea. The same fish was caught three times, and at last the saint accepted it, cooked and placed it before his guests, when the child was choked by the first mouthful, and St. Levan saw in the accident a punishment for his dissatisfaction with the fish

ST. LEVAN.

which Providence had sent him. The chad is still called here " chack-cheeld "—choke-child. The chapel has disappeared.

FOWEY : DOZMARE POOL.

Dozmare Pool (pronounced Dosmery)—*i.e.*, Dos, a drop ; Mor and Mari, the sea, from the old tradition that it was tidal—890 feet above the sea, a melancholy sheet of water, about one mile in circumference, and from 4 to 5 feet in depth. The lofty hill called Brown Willy, is the mark by which the traveller can direct his course. On the north side of the hill are the remains of an ancient village, probably of tinners or streamers, as they are locally called. Below this the pool is situated, on a tableland which borders the deep vale of the Fowey. The pool is the theme of many a marvellous tale, in which the peasants most implicitly believe. It is said to be unfathomable, and the resort of evil spirits. Begirt by dreary hills, it presents an aspect of utter gloom and desolation, and is said to have supplied some features for the "middle meer" in the Laureate's "Morte d'Arthur," into which Sir Bedivere at last flung Excalibur, having twice before concealed the "great brand"

" There in the many-knotted waterflags
That whistled stiff and dry about the marge."

The country people represent the pool as haunted by an unearthly visitant, a grim giant of the name of Tregeagle, who, it is said, may be heard howling here when wintry storms sweep the moors. He is condemned to the melancholy task of emptying the pool with a limpet-shell, and is continually howling in despair at the hopelessness of his labour. Occasionally, too, it is said this miserable monster is hunted by the devil round and about the tarn, when he flies to the Roche Rocks, some 15 miles distant, and, by thrusting his head in at the chapel window, finds a respite from his torments. Other versions of the legend place Tregeagle on the coast near Padstow, where he is condemned to make trusses of sand and ropes of sand to bind them; or at the mouth of the estuary at Helston, across which he was condemned to carry sacks of sand until the beach should be clean of the rocks.

The story of Tregeagle, however, with his endless labour, has been connected in Cornwall with a real person, the dishonest steward of Lord Robartes at Lanhydrock (where a room in the house is still called Tregeagle's), who maltreated the tenants under his charge, and amassed money sufficient to purchase the estate of Trevorder, in St. Breock, where he distinguished himself as a harsh and arbitrary magistrate.

ST. NEOT'S WELL.

St. Neot's Well, not far west from the church, was arched over in granite by the late General Carlyon, the old arched covering having fallen in many years ago. St. Neot, said to have been learned, eloquent, and intelligent, was a monk of Glastonbury, and supposed to have been brother to Alfred the Great, co-temporary with St. Dunstan; he died 890. Many sought his prayers, either for relief of their infirmities, or for spiritual comfort. Wearied of his fame he retired to his hermitage here, with one attendant, Barius. It was in this well that he stood up to his chin daily, and chanted the Psalter throughout.

Many are the wild tales of his miraculous performances at his "holy well," which an angel stocked with fish as food for St. Neot, but on condition that he took only one for his daily meal. The stock consisted but of two—some accounts say three—but of two for ever, like a guinea in a fairy purse. It happened, however, that the saint fell sick and became dainty in his appetite; and his servant, Barius by name, in his eagerness to please his master, cooked the two, boiling the one and broiling the other. Great was the consternation of St. Neot; but, recovering his presence of mind, he ordered the fish to be thrown back into the spring, and falling on his knees, most humbly sought forgiveness. The servant returned, declaring that the fish were alive and sporting in the water, and when the proper meal had been prepared, the saint on tasting it was instantly restored to health. Some fox-hunters one day entered the wood, the retreat of the saint, who fled, and lost his shoe in his hurry; the fox stole it, and was in consequence cast into a deep sleep, and died. At another time St. Neot was praying at this well, when a hunted deer sought protection by his side. On the arrival of the dogs the saint reproved them, and, behold! they crouched at his feet, whilst the huntsman, affected by the miracle, renounced the world, and hung up his bugle-horn in the cloister. Again, the oxen belonging to the saint had been stolen, and wild deer came of their own accord to replace them, and returned to their woods at night, until the stolen bullocks were restored. When the thieves beheld St. Neot ploughing with his stags they were conscience-stricken, and returned what they had stolen. Such stories as these are represented in the stained-glass window, *c.* 1500-1530, and many more may be gathered from the country people, who affirm that the church was built by night, and the materials brought together by teams of two deer and one hare. They also show in the churchyard the stone on which the saint used to stand to throw the key into the keyhole, which had been accidentally placed too high. (St. Neot was of small stature, and either this lock or another was in the habit of descending, so that his hand could reach it.)

The first three mornings in May are those on which patients should visit this well.

The old name of the parish was Neotstow, and it is said to have been in a church on this site that King Alfred was praying (during a hunting expedition into Cornwall) when a change took place in his life.

CAMELFORD : ST. BREWARD'S WELL.

This well is situated in a valley near a farm called "Chapel," close to Camelford. It is, or was, visited by sufferers from in-

ST. BREWARD'S WELL.

flamed eyes and other complaints. As an offering, the sufferer threw in a pin, or small coin, to the saint.—*Western Antiquary*, 37.

ST. COLAN : OUR LADY OF NANTSWELL.

In former days " Our Lady of Nantswell," in St. Colan's parish, near St. Columb Major, was resorted to by men, women, and children, to foreknow of the Lady of the Well, on Palm Sunday, what should befall them that year. These pilgrims bore a palm cross in one hand and an offering in the other. The offering fell to the priest's share : the cross was thrown into the well, and if it swam was regarded as an omen that the person who threw it would outlive the year; if, however, it sank, a shortly ensuing death was foreboded.

PADSTOW: TRAITOR POOL.

On the 1st of May, a species of festivity, Hitchins tells us, was observed in his time at Padstow: called the *Hobby-horse*, from the figure of a horse being carried through the streets. Men, women, and children flocked round it, when they proceeded to a place called Traitor Pool, about a quarter of a mile distant, in which the hobby-horse was always supposed to drink. The head, after being dipped into the water, was instantly taken out, and the mud and water were sprinkled on the spectators, to the no small diversion of all. On returning home a particular song was sung, which was supposed to commemorate the event that gave the hobby-horse birth. According to tradition the French once upon a time effected a landing at a small cove in the vicinity, but seeing at a distance a number of women dressed in red cloaks, whom they mistook for soldiers, they fled to their ships and put to sea. The day generally ended in riot and dissipation.

GRADE: ST. RUAN'S, OR ST. RUMON.

The well is about a quarter of a mile from Grade Church, rudely built of granite. Its water is used for all baptisms in the church. St. Rumon is believed to have come as a missionary from Ireland in the ninth or tenth century, and to have dwelt in a

ST. RUAN'S WELL, NEW GRADE CHINE.

wood near Grade Church and the Lizard Point, having a cell and chapel, and regardless of the wild beasts which then roamed there. His name excited such reverence, that his remains were removed to Tavistock Abbey.

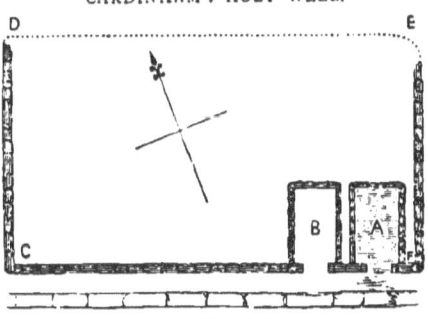

CARDINHAM : HOLY WELL.

CARDINHAM.

Cardinham, near Bodmin, has near the church its sacred well
in the corner of a walled space about 80 feet by 42 feet; the

3

water runs out into the road.   The well (A) is walled in and roofed over, and has an oratory (B) adjoining it, 14 feet by 8 feet.—E. Ashworth, " Holy Wells," paper on, p. 145.

LUDGVAN: WELL OF COLURIAN.

This well is in the parish of Ludgvan.   It was sacred before the saints.—Polwhele's *History of Cornwall.*

ST. CUTHBERT: ST. CUTHBERT'S WELL.

In this parish (St. Cuthbert) is that famous and well-known spring of water, called Holy Well, so named, the inhabitants say, for that the virtues of this water were first discovered on All Hallow's Day.   The same stands in a dark cavern of the sea cliff rocks, beneath full sea-mark on spring tides.   The virtues of the waters are, if taken inward, a notable vomit, or as a purgent.   If applied outward, it presently strikes in, or dries up, all itch, scurf, dandriff, and such-like distempers in men or women.   Numbers of persons in summer season frequent this place and waters from countries far distant.   It is a petrifying well.—*Ibid.*, 53.

CUBERT: ST. CUTHBERT'S WELL.

There is a hollow in the rock on the coast south of Creek which at high-tide is always filled by the salt water, but at low-tide the water is always fresh ; it is said to have the power of curing diseases.   The dropping water forms a stalagmite.—*Ibid.*, 147n.

MOUNT EDGECUMBE : ST. LEONARD'S WELL.

The chapel of this well is in the grounds of Mount Edgecumbe. It is a ruined cell, 6 feet by $4\frac{1}{2}$ feet.   It had an arched roof, with a central rib, part of which remains ; opposite the doorway is a niche.   The water now supplies a cattle trough.—Ashford, 147.

WADEBRIDGE : ST. MINVER'S WELL.

There is a spring in St. Minver, near Wadebridge, still in some repute for curing disorders of the eye.—*Ibid.*, 147.

JESUS WELL, ST. MINVER.

Here also is a well, or spring, known as JESUS WELL, to which children suffering from the whooping-cough are brought.—*Ibid.*, 147.

LUXULION.

In the village is a little baptistry, with a granite roof and sides.

LUXULION.

DULOE : ST. KILBY'S WELL.

Between Duloe and the village of Sand-place, on the canal, is a celebrated spring sacred to St. Cuby—believed to be St. Cuthbert —and commonly called St. Kilby's.

WELL OF ST. CRANHOCUS, CRANSTOCK.

RIALTON PRIORY.

There is a well here, an illustration of which is given below.

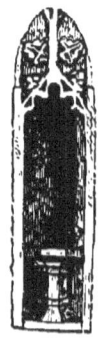

WELL IN THE COURT OF RIALTON PRIORY (WITH NICHE AT BACK OF THE
WELL).

CHAPEL COMB : ST. AGNES' WELL.

Near to Chapel Comb, Maclean tells us, is St. Agnes' Well, about which miraculous stories are told [*Parochial History of Cornwall*, p. 8]; but what these stories were, or where they are to be found, is not stated.

ST. DOMINICK'S WELL.

CHAPEL FARM : ST. DOMINICK'S WELL.

This well is situated between Chapel Farm and the Tamar.— Ashford, 147.

CRANSTOCK : ST. AMBROSE'S WELL.

Gilbert mentions this well at the west of Cranstock, near the ruins of a college, buried by the blown sand from Grannel Creek.

CUMBERLAND.

COCKERMOUTH : MOCKERKIN TARN.

A SMALL town on the left-hand side of the road leading from Cockermouth to Egremont, and near the village of Mockerkin, about four miles from Cockermouth, is said once to have been prosperous, but for some reason the waters submerged it. It is affirmed that at times the roofs and chimneys of the houses may be seen. A stream runs from it, but not into it; the springs in the tarn are probably the source of the supply. It is known as Mockerkin Tarn.

KIRKOSWALD : ST. RENALD'S WELL.

Bishop Nicholson was of opinion that the spring which issued from the west end of Kirkoswald Church was the ancient well of the Saxons, and which was afterwards exorcised and dedicated to Christian uses. It undoubtedly served the purposes of baptism. The church was built over it, and called after the saint's name. No one can visit the spot without admiring its adaptation for the site of a religious house, its retirement helping a life of piety and contemplation.—Rev. J. Wilson, *Penrith Observer.*

IRTHINGTON : HOLY WELL.

At Irthington, rising in the churchyard boundary, was the well called " How," or " Ha," evidently a corruption of " Holy " Well, which served the saint on his visit to this place for preaching and baptizing. In one of the church windows of modern date there were two medallions of St. Kentigern, one a full-length figure, and the other a representation of him preaching to the Britons. The encroachment of the river Eden at Grinsdale is said to have obliterated the well.—*Ibid.*

BROMFIELD: ST. KENTIGERN'S WELL.

In Bromfield there were plenty of legends connected with this well. It is situated in a field near the churchyard. The present vicar, the Rev. R. Taylor, with reverent care, had it cleared and enclosed with a circular vaulted dome of stone, on which he placed an appropriate inscription. Hutchinson, in his *History of Cumberland,* speaks with regret of the suppression of this well. In the beginning of the eighteenth century, one who knew St. Kentigern's Well at Bromfield, and who had a high idea of the use of such places, wrote a beautiful ballad of ten verses, from which are selected the three following :

> Look north, look south, look east, look west,
> The country smiles with plenty blest ;
> For every hill and plain and dell
> Stands thick with corn round Helly Well.

> To usher in the new-born May
> The country round came here to play ;
> But where's the tongue or pen can tell
> The feats then played at Helly Well ?

> Thrice happy people ! long may ye
> Enjoy your rural revelry ;
> And dire misrule and discord fell
> Be far—O far—from Helly Well !—*Ibid.*

DALSTON : HOLY WELL.

The Holy Well near Dalston is very interesting, and had some connection with Carlisle. It is situated in the Shawk quarries, about two miles west of the village. These quarries supplied the white freestone for building Christ Church, Carlisle, and were supposed to have been opened in Roman times for materials to build the portion of the Great Wall west of Carlisle. The Holy Well, still called Helly Well, springs out of the limestone rock. It was remarkable for the religious rites formerly performed around it on certain Sundays by the villagers in the neighbourhood. The good spirit of the well was sought out and supposed to teach its votaries the virtues of temperance, health, cleanliness, simplicity, and love. Worse customs we might have, but few, if any, persons nowadays seek its blessings, and the old faith in its powers has died out. Not far from this well at the written rocks of Shawk-beck is Tom Smith's Leap, so called from a legend of some mosstrooper who, when pursued with hottrod, jumped down and was killed rather than fall into the hands of justice.—*Ibid.*

CARLISLE CATHEDRAL.

There is a well in Carlisle Cathedral situated partially under one of the pillars. It is said the late Dean had it covered over for fear of it or the water in some way "affecting the music." Carlisle having been a border city, open to inroads of every description in early times, it is probable that the inhabitants may have fled to the cathedral sanctuary on such occasions, in which case a well of pure water would be an invaluable boon. (*Notes and Queries,* 3rd series, xii. 235.)

EDEN HALL : GIANT'S CAVE.

At Giant's Cave, near Eden Hall, it has been the custom from time immemorial for the lads and lasses of the neighbouring villages to collect together on the third Sunday in May, to drink sugar and water, when the lasses give the treat : this is called Sugar-and-Water Sunday. They afterwards adjourn to the public house, and the lads return the compliment in cakes, ale, punch, etc. A vast concourse of both sexes assemble for the above purpose. (Brand's *Pop. Ant. ;* Bohn's Ed.)

BROMFIELD : ST. CUTHBERT'S.

In the parish of Bromfield, in the neighbourhood of Blencogo, "on the common to the east of that village, not far from Ware-Brig, near a pretty large rock of granite, called St. Cuthbert's Stane, is a fine copious spring of remarkably pure and sweet water, which (probably from its having been anciently dedicated to the same St. Cuthbert) is called Helly-Well, *i.e.,* Haly or Holy Well. It formerly was the custom for the youth of all the neighbouring villages to assemble at this well early in the afternoon of the second Sunday in May, and there to join in a variety of rural sports. It was the village wake, and took place here, it is possible, when the keeping of wakes and fairs in the churchyard was discontinued. And it differed from the wakes of later times chiefly in this, that though it was a meeting entirely devoted to festivity and mirth, no strong drink of any kind was ever seen there, nor anything ever drunk but the beverage furnished by the Naiad of the place. A curate of the parish, about twenty years ago, on the idea that it was a profanation of the Sabbath, saw fit to set his face against it ; and having deservedly great influence in the parish, the meetings at Helly-Well have ever since been discontinued."—Rev. J. Wilson in *Penrith Observer.*

TORPENHOW.

At Bothel, in the parish of Torpenhow, a stream rises from a well which supplies the village with water. The proverbial "oldest inhabitant" asserted that this stream ran blood on the day of King Charles's martyrdom. He would not be surprised to hear that the "Boulder Stone" in the vicinity was carried from Norway by the fairies. If they believed the same authority, Plumbland put in a claim for the virtues of this well also, but one could not decide to which parish it belonged.—*Ibid.*

ARTHURET : ST. MICHAEL'S WELL.

Near the church of Arthuret is St. Michael's Well, which is still looked upon as the ancient place of baptism, and under the special protection of St. Michael, in whose honour the church, on account of the well, was dedicated.—*Ibid.*

KIRKANDREWS-ON-EDEN : ST. ANDREW'S WELL.

Only one well has been discovered dedicated to St. Andrew in the county, which is situate in the churchyard of Kirkandrews-on-Eden, and is not affected by the most intense frost or the longest drought. It is another of the many instances where holy wells were used for sacred purposes, placed conveniently for the service of the church.—*Ibid.*

ESKDALE : ST. CATHARINE'S WELL.

At the head of the charming valley of Eskdale stands the interesting little church dedicated to St. Catharine. Just outside the churchyard wall is St. Catharine's Well. In olden times, on the feast-day of the saint the fairs were held on the north side of the chapel yard, when the usual commodities were bought and sold by the dalesmen. The font, which is a neat specimen of Early English style, bears St. Catharine's wheel, as also does some very old glass in a few of the windows. To the north of the church is a rock called Bell Hill, where the chapel bell is said to have been hung. It is more likely a relic of the old fire-worship of Beltan, of which our pagan ancestors were so fond.—*Ibid.*

KIRKHAMPTON : TODDEL WELL.

No one now seeks Toddel Well in the township of Longrigg. It was formerly the belief in this parish that the waters of this well had a similar efficacy to the pool of Bethesda, where scrofula sores and all sorts of skin diseases could be healed. A bonfire was an annual dissipation on the eve of St. John the Baptist, the lads and lasses rushing through the smoke and flames singing " Awake, awake, for sin gale's sake."—*Ibid.*

GILCRUX : TOMMY TACK WELL.

In a field a little to the east of the village of Gilcrux there are two springs some fifty yards apart; one has fresh water, and the other salt and of medicinal qualities. The salt water well is named the "Tommy Tack," but by some " Funny Jack."—*Ibid.*

BRISCOE : ST. NINIAN'S WELL.

Miss Losh, who will be long remembered in this county for her works of piety and love, extended her protecting care to St. Ninian's Well at Briscoe, erecting over it a semicircular arch, and cutting upon it a characteristic inscription.—*Ibid.*

PENRITH WELLS.

The only church in the diocese dedicated to St. Ninian is at Penrith. Penrith was once noted, and has some fame still, for the number of its wells. The whole month of May was set apart for special observance of customs and ceremonies to be performed on each Sunday. There were four wells with a Sunday allocated for honouring each well. The Fontinalia opened at Skirsgill on the first Sunday ; then in order Clifton, afterwards the well at the Giant's Caves, supposed to be St. Ninian's ; and, lastly, at Dicky Bank, on the fellside, where the festivities were concluded. The chief of these gatherings was at Clifton on the Sunday after the Ascension. This was remarkable. The feast of the Ascension was chosen by the early Christians to commemorate the return of spring, and gatherings of this kind were used to thank God for the continuance of His providence to man. It was the special season for the dressing and decoration of wells as emblematical of immortality, when taken in connection with the Christian festival, the flowers symbolizing the transitoriness of human life. But in later years the Penrith observance was woefully debased : *corruptio optimi est pessima.* At Clifton the old custom only survived in brutal fights, both of cocks and men, as well as drinking bouts and other orgies, which would have disgraced the Floralia of the ancient Greeks. These disorders have been suppressed within living memory. The rites at the Giant's Caves were harmless enough, and similar to those at Greystoke and other places in Cumberland. The remnant of the great past appeared in the middle of this century amongst the children in the custom of "shaking bottles" over the well with certain incantations, hence the day was called "shaking bottle Sunday." It was supposed that these customs were fostered by the celebrated hermit who dwelt in these caves, and was the object of reverence throughout the district.—*Ibid.*

GILSLAND.

> " In Cumberland there is a spring,
> And strange it is to tell,
> That many a fortune it will make,
> If never a drop they sell."

The above prophetic rhymes are popularly understood to allude to Gilsland Spa, respecting which there is a very curious tradition, viz., that on the medicinal virtues being first discovered, the person who owned the land, not resting satisfied, as would appear, with his profits which the influx of strangers to the place had caused, built a house over the spring, with the intention of selling the waters. But his avarice was punished in a very singular manner, for no sooner had he completed his house than the spring dried up, and continued so till the house was pulled down ; when lo ! another miracle, it flowed again as before. Whether true or false, this story of antiquity enforces a most beautiful moral and religious precept.—Clarke's *Survey of the Lake.*

COWT OF KEILDAR'S POOL.

The Cowt of Keildar was a powerful chief in the district wherein Keildar Castle is situated, adjacent to Cumberland. He was the redoubtable enemy of Lord Soulis, and perished in an encounter on the banks of the Hermitage. Being encased in armour, he received no hurt in battle, but falling in retreating across the stream, his opponents, to their everlasting shame be it written, held him beneath the water till he was drowned. That portion of the river in which he perished is to this day known as the Cowt of Keildar's Pool.

CALDEW : ST. KENTIGERN'S WELL.

St. Kentigern's Well is still *in statu quo,* near the churchyard. Steps to this well were formerly constructed out of the relics of an old font. The Rev. James Thwaites, a former rector, had these restored to their proper use.—Rev. J. Wilson, *Penrith Observer.*

GREYSTOKE : ST. KENTIGERN'S WELL.

In Greystoke, about a mile away on the borders of this parish, there seemed to be a most interesting memorial of St. Kentigern in a well much visited by strangers and farmers called "Thanet Well." His mother's name was "Thenew." Fordun called her "Thanes," and Camerarius "Themets" or "Thennet," so the change from this last name to "Thanet" was not by any means so violent as that which had converted her church in Glasgow into St. Enoch's! The connection of the Earls of Thanet with this country was of far too recent a date for this name to have been attached to an ancient well, and one too far away from their possessions.—*Ibid.*

CASTLE-SOWERBY : ST. KENTIGERN'S WELL.

There was an ancient well in the vicarage garden at Castle-Sowerby, which probably once bore the saint's name, but was now forgotten. It had been carefully cased with hewn stones, to which there seemed to have been formerly a roof.—*Ibid.*

MELMERBY : ST. JOHN THE BAPTIST'S WELL.

Richard Singleton, the rector of Melmerby, who died in 1684, wrote as follows (Machell MSS.) :

"Wee have sev'all wells in the parish, whereof 4 are more remarkable than the rest. Imp. Margett Hardies well, which is in the Gale intack : some say it will purge both waies, but this I am sure of that if any drink of it (as I have done when hunting) they will presently become very hungry. It was so called from a woman of that name who frequented it daily, and lived to a great age : they report her to have been a witch. Secondly, Fen hiey well, ffamous for Sir Lancelott's (Threlkeld) father frequenting it, and this they say will cure the . . . or . . . Thirdly, Kep-gob-well, which is upon the mountains, and in the drought of summer is a great relief to man and horse when we bring downe our peates. Fourthly, The Ladies well, which is in the Lord's parke, and is good for dressing butter with."—*Ibid.*

HUTTON : COLLINSON'S WELL.

The church was dedicated in honour of St. John the Baptist. Little remains to tell either of the castle or well on Hutton

Common, but both were popularly known as having been named after one Collinson. There was a tradition, with every probability of truth, that when King Charles marched his men on the road through this parish he turned aside and drank out of Collinson's Well. He had been unable to connect these wells with the saint's name to whom the churches were dedicated.—*Ibid.*

ASPATRIA : BISHOP'S WELL.

There was formerly a well in the glebe field near the church, by some called the Bishop's Well.—*Ibid.*

PATTERDALE : ST. PATRICK'S WELL.

St. Patrick's Well is situated near the chapel in Patterdale.

CASTERTON : ST. COUME'S OR COLUMBA'S WELL.

The well dedicated to this saint is near the chapel.

DERBYSHIRE.

HAYFIELD : MERMAID'S POOL OR WELL.

NEAR Downfall, a short walk from the Old Oak Wood, not far from Hayfield, is the Mermaid's Pool. There is a local tradition that a beautiful nymph lives in the side of the Scout, who comes to bathe daily in the Mermaid's Pool, and that the man who has the good fortune to see her whilst bathing will become immortal.

The old folk of Hayfield, moreover, have a long story of a man who, some time in the last century, went from Hayfield over the Scout, and was lucky enough to meet this mountain nymph, by whom he was conducted to a cavern hard by. Tradition adds that she was pleased with this humble mortal, and that he lingered there for some time, when she conferred on him the precious gift of immortality.

ASHFORD-IN-THE-WATER : SKINNER'S WELL.

This well or spring of water is situated in a little dell at the foot of Great Shacklow, a perfect cavern or grotto overgrown with moss and verdure. It was customary here on Easter morning, as at Tideswell, to drink of this water after putting in some sugar.

WILNE: ST. CHAD'S WELL.

The church of St. Chad at Wilne is a remarkable specimen of mediæval architecture, and its massive tower is a notable feature in the lower part of the Derwent Valley, being about a mile above the estuary of that river with the Trent. The interior of the church has a font which is altogether unique, while the Willoughby Chapel contains the remains of a noble family who once resided in the parish, which at one time included, besides the hamlets of Wilne or Wilton, on each side of the Derwent, the townships or chapelries of Sawley, Long Eaton, Breaston Risley, and the places of Draycott, Hopwell, and Wilsthorpe. Near the church are some farm buildings where was a well, now, it is said, closed, but which is stated to be the well of St. Chad, the first Bishop of Lichfield, who ruled over the diocese from A.D. 669 to A.D. 672. Repingdon, Repington, afterwards called Repton, had been previously the headquarters of Christianity for what was then termed mercie, *i.e.*, the "marches," or districts bordering upon Wales. Previous to this time the Britons, the former inhabitants, had been driven westwards by the advancing tide of Teutons, or Angles and Saxons, and many were the struggles between the rival races ere the conflict ceased. For many years the Celts maintained their footing in some portions of the country, but in time the whole of the large district of which St. Chad's diocese consisted, and which is said at one time to have held in its limits no less than nineteen counties, became Anglicised. Of St. Chad previously but little is known. During his episcopate, which lasted but two and a half years, his piety and zeal for the spread of the Gospel shone out with effulgence. It was his custom, as of others in those times of strife, to missionize, and this he did on foot until compelled by the metropolitan to ride on horseback. It is supposed that Christianity was thus first planted at Wilne, and that the well at that place was used for the purpose of baptizing the early converts. St. Chad, as might be expected, has numerous churches dedicated to his memory, amongst which may be mentioned the venerable church of St. Chad (Stowe), Lichfield, and the round church at Shrewsbury, besides the recently-erected church of St. Chad at Derby.

Well Dressing.

The custom of " well-flowering " is common in Derbyshire.

Custom of Decorating Wells.

At the village of Tissington, near Ashborne, in Derbyshire, the custom of well-flowering is still observed on every anniversary of the Ascension, or Holy Thursday. On this occasion the day is regarded as a festival; the villagers array themselves in their best attire, and keep open house for their friends. All the wells in the place, which are five in number, are decorated with wreaths and garlands of newly-gathered flowers disposed in various devices. Boards are sometimes used, cut into different forms, and then covered with moist clay, into which the stems of flowers are inserted to preserve their freshness, and they are so arranged as to form a beautiful mosaic work. When thus adorned, the boards are so disposed at the springs that the water appears to issue from amidst beds of flowers. After service at church, where a sermon is preached, a procession is made, and the wells are visited in succession: the psalms for the day, the epistle and gospel are read, one at each well, and the whole concludes with a hymn, sung by the church singers, accompanied by a band of music. Rural sports and holiday pastimes occupy the remainder of the day. (*Notes and Queries*, 2nd Series, x., p. 38.)

The custom was common with the ancient Greeks and Romans. The ode of Horace to the fountain of Blandusia is well known :

> O fons Blandusiæ, splendidior vitro,
> Dulci digne mero, non sine floribus.

" Where a spring or a river flows," says Seneca, " there should we build altars and offer sacrifices."

Various are the conjectures respecting this ceremony; some supposing it to be the remains of a heathen worship, observed the four last days of April, and first of May, in honour of the goddess Flora, whose votaries instituted games called Florales or Floralia, to be celebrated annually on her birthday. But because they appeared impious and profane to the Roman Senate, which was the case, they covered their design, and worshipped Flora under the title of " Goddess of Flowers ;" and pretended that they offered sacrifice to her, that the plants and trees might flourish. While these sports were celebrating, the officers or ædiles scattered beans and other pulse among the people. These games were proclaimed and begun by sound of trumpet, as we find mentioned in Juvenal, Sat. 6; and had they been divested of obscene and lewd practices, so far from incurring censure, they would have handed down to posterity admiration at the innocent pastimes of the ancients, instead of regret, that such proceedings should have been countenanced by the great. From the above being recorded, it is not unlikely that the custom originated, in some parts of England, of the youth of both sexes going into the woods and fields on the first of May, to gather boughs and flowers, with which they make garlands, and adorn their doors and windows with nosegays and artificial crowns. Triumphing thus in the flowery spoil, they decked also with flowers a tall pole, which they named the Maypole, and which they placed in some convenient part of the village, and spent their time in dancing round it, consecrating it, as it were, to the Goddess of Flowers, without the least violation being offered to it through the circle of the whole year. Nor is this custom alone observed in England, but it is done in other nations, particularly Italy, where young men and maidens are accustomed to go into the fields on the calends of May, and bring thence the branches of trees, singing all the way as they return, and so place them on the doors of their houses (A full account of the well-dressing here in 1823 will be found in the *Gentleman's Magazine Library*, Pop. Sup., 144, and an illustration in Chambers's *Book of Days*, 1.)

BASLOW-PILSLEY KIT-DRESSING.

In 1855, while passing an evening hour at a garden-gate in the village of Baslow, a youth arrived bearing on his arm a very large basket, well garnished with flowers of divers kinds and colours, an increase of which he solicited by a selection from my friend's garden—such as had already been granted him by others in the village. Upon inquiring, with the thirstiness of an antiquary, the meaning of this goodly basket of flowers, I was informed that young Corydon was collecting them for the Pilsley "Well" or "Tap" dressing. When all was ready, I visited Pilsley to join in the festival, and found that it answered exactly to an account in a letter written to me by a brother in 1851, describing the "Well" dressing which he witnessed at the above-named place. It was as follows :

"After tea, we all went up to Pilsley to witness a 'Village Festival,' or 'Wake,' as it is called. . . . In the morning a procession passed thro' Baslow on its way to Pilsley. It consisted of

nine carts and wagons of all shapes and sizes, containing the boys
and girls of Eyam School, with their dads and mams, uncles and
aunts, brothers and sisters, cousins and friends ; a few flags, and
headed by some stout fellows armed with cornopeans and trom-
bones, blowing discordant sounds, and 'making *day* hideous.'
They march round the village where the 'well-flowering' takes
place, carrying their flags, and headed by their bands. In the
afternoon we saw them come back, the chaps in the cart blowing
away as fresh as ever. When we went up in the evening, we
found quite 'a throng' in the village. People come from all
parts ; and it seems to be the custom, with those who can afford
it, to keep open house for the day. A great deal of taste and
fancy is exhibited in the 'well-flowering,' or 'well-dressing,' or
'tap-dressing,' as it is variously called. Behind two of the taps
that supply water to the village, was erected a large screen of
rough boards ; the principal one was about 20 feet square. The
screen is then plastered over with moist clay, upon which the
Duke of Devonshire's arms, and a great variety of fanciful devices
and mottoes, are executed in various colours by sticking flowers
and buds into the clay, by which means they keep fresh for
several days. The background to the device is formed with the
green leaves of the fir. Some of the ornaments are formed of
shells stuck into the clay. Branches of trees are arranged at the
sides of the screen, and in front of the screen a miniature garden
is laid out, with tiny gravel walks, and flower-beds with shell
borders, and surrounded by a fence of stakes and ropes. Opposite
the principal screen they had gone a step further, and attempted
a fountain, formed by the figure of a duck with outstretched
wings, straight neck, and bill wide open, from which a stream of
water shot up about a yard high. . . . There was a handsome flag
flying on the village green, and the same at the inn, and a pole
decorated with flowers, and a young tree tied to the lower part ;
and a few stalls for nuts and gingerbread."—*Notes and Queries*,
2 S., ix. 430.

BUXTON WELL-DRESSING.

An account of the Buxton well-dressing, 1846, in a local news-
paper, speaks of it as a long-established fête :

"'The fountain was, as usual, the centre of attraction. The
great difficulty was to obtain a novel design, and a sort of Chinese
figure was selected for the front of the cenotaph, while from each

corner of railing pillars sprung, profusely decorated with ever-
greens, and united in a sort of arch at the top, on which the velvet
cushion was placed. The principal decoration had a railed-in
grassplot in front, with four several fountains throwing up water—
two from handsome vases on each side, one from a very good
model of a duck, and another from a sort of shallow basin, from
which a variety of beautiful jets were thrown by altering the
arrangement of the orifice." A band of morris dancers, whose
"graceful evolutions" are described, formed part of the proceedings.

BUXTON : ST. ANNE'S WELL.

The waters of Buxton and their healing properties were well
known to the Romans, as has been proved by the remains of
their baths on the site of the warm springs. In mediæval days
the well was dedicated to St. Anne. The actual well remained
in a comparatively untouched condition, lined with Roman lead,
and surrounded with Roman brick and cement, down to the year
1709, when Sir Thomas Delves, a gentleman of Cheshire, who
had received benefit at the spring, removed the old work, and
erected over it a stone alcove, or porch. But for several centuries
before the Reformation, a chapel existed closely adjoining the
spring, a little to the east, and with probably an ante-chapel over
the water. The first historical allusion to this chapel, says Rev.
Dr. Cox in his *Churches of Derbyshire*, occurs in the *Valor
Ecclesiasticus* (27 Henry VIII.), wherein is the following entry,
under the parish church of Bakwell : "Capella de Bukstones in
parochia de Bakwell. In oblationibus ibidem ad Sanctum Annan
coram nobis dictis commissionariis non patet." It is not to be
wondered at that there was a difficulty in supplying the commis-
sioner with the value of the offerings made to St. Anne, as they
must have fluctuated considerably according to the social position
of the patient and the completeness of the cure. A few years later
the superstitious reverence that associated the healing properties
of the water with St. Anne was rudely crushed by one of the agents
of Henry VIII. In his zeal to do his masters' bidding, he not
only closed the chapel and removed the image, but even deprived
the sick for a time of all access to the waters. The following
letter from Sir William Bassett to Lord Cromwell will be read with
interest :

" Right Honourable my in especial good Lord,

" According to my bounden duty, and the tenor of your lordship's letters lately to me directed, I have sent your lordship by this bearer, my brother Francis Bassett, the images of St. Anne, of Buxton, and St. Andrew of Burton-upon-Trent, which images I did take from the places where they did stand and brought to my own house, within forty-eight hours after the contemplation of your said lordship's letters, in as sober a manner as my little and rude wits would serve me. And for that there should be no more idolatry and superstition there used, I did not only deface the tabernacles and places where they did stand, but did also take away crutches, shirts, and shifts, with was offered, being things that allure and entice the ignorant to the said offering, also giving the keepers of both places orders that no more offerings should be made in those places till the king's pleasure and your lordship's be further known on their behalf.

" My lord, I have locked and sealed the baths and wells at Buxton, that none shall enter to wash there till your lordship's pleasure be further known. Whereof I beseech your good lordship that I may be ascertained again at your pleasures, and I shall not fail to execute your lordship's commandments to the utmost of my little wit and power. And my lord, as touching the opinion of the people, and the fond trust they do put in those images, and the vanity of the things ; this bearer can tell your lordship better at large than I can write, for he was with me at the doing of all this, and in all places, as knoweth good Jesus, whom ever have your good lordship in his blessed keeping.

" Written at Langley with the rude and simple hand of your assured and most faithful orator, and as one ever at your commandment next unto the king's, to the uttermost of his little power.

" WILLIAM BASSETT, Knight.

" To Lord Cromwell."

It would seem that the old chapel of St. Anne was demolished with the idea of eradicating superstitious notions shortly after the receipt of Lord Cromwell's letter. The foundations of the chapel were uncovered in 1698. When Dr. Jones wrote a little treatise on *The Benefit of the Ancient Bathes of Buckstone*, in 1572, the chapel did not exist, and the crutches and other tokens of restored health were hung up on the walls of a public room erected by the Earl of Shrewsbury not far from the baths.   He mentions, also, the legend that the image of St. Anne had been miraculously found in the well, and thus given it her name.

Various of our earlier writers testify to the repute of Buxton waters, two of which, that have not found their way into local guides, shall here be quoted.

In John Heywood's play of *The Four P.P.*, the palmer, recounting his wanderings, says :

> Then at the Rhodes also I was ;
> And round about to Amias
> At St. Uncumber and Trunnion ;
> At St. Botoph and St. Annie of Buxton.

Drayton, in the *Polyolbion*, says :

> I can again produce those wondrous wells
> Of Bueston, as I have, that most delicious fount
> Which men the second Bath of England do account,
> Which in the primer reigns, which first this well began
> To have her virtues known, unto the blest St. Anne,
> Was consecrated then.

WIRKSWORTH TAP-DRESSING.

This beautiful custom is observed here with great gusto, though said to be of comparatively late origin.   It is very similar to that which obtains at Tissington in all its details, and attracts hundreds of sight-seers.

BELPER WELL-DRESSING.

The first attempt at well-dressing at Belper was made at the wakes, in July, 1838, by a few young men residing in the town, who made a bower of small dimensions over the Mill Lane Well on the road leading to the Park.   Inside the bower was a design made of flowers, moss, etc., something after the style of the Tissington well-dressings.   The following year the Manor Well, the Victoria Well, and the Green Well were all dressed, with much rivalry among their respective artists.   The custom has been since occasionally continued.

BELPER.

Our Lady's Well.

Of all Belper wells, the well *par excellence* is " The Lady Well," or " Our Lady's Well."   Was the Lady Well famous in days gone by for saintly and medicinal properties ?   If so, its fame still lingers, unconsciously perhaps, in the minds of the people, for they still make journeys of a mile or two, carrying with them a glass or a mug, to drink its waters. From Duffield, and other places round about, people used to come, years ago, in parties to the Lady Well, bringing not only vessels from which to drink the water, but "noggins" in which to carry back a supply for home drinking. Afflicted persons have been seen bathing their limbs in the cold running water, and heard to say they were benefited by repeated applications. All this must be the remains of some old superstition connected with Our Lady's Well.

Belper children used to carry—at any time when they thought fit, and could get permission from their mothers—a mug or porringer, and a paper containing oatmeal and sugar, to the Lady Well, and there drink the mixture of meal, sugar, and water. This was the chief item of the afternoon's outing. (See similar custom at Tideswell.) Perhaps the only custom now associated with the Lady Well is the annual gathering round the well on Whit Monday of Sunday-school scholars. A local poet, Mr. Thomas Crofts, has often sung the praises of this well in the Derbyshire newspapers.

Paddle Well.

In the old cotton mill yard was a well called the "Paddle Well." It is believed to be the only well in Derbyshire from which water used to be raised paddle-wheel fashion, hence its name. It was done away with in consequence of a suicide, or an attempt at suicide, by a woman who had quarrelled with her husband.

Jacob's Well.

It is situated on the north side of the coppice ground, and was, the last time I saw it, in a sorry condition, stony, weedy, and half filled up. Yet once upon a time its water was of good repute.

CHAPEL-EN-LE-FRITH, MERMAID'S POOL, MILL HILL.

On Easter Eve, at twelve o'clock, when Easter Day is coming in, if you look steadfastly into the pool, you will see a mermaid.

DALE ABBEY : HOLY WELL.

A hermit once going through Deep Dale being very thirsty, and for a time not able to find any water, at last came upon a stream, which he followed up to the place where it rose ; here he dug a well, returned thanks to the Almighty, and blessed it, saying it should be holy for evermore, and be a cure for all ills.   Another version is that the famous Hermit of Deep Dale, who lived in the Hermitage which is close by the well, discovered this spring and dug the well, which never dries up, nor does the water diminish in quantity, however dry the season, and blessed it. Many marvellous cures are still ascribed to its waters.   It is also used as a wishing well.   The *modus operandi* is to go on Good Friday, between twelve and three o'clock, drink the water three times, and wish.

Another Version.

There was a baker in Derby, in the street which is called after the name of St. Mary.   At that period the church of the Blessed Virgin at Derby was at the head of a large parish, and had under its authority a church *de onere* and a chapel.   And this baker, otherwise called Cornelius, was a religious man, fearing God, and, moreover, so wholly occupied in good works and the bestowing of alms, that whatsoever remained to him on every seventh day beyond what had been required for the food and clothing of himself and his, and the needful things of his house, he would on the Sabbath day take to the church of St. Mary, and give to the poor for the love of God, and of the Holy Virgin.

It happened on a certain day in autumn, when he had resigned himself to repose at the hour of noon, the Blessed Virgin appeared to him in his sleep, saying, "Acceptable in the eyes of my Son and of me are the alms thou hast bestowed.   But now, if thou art willing to be made perfect, leave all that thou hast, and go to Depedale, where thou shalt serve my Son and me in solitude; and when thou shalt happily have terminated thy course thou shalt inherit the kingdom of love, joy, and eternal bliss which God has prepared for them who love Him."

The man, awakening, perceived the divine goodness which had been done for his sake; and, giving thanks to God and the Blessed Virgin, his encourager, he straightway went forth without speaking a word to anyone.

Having turned his steps towards the east, it befel him, as he was passing through the middle of the village of Stanley, he heard a woman say to a girl, "Take our calves with you, drive them as far as Depedale, and make haste back."

Having heard this, the man, admiring the favour of God, and

believing that this word had been spoken in grace, as it were, to him, was astonished, and approached near, and said, "Good woman, tell me, where is Depedale?" She replied, "Go with this maiden, and she, if you desire it, will show you the place."

When he arrived there, he found that the place was marshy, and of fearful aspect, far distant from any habitation of man. Then directing his steps to the south-east of the place, he cut for himself, in the side of the mountain, in the rock, a very small dwelling, and an altar towards the south, which hath been preserved to this day; and there he served God, day and night, in hunger and thirst, in cold and in meditation.

And it came to pass that the old designing enemy of mankind, beholding this disciple of Christ flourishing with the different flowers of the virtues, began to envy him, as he envies other holy men, sending frequently amidst his cogitations the vanities of the world, the bitterness of his existence, the solitariness of his situation, and the various troubles of the desert. But the aforesaid man of God, conscious of the venom of the crooked serpent, did, by continual prayer, repeated fastings, and holy meditations, cast forth, through the grace of God, all his temptations. Whereupon the enemy rose upon him in all his might, both secretly and openly waging with him a visible conflict. And while the assaults of his foe became day by day more grievous, he had to sustain a very great want of water. Wandering about the neighbouring places, he discovered a spring in a valley not far from his dwelling, towards the west, and near unto it he made for himself a cottage, and built an oratory in honour of God and the Blessed Virgin. There, wearing away the sufferings of his life, laudably, in the service of God, he departed happily to God, from out of the prison-house of the body. (*Chronicle of Thomas de Musca,* quoted by Glover in *History of Derbyshire,* ii. 340·41.)

DERBY.

Well of St. Alkmund's.

St. Alkmund, a Northumbrian prince, was treacherously slain by the Danes in 819, and buried at Lilleshall, Salop. But soon afterwards, through fear of the Danes, his remains were hastily removed and translated to Derby, where he was honoured on March·19 (the day of his translation) as patron saint of the town, a church being built over the shrine. Situated close by the side

BECKET'S WELL, DERBY, SHOWING PRESENT MASONRY.

of one of the most important roads in the kingdom, the fame of
St. Alkmund's shrine appears to have been vividly retained long
after the Reformation. As late as 1760 north countrymen were in
the habit of inquiring for the tomb, and rested their packs upon
it. A well, a short distance to the north of the church of St.
Alkmund's, is still known by the name of "St. Alkmund's Well."
The ancient custom of dressing this well with flowers was revived
in 1870, and is now annually observed, the clergy and choir of
St. Alkmund's meeting at the church and walking there in procession. The street leading down to St. Mary's Bridge, past
St. Alkmund's, formed, until quite a recent date, the northern
boundary of the town. The well is beyond this—outside the
walls of the old borough. It is said that when the pious company
bearing the relics of St. Alkmund reached the outskirts of the
town, they laid down their precious burden by the side of this
well, whilst they treated with the townspeople for their safe admission within the walls. From that time the waters of the well were
blessed with special curative powers, and the well itself has been
ever since known by the name of St. Alkmund. Long after the
Reformation, a belief in the special virtues of this water lingered
in the minds of even well-educated people, a belief not altogether
exploded at the present day. Mr. Cantrell, writing in 1760, records
how the late Vicar of St. Werburgh's (Rev. William Lockett), being
in a low consumption, constantly drank water of St. Alkmund's
well, and recovered his health.

The well (*fons*) of St. Alkmund is mentioned in a fourteenth-
century charter, between the Abbey of Darley and the Hospital of
St. Helen, wherein it is described as lying between the well of St.
Helen and a meadow pertaining to one William Greene. These
particulars are taken from the fourth volume of Cox's *Churches of
Derbyshire*.

St. Thomas à Becket's Well.

Another well in Derby of mediæval repute bore the name of
the murdered archbishop. There was a chapel over it, or close
by its side. The foundations of the walls are marked H H on the
plan, p. 58. In 1652, a small building was again erected over it.
The water is still much valued, and the small building was restored
by Mr. Keys in 1889. An exhaustive illustrated article on this
well, from the pen and pencil of Mr. G. Bailey, appears in the
just-issued twelfth volume of the Journal of the *Derbyshire Archæological Society*.

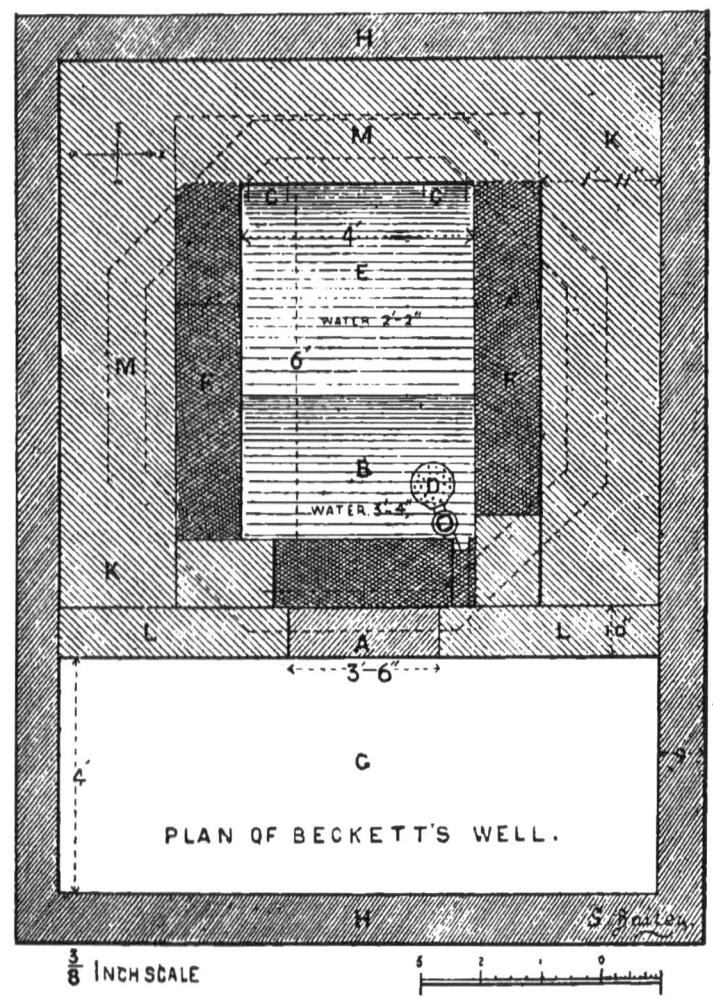

PLAN OF BECKETT'S WELL.

⅜ INCH SCALE

Other Wells in Derby.

Other old "wells" of sacred association in Derby were St. Helen's, near the modern Grammar School ; the Pilgrim's Well, Normanton Road, now destroyed ; the Virgin's, Abbey Street ; and St. Peter's, near the church of that name, now filled up

KEDLESTON AND QUARNDON.

In the *Diary of a Journey to Glastonbury Thorn*, written in 1765, and printed in vol. xv. of the *Reliquary*, occurs the following :

"Sunday, the 19th day of November. I called at Higham Hills, at Richard Lee's, and there I am told of a well near Duffield, where it is said that the cripples are cured, and some have left their crutches."

This may have been either Kedleston or Quarndon mineral springs.

The mineral wells of Quarne and Kedleston seem to have been the oldest used in the county next to Buxton. In Philip Kinder's MS. *Historie of Darbyshire*, written in 1663, is the following :

" At Keddleston and at Quarne a vitrioll could spring, which is good against vomitting, comforts ye stomach, cures ye ulcers of ye bladder, stopps all fluxes, helps conception, stays bleeding in the breast and at ye srige. The Iron mixt with both is good for ye Splen and Urines, is good against ye Colick, and ache in Joynts, cures tertian and quartan feavers and y^e stone, and all these more effectually than y^e Tincture of Lilium, or y^e Milke of Pearle."

KING'S NEWTON.

The well here is of some antiquity; an illustration of it is appended.

KING'S NEWTON.

ILKESTON.

Some few years ago a body was drowned in the canal near Ilkeston ; the means taken to discover it was as follows : A penny

loaf of bread was procured, the inside scooped out, and the
vacuum filled with quicksilver ; the loaf was then put into the
water, and allowed to float down with the current, the superstition
being that, when it came to the spot where the body lay, it would
stop.   (See *Notes and Queries* for similar cases elsewhere.)

MILFORD : RIVER SUPERSTITION.

A painfully grotesque scene was witnessed on the river Derwent,
at Milford, Derbyshire, on July 22, 1882.   The river having been
unsuccessfully dragged several days for the body of a young
woman named Webster, who was drowned, a drum was loudly
beaten for several hours on the river.   It is a superstitious belief
that, when a drum is so beaten, it will cease to emit any sound
when the boat containing it passes over the place where the
drowned person lies.

NORTH LEES : TRINITY WELL.

A little to the south-west of the ruined chapel of the Holy
Trinity at North Lees, in the parish of Hathenage, is a good clear
spring called Trinity Well, sheltered by four slabs of gritstone, one
as the bed, two as upright stones, and the fourth as a covering.
Close by the well is a flat stone, on which are rudely sculptured a
small cross, and the letters T. S.   This chapel was built by the
Italian Mission in the time of James II., and destroyed by a
protesting mob when William III. came to the throne.

STONY MIDDLETON : ST. MARTIN'S WELL.

The Romans had a bath here in connection with the mineral
waters.   In early mediæval days a well-chapel was erected and
dedicated to St. Martin.   The legend says that a Derbyshire
Crusader of the name of Martin was here healed of his leprosy,
and that in gratitude he built a chapel in honour of his patron
saint.   It is supposed that the present church stands on the site
of the old well-chapel.

TIDESWELL : DROPPING WELL.

Sugar-cupping is another ancient custom which survives here.
On Easter Day young people and children go to the Dropping
Well, near Tideswell, with a cup in one pocket and a quarter of a
pound of sugar [? honey] in the other, and having caught in their

cups as much water as they wished from the droppings of the Tor-spring, they dissolved the sugar in it.—Glover, *History of Derbyshire*, 8vo., vol. i. 307.

OTHER DERBYSHIRE WELLS.

Rev. Dr. Cox enumerates the following old wells in the county, dedicated to saints, in addition to those already given : St. Osyth, Sandiacre ; St. Thomas à Becket, Linbury ; St. Thomas and St. Anne, Repton ; the Mary Well, "Capersuck," Allestree ; and St. Cuthbert's, Dovebridge.

DEVONSHIRE.

MORWENSTOWE : ST. MOORIN'S WELL.

THE following curious tradition has been preserved among some valuable MSS. belonging to the Coffins, of Porteldge. They were collected by an antiquary of that family above 250 years since. "Moorwinstow, its name, is from St. Moorin. The tradition is, that when the parishioners were about to build their church this saint went down under the cliff and chose a stone for the font, which she brought up upon her head. In her way, being weary, she lay down the stone and rested herself, out of which place sprang a well, from thence called St. Moorin's Well. Then she took up the stone and carried it to the place where now the church standeth. The parishioners had begun their church in another place, and there did convey this stone, but what was built by day was pulled down by night, and the materials carried to this place ; whereupon they forbare, and built it in the place they were directed to by a wonder."

MORWENSTOWE : WELL OF ST. JOHN-IN-THE-WILDERNESS.

The following is recorded in the endowment deed, dated 1296, regarding this well on the eastern boundary of Morwenstow Glebe. It is preserved in Bishop Brantingham's Register : "The church land is said to extend eastward *ad quendum fontem Johannis.* Water wherewithal to fill the font for baptism is always drawn from this well by the sacristan, in pitchers set apart for this purpose. It stands midway down the cliff on the present glebe : around it on either hand are rugged and sea-worn rocks, before it

ST. JOHN'S WELL ON MORWENSTOW GLEBE.

the wide sea." This hallowed spot has been made by Mr. Hawker the subject of the following lines :

> Here dwelt in times long past, so legends tell,
> Holy Morwenna, guardian of this well ;
> Here on the foreheads of our fathers pour'd
> From this lone spring the laver of the Lord !
> If, traveller, thy happy spirit know
> That awful font whence living waters flow,
> Then hither come to draw—thy feet have found
> Amid these rocks a place of holy ground !
> Then sigh one blessing ! breathe a voice of praise
> O'er the fond labour of departed days !
> Tell the glad waters of their former fame,
> And teach the joyful winds Morwenna's name.

PLYMOUTH.

The source of the Plymouth leat is visited annually by the Mayor and Corporation, who there drink in water "to the pious memory of Sir Francis Drake," and then in wine, "May the descendants of him who brought us water never want wine." The legend runs that the inhabitants, or rather laundresses, being much inconvenienced from want of water, Sir Francis Drake called for his horse, and riding into Dartmoor, searched about until he had found a very fine spring, when he bewitched it with magical words, and, starting away at a gallop, the stream followed his horse's heels into the town.

CRANMERE POOL.

Cranmere Pool is believed to be a place of punishment for unhappy spirits, who are frequently to be heard wailing in the morasses which surround it.

FITZ'S WELL, NEAR PRINCE TOWN.

John Fitz, of Fitzford, near Tavistock, who was one day riding with his wife, lost his way on the moor. After wandering in vain to find the right path, being thirsty and fatigued, he at last found a delicious spring of water, whose powers seemed to be miraculous, for no sooner had he partaken thereof than he was enabled to trace his steps correctly homewards. It is still believed to possess many healing virtues. In gratitude John Fitz erected the memorial-stone marked I. F., 1568, which, with a few other slabs of granite, protects it, for the advantage of all *pixy-led* travellers. It is about 3 feet deep, and lies in a swamp near the remains of an ancient bridge, or *clam*, the bridge being partly swept away by a flood in 1873.

CHIPPING TAWTON : PROPHETIC SPRING.

There is a pool here, usually dry in summer, but before the death of a royal personage, or any great accident, is said—even in the driest season—to become full of water, and so continue till the event thus foretold is fulfilled.

CLACYWELL OR CLASENWELL POOL.

This pool is believed to be bottomless ; it, however, really fills the shaft of an early mine.

NORTH MOLTON : HOLY WELL REVEL.

At daybreak on Ascension morning (1882), two men, and a woman carrying a child, were seen hurrying towards the celebrated well at North Molton, each trying to outrun the others, so as to be the first to bathe, and to be cured of some ailment. Later in the day merry groups of children and picnic parties enlivened the glen in which the well is situated. An old chapel, with a cemetery attached, is said to have formerly occupied the ground surrounding the far-famed spring. Every year pilgrims full of faith in the miraculous power of the water visit the spot for bathing, and jars of the water are carried by some of them to their homes ; indeed, believers prize this water, which they carry back with them, as much as ever did any pilgrims of old value the leaden bottle of liquid obtained from Beckett's tomb at Canterbury.—*Folk-lore Record*, v., 160.

The *North Devonshire Herald*, May 25, 1884, records a pilgrimage having just been made to the well on the morning of Ascension Day.

DEAN COMBE : THE POOL OF THE BLACK HOUND.

In the parish of Dean Combe is a narrow wooded valley, watered by a streamlet, that in two or three places falls into cascades of considerable beauty. At the foot of one of these is a deep hollow called the Hound's Pool. Its story is as follows : There once lived in this hamlet a weaver of great fame and skill. After long prosperity he died, and was buried. But the next day he appeared sitting at the loom in his chamber, working diligently as when he was alive. His sons applied to the parson, who went accordingly to the foot of the stairs, and heard the noise of the weaver's shuttle above. " Knowles !" he said, " come down ; this is no place for thee." "I will," said the weaver, "as soon as I have worked out my quill " (the quill is the shuttle full of wool). " Nay," said the Vicar, "thou hast been long enough at thy work ; come down at once !" So when the spirit came down, the Vicar took a handful of earth from the churchyard and threw it in his face. And in a moment it became a black hound. " Follow me," said the Vicar, and it followed him to the gate of the wood. And when they got there, it seemed as if all the trees in the wood were " coming to-gether," so great was the wind. Then the Vicar took a nutshell with a hole in it, and led the hound to the pool below the water-fall. " Take this shell," he said, " and when thou shalt have dipped out the pool with it, thou mayest rest, not before." And at mid-day or at midnight the hound may still be seen at its work. —*Notes and Queries*, 1 S., ii. 515.

EXETER : ST. ANNE'S WELL.

St. Anne's Well was formerly known as Lion's Holt Well ; it anciently supplied the city with water. Its history is of consider-able antiquity.

On the spot where St. Sidwella is reputed to have been martyred is the well dedicated in her honour ; it is situated on the left-hand of the Exeter side of the tunnel leaving the city, at a place called Lion's Holt.

St. Sidwella, virgin martyr 740, was buried near St. Sidwell's Church, Exeter. William of Worcester speaks of her thus : "Sancta Satwola virgo canonizata ultra portam orientalem." She is commemorated on December 18.

A fine spring near the church supplied the ancient well bearing her name, by which, tradition has it, she lived the life of a recluse.

In the east window of Exeter Cathedral she is represented with a scythe in her hand, and a well behind her, probably but a rebus on her name Sithewella ; she also figures on one of the columns in the cathedral, carrying her head in her hands (*Cal. Ang. Ch*, 287).

Bishop Grandison, in his *Legenda Sanctorum*, states that St. Sidwella was the eldest of four devout sisters, daughters of Benna, a noble Briton residing in Exeter. On his death, her cruel and covetous stepmother, envious of the fortune of St. Sidwella, who inherited considerable property in the eastern suburbs of the city, engaged one of her servants, a reaper or mower, to become her assassin, which he did, whilst she was occupied in her devotions, near the well in Hedewell Mede, at a little distance from the parish church which still bears her name.

The locality of the spring agrees very well with this, as it is situated in what is now called Well Lane. Some time hence people may wonder why this street is so called, as the well is not now to be seen ; it has been destroyed, and the site is occupied by a house which has been built over it. The well, however, is distinctly marked on Rogers' map of Exeter, dated 1744, as " Sidwell's Well."—*Trans. and Reports Dev. Ass.*, xii. 449.

One and a half miles north of Dartmoor Prison is the above well, protected by rude slabs of granite, bearing the initials I. F., and date 1568. It is said to possess many healing virtues, and to have been first brought into notice by John Fitz, of Fitzford, near Tavistock, who accidentally discovered it when, riding with his wife, he had lost his way on the moor. The legend runs that,

"After wandering in the vain effort to find the right path, they felt so fatigued and thirsty that it was with extreme delight they discovered a spring of water, whose powers seemed to be miraculous ; for no sooner had they satisfied their thirst than they were enabled to find their way through the moor towards home without the least difficulty. In gratitude for this deliverance, and the benefit they had received from the water, John Fitz caused a stone memorial to be placed over the spring, for the advantage of all *pixy-led* travellers." It is about 3 feet deep, and lies in a swamp at a short distance from the remains of an *ancient bridge*, or *clam*, on the Blackabrook. The bridge was swept away by a flood " (1873). —*Murray's Guide*, 207.

NORTH TAWTON.

In the parish is the barton of Bath, and famous for a pool which was usually dry in summer, but which " before the death of any great prince or other strange accident " would in the driest time become full of water, and so continue until the matter happened that it thus foretold : so says Westcote, writing about 1630. The pool is on the left of the road from Bowr to Okehampton.— *Ibid.*, 217.

BRAUNTON : ST. BRANOCK'S WELL.

"I forbear," says Leland (*Itin.*), "to speak of St. Branock's cow, his staff, his oak, his well, and his servant Abel, all of which are lively represented in a glass window of that church."—*Ibid.*, 256.

DORSETSHIRE.

UPWEY : WISHING WELL.

THERE is a spring or well at Upwey, a few miles from Weymouth ; it is a wishing well. There is always a person near with glasses from which to drink the waters, wish, and throw the remainder over the shoulder. It is really the source of the Wey, a fine spring of clear water coming out of the ground, and flows on until it becomes the river at Weymouth. There is a church a few yards higher up.—[George Bailey, Derby], *Antiquary*.

At the north side of the churchyard is a spring which bursts out
of the rock dedicated to St. Eustachius. It is locally called Stachy's
Well, or the Waterpond.—Hutchins' *History of Dorset*, iv. 361.

ABBOTSBURY : WISHING WELL.

On a certain day every year the young women of Abbotsbury
used to go up to the Norman chapel of St. Catharine, Melton
Abbey, where, after drinking the water of the Saint's well, they
made use of the following invocations :

> A husband, St. Catharine.
> A handsome one, St. Catharine.
> A rich one, St. Catharine.
> A nice one, St. Catharine.
> And soon, St. Catharine.

ELMORE.

It has been the custom in the tithing of Motcombe, time out of
mind, on the Sunday next after Holy Rood Day, in May every year,
for each parish within the borough of Shaston to come down
that day to Elmore, or Enmore Green, at one o'clock in the afternoon, with their minstrels, and play with games, and from one to
two o'clock—one whole hour—to dance. The Mayor of Shaston
was to see that the Queen's Bailiff had a penny loaf, a gallon of
ale, and a calf's head, with a pair of gloves ; to see the order of
the dance that day, and if the dance failed any day and the bailiff
had not his due, the bailiff and his men stopped the water from
the four wells at Elmore which supplied the borough.

A slightly different account of this is given in Dyer's *Brit. Pop.
Customs*, pp. 205-6.

CERNE : ST. AUGUSTINE'S WELL.

St. Augustine destroyed the idol Heil or Heile, or, according to
Leland, Helith, the Saxon Æsculapius, or preserver of health, who
was worshipped here at that time. This saint's company being
weary and thirsty, he stuck his staff in the ground, and fetched
out a crystal fountain, whence this place was called Cernel, from
Cerno and El.   Fuller thinks it should be Cerneswell, behold the
fountain, or Cerne Heal, *i.e.*, see the destruction of the idol.—

Author of *Flores Sanctorum in Life of St. Augustine* (pp. 515, 516);
Fuller's *Ch. Hist.* (pp. 66, 67); Dugdale (ii. 621).

WAREHAM: ST. EDWARD'S WELL.

This well, of miraculous virtue, is said to have sprung up on
the spot where St. Edward the Martyr, King of England, died 979.

DURHAM.

LAMBTON: WORM WELL.

THE park and manor-house of Lambton, belonging to a
family of the same name, lie on the banks of the Wear,
to the north of Lumley. The family is a very ancient
one, much older, it is believed, than the twelfth century, to which
date its pedigree extends. The old castle was dismantled in 1797,
when a site was adopted for the present mansion on the north
bank of the swiftly-flowing Wear, in a situation of exceeding
beauty. The park also contains the ruin of a chapel, called
Brugeford, or Bridge-ford, close to one of the bridges which span
the Wear.

Long, long ago—some say about the fourteenth century—the
young heir of Lambton led a careless and profane life, regardless
alike of his duties to God and man, and in particular neglecting
to attend Mass, that he might spend his Sunday mornings in fishing. One Sunday, while thus engaged, having cast his line into
the Wear many times without success, he vented his disappoint-
ment in curses loud and deep, to the great scandal of the servants
and tenantry as they passed by to the Chapel at Brugeford.

Soon afterwards he felt something tugging at his line, and,
trusting he had at last secured a fine fish, he exerted all his skill
and strength to bring his prey to land. But what were his horror
and dismay on finding that, instead of a fish, he had only caught
a worm of most unsightly appearance ! He hastily tore the thing
from his hook, and flung it into a well close by, which is still
known by the name of the Worm Well.

The young heir had scarcely thrown his line again into the
stream when a stranger, of venerable appearance, passing by,

asked him what sport he had met with, to which he replied,
" Why, truly, I think I have caught the devil himself. Look in,
and judge." The stranger looked, and remarked that he had
never seen the like of it before ; that it resembled an eft, only it
had nine holes on each side of its mouth ; and, finally, that he
thought it boded no good.

The worm remained unheeded in the well, till it outgrew so
confined a dwelling-place. It then emerged, and betook itself by
day to the river, where it lay coiled round a rock in the middle of
the stream, and by night to a neighbouring hill, round whose base
it would twine itself ; while it continued to grow so fast that it
soon could encircle the hill three times. This eminence is still
called the Worm Hill. It is oval in shape, on the north side of
the Wear, and about a mile and a half from old Lambton Hall.

The monster now became the terror of the whole country side.
It sucked the cows' milk, worried the cattle, devoured the lambs,
and committed every sort of depredation on the helpless peasantry.
Having laid waste the district on the north side of the river, it
crossed the stream and approached Lambton Hall, where the old
lord was living, alone and desolate. His son had repented of his
evil life, and had gone to the wars in a distant country. Some
authorities tell us he had embarked as a crusader for the Holy
Land.

On hearing of their enemy's approach, the terrified household
assembled in a council. Much was said, but to little purport, till
the steward, a man of age and experience, advised that the large
trough which stood in the courtyard should immediately be filled
with milk. This was done without delay ; the monster approached,
drank the milk, and, without doing further harm, returned across
the Wear to wrap his giant form around his favourite hill. The
next day he was seen recrossing the river ; the trough was hastily
filled again, and with the same results. It was found that the
milk of "nine kye" was needed to fill the trough ; and if this
quantity was not placed there every day regularly, and in full
measure, the worm would break out into a violent rage, lashing its
tail round the trees in the park, and tearing them up by the roots.

After seven long years, however, the heir of Lambton returned
home, a sadder and a wiser man—returned to find the broad
lands of his ancestors waste and desolate, his people oppressed,
and well-nigh exterminated, his father sinking into the grave, over-

whelmed with care and anxiety. He took no rest, we are told, till he had crossed the river and surveyed the worm as it lay coiled round the foot of the hill; then, hearing how its former opponents had failed, he took counsel in the matter from a sibyl, or wise woman.

At first the sibyl did nothing but upbraid him for having brought this scourge upon his house and neighbourhood; but when she perceived that he was indeed penitent, and desirous, at any cost, to remove the evil he had caused, she gave him her advice and instructions. He was to get his best suit of mail studded thickly with spear-heads, to put it on, and thus armed, to take his stand on the rock in the middle of the river, there to meet his enemy, trusting the issue to Providence and his good sword. But she charged him, before going to the encounter, to take a vow that, if successful, he would slay the first living thing that met him on his way homewards. Should he fail to fulfil this vow, she warned him that for nine generations no lord of Lambton would die in his bed.

The heir, now a belted knight, made the vow in Brugeford Chapel; he studded his armour with the sharpest spear-heads, and, unsheathing his trusty sword, took his stand on the rock in the middle of the Wear. At the accustomed hour the worm uncoiled its "snaky twine," and wound its way towards the hall, crossing the river close by the rock on which the knight was standing eager for the combat. He struck a violent blow upon the monster's head as it passed, on which, the creature, "irritated and vexed," though apparently not injured, flung its tail round him, as if to strangle him in its coils.

In the words of a local poet:

> The worm shot down the middle stream
>   Like a flash of living light,
> And the waters kindled round his path
>   In rainbow colours bright.
>
> But when he saw the armed knight
>   He gathered all his pride,
> And, coiled in many a radiant spire,
>   Rode buoyant o'er the tide.
>
> When he darted at length his dragon strength
>   An earthquake shook the rock,
> And the fire-flakes bright fell round the knight
>   As unmoved he met the shock.

Though his heart was stout it quailed, no doubt ;
His very life-blood ran cold
As round and round the wild worm wound
In many a grappling fold.

Now was seen the value of the sibyl's advice. The closer the worm wrapped him in its folds, the more deadly were its self-inflicted wounds, till at last the river ran crimson with its gore. Its strength thus diminished, the knight was able at last with his good sword to cut the serpent in two ; the severed part was immediately borne away by the swiftness of the current, and the worm, unable to reunite itself, was utterly destroyed.

During this long and desperate conflict, the household of Lambton had shut themselves within doors to pray for their young lord, he having promised that, when it was over, he would, if conqueror, blow a blast on his bugle. This would assure his father of his safety, and warn them to let loose the favourite hound, which they had destined as the sacrifice on the occasion, according to the sibyl's requirements and the young lord's vow. When, however, the bugle notes were heard within the halls, the old man forgot everything but his son's safety, and, rushing out of doors, ran to meet the hero and embrace him. The heir of Lambton was thunderstruck. What could he do ? It was impossible to lift his hand against his father ; yet how else to fulfil his vow. In his perplexity he blew another blast ; the hound was let loose, it bounded to its master ; the sword, yet reeking with the monster's gore, was plunged into its heart ; but all in vain. The vow was broken, the sibyl's prediction fulfilled, and the curse lay upon the house of Lambton for nine generations.—*Bishoprick Garland.*

Worm Well is a wishing well, wherein pins are dropped as offerings.

DARLINGTON : HELL-KETTLES.

The above is the name of three deep pits at Oxen-le-Hall, in the parish of Darlington. Many fabulous traditionary tales are told of them. It is said that they are bottomless ; that the water is hot in consequence of reverberation ; that geese and ducks thrown therein have discovered subterraneous passages to the river Tees, etc. Harrison (1577) calls them "three little poles, w'ch the people call the Kettles of Hell, or ye Devil's Kettles, as if he should seethe soules of sinfull men and women in them ;

they adde also that ye spirits have oft beene harde to cry and yell about them."

Many centuries ago the owner, or occupier, of the fields where the Hell-Kettles are situate, was going to lead his hay on the *feast day* of St. Barnabas (June 11), and being remonstrated with on the impiety of the act by some more pious neighbour, he used the rhymes :

> Barnaby yea ! Barnaby nay !
> A cartload of hay, whether God will or nay,

when instantly he, his carts and horses, were all swallowed up in the pools ; where they may still be seen, on a fine day and clear water, many fathoms deep.—*Denham Tracts.*

PIERSE BRIDGE : PEG POWLER.

The spirit, nymph or demon who inhabits the river Tees is known as Peg Powler. Wonderful stories are told at Piersebridge, of her dragging naughty children into its deep waters when playing, despite the orders and threats of their parents, on its banks, especially on Sunday.—*Ibid.*

JARROW : BEDE'S WELL.

About a mile to the west of Jarrow, near Newcastle-on-Tyne, there is a well called Bede's Well, to which, as late as the year 1740, it was a prevailing custom to bring children troubled with any disease or infirmity ; a crooked pin was put in, and the well laved dry (*sic*) between each dipping. My informant has seen twenty children brought on a Sunday to be dipped in this well, at which also, on Midsummer Eve, there was a great resort of neighbouring people, with bonfires, music, etc.—Brand's *H. of Newcastle*, ii., 54.

ESSEX.

FOUNTAIN OF ST. OSYTH.

S T. OSITHA was the daughter of Redoald or Frewald, the first Christian King of the East Angles, by Wilburga, daughter of Penda, King of the Mercians. She was born at Marendon, in the county of Bucks, and, according to the legend, took a vow of perpetual virginity at an early age. She was

compelled, however, to marry Sighere, the Christian King of the
East Saxons. The marriage was not consummated, for in her husband's absence she assumed the veil, and afterwards obtained his
consent to the fulfilment of her vow. Sighere gave her the village
of Cise or Chich, in the Tendring Hundred of Essex, ten miles
south-east from Colchester, and sixty-one from London ; now called
St. Osyth, or, according to the natives, Toosy. Here she founded
a church of St. Peter and St. Paul, and instituted a nunnery, supposed to be the most ancient monastic establishment in England.
She was beheaded by the Danes, and the legend runs that at the
place of her martyrdom a fountain sprang up, which continues to
this day as a sovereign remedy for many diseases ; her head was cut
off ; the body rose, and taking the head in her hand walked—guided
by angels—to the church. Here it knocked at the door, and then
fell to the ground. The stream was afterwards collected by the
monks in a long pipe. "But a few years ago," says Mr. Watson
(*Tendring Hundred in the Olden Time*), "a modern goth, wanting
ballast for his yacht, tore up and utilised the leaden pipes, and
thus destroyed the pride of ages."—*Communicated.*

St. Osyth was commemorated October 7.

Another account is as follows :

ST. OSYTH'S GHOST.

If what honest Capgrave tells of St. Osyth be correct, it is
scarcely wonderful that her restless spirit should "walk" at certain
approved times of the year. She seems to have met with nought
but ill-luck from her infancy. When a child she was sent with a
book by St. Edith to St. Modwen, at Pollesworth, in Warwickshire,
but on her way fell into a river and was drowned, but restored to
life after three days at the intercession of the latter. Against her
will she was betrothed to Sibere, prince of the East Saxons, but
giving him the slip, she took the veil, and then prevailed upon
her disappointed lover to give her the land whereon to build a
nunnery. Here she reigned as Abbess, till in A.D. 653 some
roving Danes landed on the coast of Essex, destroyed the convent, and cut off St. Osyth's head. Had her old friend St. Modwen
been at hand, or that St. Beuno who successfully repaired St. Winifred after a similar calamity, she might yet have defied her fate ;
but they were not, and, left to her own resources, she picked up
her head, and, carrying it in her hands, made off to the nearest

church.   She reached the sacred portal, struck the door with her blood-stained sconce, and, fairly overcome, fell prostrate, and so expired.   Where she received the fatal blow a fountain gushed forth, famed in after days as St. Osyth's well, and blessed by many a sufferer who found there a medicine for his ills.   Her body, removed to Aylesbury and there buried, was miraculously brought back to the church to which she made her last and certainly most remarkable journey, and till very lately there was a legend that the murdered abbess, head in hand, visited again well, and wood, and church, scaring the traveller who was so unfortunate as to be belated in Nun's Wood.   Scoffers have said that the sign of the " Good Woman " at Widford owes its origin to the legend of the headless Saint, but this is too deep a subject to be discussed here. —*East Anglian Handbook*, 1885, p. 69.

GLOUCESTERSHIRE.

WINCHCOMBE : ST. KENELM'S WELL.

W HILE the body of St. Kenelm was being brought to Winchcombe, the bearers, becoming very weary and thirsty, were obliged to stop and rest on a high down on the east side of the town.   There being no water, they prayed to the Almighty, who heard their request, and answered by causing a well or spring to rise on the spot, near which was built St. Kenelm's Chapel.

CONDICOTE : FLOWING WELL.

There is a beautiful old well flowing from under a wayside cross here, close to the church.   The cross and well were restored by the late rector, Rev. H. Van Notten Pole.

EYEFORD : MILTON'S WELL.

The following charming embodiment of the local tradition and description of the well and its situation is still to be seen, inscribed in 1866 on the wall near the well, which is covered in by a dome above.   The punctuation and spelling are copied exactly.

Milton's Well.

Tis said amidst these lovely glades
These crystal streams these sylvan shades
Where feathered songsters on their wing
In heavenly chorus join and sing
That Milton penned immortal lays
On Paradise and Heaven's praise.
Each object here that greets the eye
Raises the Poets thoughts on high
No earthly things their cares intrude
On lovely Ey ford's solitude
But beauteous Nature reigns supreme
And Paradise is all his theme.

W. H. C. PLOWDEN, ESQ.

The above lines were written by a friend
for Mrs. Somerset D'Arcy Irvine.
Who Restored and Embelished [*sic*]
this Ancient Well in the year 1866
Beside this spring Milton wrote *Paradise Lost.*
A. R. Shilleto : *Notes and Queries,* 7th S., ii. 246.

LANTONY : "OUR LADY'S WORKHOUSE."

Near Lantony Abbey is an old conduit which used to be styled
Our Lady's Workhouse. Its waters were reputed to be medicinal ;
on the east side is a carving showing the Virgin addressed by
kneeling figures. The edifice is about 6½ feet square ; many who
washed in the waters were relieved of their infirmities.

WANSWELL : WODEN OR HOLY WELL.

Smyth, the learned historian of the great house of Berkeley,
tells us that at Wanswell, a fount, in his days called Holy Well,
had anciently been named Woden or Woden's Well. This spring,
we imagine, could be easily identified, for Smyth proceeds to tell
his readers that "this faire springe havinge in its course watered
the meadowe grounds belowe it, compasseth well nigh three-fourth
parts of Berkeley Towne and Castle, and that done falls into
Berkeley haven, where its freshnes turneth salt."—*Berkeley
Manuscripts,* vol. iii., p. 372.

BONCHURCH: ST. BONIFACE'S WELL.

I N ancient days, when sailors passed within sight of the island near this place, it was customary for them to lower the topmast in reverence to St. Boniface. The wishing well is near the summit of St. Boniface, interesting to the geologist from the unusual elevation at which it bursts forth, and to the lover of old superstitions from the reverence formerly paid to it, on account of a popular belief that, if one walked backward to the spring, any wish formed while drinking of its waters would be granted. As late as last century it was customary for the youth of both sexes to assemble at the well on St. Boniface's Day and decorate it with chaplets of flowers, and many good "wishes" were interchanged at these annual gatherings. An account of this well is given in Tomkins' *History of the Isle of Wight*, vol. ii., p. 121.

SOBERTON: ST. CLARE'S WELL.

On the mainland, to the south, is a pool or well called St. Clare's Well.

STEEP: ST. MARY'S WELL.

Near here, in St. Mary's Well Hanger, is St. Mary's Well, 172 feet above the sea.

WATERSWELL: WATER CROSS WELL.

About half a mile south of Tangley, on the north-west border of Hampshire, is the hamlet of Waterswell Cross, a name probably derived from a cross in ancient days placed over a well in a dry chalk country.

ST. LAWRENCE'S WELL.

Another ancient holy well in the Isle of Wight was St. Lawrence's Well. Henry Brinsley Sheridan wrote a poem on "A Legend of St. Lawrence's Well." It is now cleared away.

ALTON: THE HOLYBOURNE.

The Holybourne is supplied by a spring from the chalk near the upper green sand outcrop. The spring has an elevation of about 350 feet, and is close to the churchyard. Formerly the water issued from its natural spring almost opposite the west door of the church, and about 20 yards from it; but when the churchyard was enlarged, the spring-head and stream were culverted for about 30 or 40 yards to the pond. What its ancient sanctity was derived from, it is, perhaps, now difficult to say.—*Hampshire Field Club*, ii., pt. i., p. 51.

SHEET : ST. MARY'S WELL.

There was a well dedicated in honour of St. Mary, at Sheet, near Petersfield.

HENSTING : JACOB'S WELL.

Near Hensting is a well surrounded with yew-trees, called Jacob's Well.—*Ibid.*, p. 44.

FRITHAM : LEPERS' OR IRON'S WELL.

The water from this spring is chalybeate, but by rapid oxidation its iron is deposited along the banks of the stream. The widespread prevalence of leprosy in Hampshire in ancient days is beyond dispute. The lepers' hospitals at Winchester, Southampton, Christchurch, and near Carisbrook, in the Isle of Wight, sufficiently prove this. That the lepers sought relief by ablutions in the ferruginous water of some of our Hampshire springs is probable, and this Lepers' Well is, according to tradition, one of these springs. From lepers to mangy dogs is a considerable change, but this change has occurred in the curative uses of the water at Iron's Well. We have no longer lepers, but we have dogs afflicted with the mange, a disease which causes the hair partly to fall off. Iron's Well, by common repute, is useful in curing these dogs. The spring has a little wooden structure over and round it, with a board wanting at the top, by which you may drop your dog into the chalybeate water; and a convenient arrangement exists by which, after he has finished his ablutions, he may scramble out on the other side.—*Ibid.*, p. 46.

BUCKLAND SPRING.

Near Buckland, north of Lymington, there was a small spring to the north of the great earthwork which was for generations held in great estimation for its reputative curative properties in ophthalmic disorders.—*Ibid.*, p. 47.

STANPIT : TUTTERS' WELL.

The well at Stanpit, near to Christchurch, known as Tutters' Well, was celebrated for the cure of sore eyes.

HEREFORDSHIRE.

MARDEN : ST. ETHELBERT'S WELL.

THERE is a well in the church of Marden, Herefordshire. It is near the west end of the nave, defended by circular stone-work, about ten inches in diameter, and enclosing a spring, supposed to arise from the spot in which the body of King Ethelbert was first interred, and is called St. Ethelbert's Well (*Notes and Queries*, 3 S., viii. 235).

PETERCHURCH : THE GOLDEN WELL.

Tradition has it that a fish was once caught in the river Dore, with a golden chain round its body, which was afterwards kept in the Golden Well, from whence the river rises.

Let into the south wall of the nave of the church is a sculptured stone painted, said to have been copied from an older one, representing a fish having a golden chain hanging from its mouth.

"The term 'Golden,' as applied to the valley in which Peterchurch is situate, and also, perhaps, to the well, is no doubt a Norman corruption of the British word *dwr* = water. The Golden or Gilden Vale of Camden and others, is the valley of the *Dwr*, or, as the stream is now often pronounced, Doyer, *i.e.*, water."— H. W. Phillott, Hereford.

HERTFORDSHIRE.

ST. ALBANS : ST. ALBAN'S WELL.

THE particulars of the life of St. Alban are but little known, except through the ecclesiastical history of the Venerable Bede, who, for want of better information, or from actual belief in the legends he had recourse to, and for which credence the general sentiments of the times must be pleaded for his weakness, has afforded the following miraculous statement of the Saint's martyrdom :

"Being yet a Pagan (or at least it not being known that he was a Christian), he entertained Amphibalus in his house, of which the Roman governor being informed, sent a party of soldiers to apprehend Amphibalus; but Alban, putting on the habit of his guest, presented himself in his stead, and was carried before the magistrate. The governor having asked him of what family he was, Alban replied: 'To what purpose do you inquire of my family? if you would know my religion, I am a Christian;' then being asked his name, he answered: 'My name is Alban, and I worship the only true and living God, who created all things.' The magistrate replied: 'If you would enjoy the happiness of eternal life, delay not to sacrifice to the great gods.' Alban replied: 'The sacrifices you offer are made to devils, neither can they help the needy, nor grant the petitions of their votaries.' This behaviour so enraged the governor, that he ordered him immediately to be beheaded. In his way to execution he was stopped by a river, over which was a bridge so thronged with spectators, that it was impossible to cross it; when the Saint, as we are told, lifting up his eyes to Heaven, the stream was miraculously divided, and afforded a passage for himself and a thousand more persons. This wonderful event converted the executioner on the spot, who threw away his drawn sword, and falling at St. Alban's feet, desired he might have the honour to die with him: and thus the execution being delayed until another person could be got to perform the office, St. Alban walked up to a neighbouring hill, where he prayed for water to quench his thirst, and a fountain of water sprang up under his feet. Here he was beheaded on June 23, A.D. 303. The executioner is said to have been a signal example of Divine vengeance; for as soon as he gave the fatal stroke, his eyes dropt out of his head!"—*Clavis Calendaria*, ii. 50.

HEXTON: ST. FAITH'S WELL.

There is a small parcel of ground adjoining the churchyard called "St. Faith's Wick Court," about a pole in measurement, anciently divided from Malewick by a ditch in the same place where now a large moat is made. The greatest part of this Wick lying upon a bed of springs, and undrained, was very boggy towards the churchyard; but the west side being higher, the ground was well planted with oaks, willows, and bushes, near adjoining unto which, writeth a narrow-minded Pharisee, "the crafty priests had made a well about a yard deep, and very clear at the bottom, and curbed about, which they called St. Faith's Well. Now over this well they built a house, and in the house they placed the image and statue of St. Faith, and a causy they had mad (which I found when I digged and levelled the ground) for the people to pass who resorted thither from far and near to visit our Lady, and to perform their devotions reverently, kissing a fine-coloured stone placed in her toe. This Lady was trimly apparelled, and I find in an old book of churchwarden's accounts, in the reign of Henry VIII., that they had delivered unto the St. Faith a cote and a velvet tippet. The Lady had no land to maintain her, that I know of, more than 1 acre lying in Mill Field, called at this day St. Faith's ½ acre, which, as being given to superstitious uses, came to the King's hands at the dissolution, and is now parcel of the demesnes. The house being pulled down, and the idol cast away, the well was filled up, yet an apparent mention of the place remained till my time, and St. Faith's Well continued as a waste and unprofitable and neglected piece of land till such time as the footpath was turned through the midst of it to the outside on the south by the highway, and their clearing and levelling the ground, having been drained, and sunk the spring, I converted the same, in the year of our Lord 1624, into a little orchard. The Lady Faith was a Virgin and Martyr of Agenne, in France, A.D. 1290." —MS. account of Hexton, by Francis Taverner. Her feast-day in the Calendar of Saints is October 6.

KENT.

HARBLEDOWN : LEPER'S WELL.

THERE is a Leper's Well here, in which Edward the Black Prince bathed for his leprosy.—G. L. Gomme, F.S.A.

KESTON NEAR HAYES : CÆSAR'S WELL.

This well, the source of the river Raven's Bourne, is so called, because when Cæsar's legions were marching along that way to London, being destitute of water, a huge raven settled down upon this well, which is said to possess healing properties.

KENT.   81

WITHERSDEN : ST. EUSTACE.

Called from Eustachius, Abbot of Flai, who is mentioned by
Matt. Paris (p. 169, an. 1200), to have been a man of learning and
sanctity, and to have come and preached at Wye, and to have
blessed a fountain there, so that afterwards its water was endowed
with such miraculous power, that by it all diseases were cured.—
Hasted's *Kent*, iii. 176.

LANGLEY : PROPHETIC SPRING.

Warksworth, in his *Chronicle* (pp. 23, 24), in recording the occurrence, in the 13th year of Edward IV., of a "gret hote somere,"
which caused much mortality and "unyversalle fevers, axes, and
the bloody flyx in dyverse places of Englonde," and also occasioned great dearth and famine "in the southe partyes of the
worlde," remarks that "dyverse tokenes have be schewede in
Englonde this year for amendynge of mennys lyvynge," and proceeds to enumerate several springs or waters in various places
which only ran at intervals, and by their running always por-
tended "derthe, pestylence, or grete batayle." After mentioning
several of these, he adds :

"Also ther is a pytte in Kent, in Langley Parke ; ayens any batayle he
wille be drye, and it rayne neveyre so myche ; and if ther be no batayle
toward, he wille be fulle of watere, be it neveyre so drye a wethyre ; and
this yere he is drye."

The state of the stream was formerly looked upon as a good
index of the probable future price of corn.—*Choice Notes and
Queries* (*Folk-Lore*), 206.

LEWISHAM : LADY WELL.

These wells were no doubt celebrated in times anterior to the
Reformation, as indicated by the name Lady Well, which still
designates the spot; but we do not possess any clear historic
evidence until the year 1648, when an event occurred which made
their virtues famous.

The manner in which the virtues of the water were discovered
is curious. A poor woman afflicted with a loathsome disease,
whose case had been given up as hopeless by the doctors, was
advised to try the water, not because of any known virtues therein,
but because her habitation was near by the springs. She used

6

the water outwardly and internally with such good effect, that, although her distemper had assumed serious and malignant symptoms, she found herself quickly restored by its daily use. From this circumstance the spot acquired some popularity and patronage.   The waters were given gratis to all comers, " as God hath freely bestowed His favours upon this water, so it is now dispensed *gratis* to any that desire it, either to themselves, or to any they shall send for it, everyone being left at liberty to gratifie the Poor people (that attend there dayly to cleanse the Wells, that the water may be taken up fresh and pure), as they shall think fit, there being no customary usuage, or fixt gratuity apportioned." An attempt to enclose the wells with a brick wall, and to give the profits of such monopoly for the " Poor's use," was frustrated by the Divine hand in a striking manner.   The water lost its virtue, " taste, its *odour,* and effects," proving that " *in behalf of the Poor (incapacitated to right themselves) God sometimes immediately steps in for their assistance.*"   The scheme of enclosure was abandoned. The wells were situated at Westwood Common, about two miles west of the parish church.   Other wells mentioned by Allen, and described as being "at the Foot of a heavy Claiy Hill, about 12 in Number," were situated near Lady Well Station.   Two of the old wells were in existence until about the year 1866, when they were ignominiously destroyed by the construction of a sewer.   An illustration of the Lady Well is preserved in Charles Knight's *Journey-Book of Kent,* p. 59.   For fuller account see *Antiquary,* xii. 56-8.

BROMLEY: ST. BLAIZE'S WELL.

Within the demesne land of the manor, and near the palace, is an ancient well, which from time immemorial has been dedicated in honour of *St. Blaize,* there having been a shrine attached to the well, to which pilgrimages were encouraged by promise of indulgences to those who worshipped there on certain occasions. —*Archæologia Cantiana,* xiii. 155.   This well is probably the same as Bishop's Well, a full account of it, with illustration, will be found in Hone's *Table Book,* pt. ii., 65-8.

SITTINGBOURNE: NAILBOURNS.

In the parts eastwards of Sittingbourne there are Nailbourns, or temporary land-springs, " their time of breaking forth, and continuance of running, is very uncertain ; but whenever they do break forth, it is held by the common people as the forerunner of scarcity and dearness of corn and victuals. Sometimes they break out for one, or, perhaps, two, successive years, and at others with two, three, or more years' intervention, and their running continues sometimes only for a few months, and at others for three or four years."—Hasted's *H. of Kent*, iii. 333.

LANCASHIRE.

WAVERTREE.

A T Wavertree, near Liverpool, is a well bearing the following inscription : " *Qui non dat quod habet, Dæmon infra videt,* 1414." Tradition says at one period there was a cross above it, inscribed " *Deus dedit, homo bibit ;*" and that all travellers gave alms on drinking. If they omitted to do so, a devil who was chained at the bottom laughed. A monastic building stood near, and the occupants received the contributions.—*Choice Notes and Queries (Folk-Lore)*, 205.

EVERTON.

There is a well here which has the reputation of being haunted, a fratricide having been committed there. It was a haunt of pick-pockets and other disorderly characters. It is now built over, and in a few short years the subterranean passage leading to the well will be forgotten.—*Ibid.*, 206.

SEFTON : ST. HELEN'S WELL.

There is a well here called St. Helen's Well, after the patron Saint of the parish church, at which people try their fortunes. It is now a stone reservoir, in and out of which the water perpetually flows. It was customary for passers-by to drop in a new pin "for good luck," or to secure the favourable issue of an expressed wish. Also conclusions were drawn as to the fidelity of their lovers, date of marriage, etc., by the turning of the pin-point to the north or any other point of the compass. Very few pins were then in it, but a few years ago, before it was cleared,

the bottom was covered with them. The tradition is, that, perhaps before the church was built, baptism was given at this well ;
it is near the Roman Catholic Chapel, township of Ince-Blundell.
It is not very far from the church on the road to Ince-Blundell,
a Roman Catholic township in Sefton parish, about twenty yards
south of the road.—Baines, iii. 497. *Notes and Queries*, 5 S. X.
158.

BRINDLE : ST. ELLEN'S WELL.

In Brindle parish, to which the vulgar neighbouring people
of the Red Letter do much resort with pretended devotion on
each year upon St. Ellin's Day, where and when, out of a foolish
ceremony, they offer, or throw into the well, pins, which there being
left may be seen a long time after.—*From Parish Register.*

CARTMELL : HOLLY OR HOLY WELL.

At Cartmell is a brackish spring, celebrated as a remedy for
stone, gout, and cutaneous complaints. The water issues from
a projecting rock of limestone called Humphrey Head, and its
medicinal qualities occasion a considerable influx of company to
Cartmell, Flookborough, Kents Bank, and Grange, during the
summer months. At Pit-farm, in the parish, is an interesting
spring, less celebrated, though of the same nature, as the Giggleswick Well in Yorkshire.

BOTTOM HALL : PUDSEY WELL.

A well adjoining to Bottom Hall still retains the name of Sir
Ralph Pudsey. He is said to have ordered it to be dug and
walled round for a bath ; and it is much venerated by the country
people to this day, who say that many remarkable cures have
been wrought there.

WINWICK : ST. OSWALD'S WELL.

This well is about half a mile from St. Oswald's Church, Winwick, and three miles from Warrington. In common with the
one bearing the same name at Oswestry, it is said to mark the
spot where St. Oswald fell when defending his kingdom against
the attack of the fire-eating old tyrant, Penda, King of the
Mercians. It is at Woodhead, near Winwick, situated in a field

on the Hermitage Farm, within a few yards of the lane, and presents a very modest appearance for so famous a spot, looking
merely like a hole in the hill-side. Passing through a small
cottage-garden, a well-trodden path leads to the well. The water
is not very bright, but the well is substantially walled inside, and
two or three deeply-worn steps lead to the water. On a recent
visit a number of beautiful ferns were growing inside from the
corners and sides of the slabs which cover in the water. Some of
the stone-work thus used is grooved and carved in a manner
which shows that at some period the well was protected, and by a
handsome and substantial erection; but most of this was taken
away many years ago, the existing rustic protection having been
fixed up about twenty years ago by the present tenant of Hermitage
Farm. Baines, in his History, speaks of Winwick as the true
scene of Oswald's death, and urges in favour that Bede describes
the well as being formed by the carrying away of earth by the
people, thus making a deep hole, which was formed into a well,
whilst the well at Oswestry is a clear sparkling spring. Not only
was the earth carried away by pious people after his death, but for
ages since, and even up to the present day the water has had
ascribed to it wondrous healing powers, though to the irreverent
mind it is very ordinary water to look at. By our reverential but
superstitious forefathers the water was carried great distances and
administered as a medicine in case of disease; and Bede relates
several miracles which he had been informed were worked in the
vicinity, and by earth or water taken from the well. At the
present day there are people who use the water as a cure for sore
eyes; and if not used at the present time, certainly within the last
twenty years it was used in the surrounding Catholic chapels. The
'Abbot's House' and 'Hermitage,' and other names, and the fact
that at one time there was a considerable ecclesiastical establishment in the vicinity, sufficiently indicate the reverence in which
our Catholic forefathers held the spot.—See *Antiquary*, iii. 260-62.

LEICESTERSHIRE.

LEICESTER: ST. AUSTIN'S WELL.

I N the western suburbs of the town of Leicester, by the side of
the ancient *Via Vicinalis*, leading from the Roman *Rata* to
the *Vosse Road*, and about seventy yards beyond the old Bow
Bridge (so romantically associated with the closing scenes in the
eventful life of Richard III.), rises a constant spring of beautifully
limpid water, and known as St. Augustine's, or more commonly,
St. Austin's Well.   It derived its designation from its vicinity to
the Augustine monastery, situated immediately on the opposite
side of the river Soar.   The well is three-quarters of a yard broad,
and the same in length within its enclosure ; the depth of its
water from the lip, or back-edging on the earth, where it commonly
overflows, is half a yard.   It is covered with a millstone, and
enclosed with brick on three sides ; that towards the Bow Bridge
and the town is open.   The water from this well was formerly in
great repute as a remedy for sore eyes, and since the well has
been covered and enclosed many applications for water from the
pump erected in the adjoining ground have been made for the
same purpose.   As an instance of the strange metamorphoses
which proper names undergo in the oral traditions of the people,
on making some inquiries a few years ago of "the oldest inhabitant" of the neighbourhood respecting St. Augustine's Well, he
at first pleaded ignorance of it, but at length, suddenly enlightened,
exclaimed : "Oh, you mean Tostings's Well !"—*Choice Notes and
Queries*, 204.   See also Nichols' *H. of Leicester*, vol. i. 300.

LEICESTER: ST. JAMES'S WELL.

In addition to the above holy well, there is also another in the
town, called St. James's Well ; but I am not aware that there is
any legend connected with it, except that it had a hermitage
adjoining it, or that any particular virtue was attributed to it.—
Ibid., 205.

CHARNWOOD FOREST: HOLY-WELL-HAW.

We have on Charnwood Forest the well giving its name to
Holy-Well-Haw, and the spring on Bosworth Field, illustrated in

Hone's *Every Day Book*, ii. 1100, rendered famous by the tradition of Richard III. having drunk at it during the battle, and which is surmounted by an inscription to that effect from the pen of the learned Dr. Parr.—*Ibid.*, 205.

HINCKLEY: ST. MARY'S OR OUR LADY'S WELL.

There is a well here known as St. Mary's Well, or more commonly as Our Lady's Well; it still supplies most excellen water to all the neighbourhood.

RATBY: HOLY WELL.

At Ratby, four miles north-west of Leicester is a place called the *Holy Well;* the waters are anti-scorbutic.

LINCOLNSHIRE.

HEBBALDSTOW: JULIAN'S STONY WELL.

H ERE are two springs, one called Julian's Stony Well, the other Castleton Well.

ALLINGTON: HAGSTON WELL.

There is a spring here called Hagston Well (*lapis ad aggerem*), on the way to Sho Lane.—Stukeley's *Diaries*, j. 296—Surtees Soc., 76.

GREAT COTES, ULCEBY.

Here is a spring celebrated locally for its healing properties. It rises from the side of a bank in a plantation, and is over-shadowed by an ancient thorn, on the branches of which hang innumerable rags, fastened there by those who have drunk of its waters.

WINTERTON: HOLY WELL DALE.

There is a spring at Holy Well Dale, near Winterton, in North Lincolnshire, formerly celebrated for its healing properties; and the bushes around used to be hung with rags.

Here is the " Bye Well," or village well, interesting as retaining
the old Danish By or Bye in a separate form.   The village of
Byewell, in Northumberland, is most probably named from some
such well.

A deep circular pit, the water of which rises to the level of
the surface but never overflows.   It is considered bottomless
by the superstitious.

In Glentham Church there is a tomb with a figure known as
Molly Grime.   Formerly this figure was regularly washed every
Good Friday by seven old maids of Glentham with water brought
from Newell Well, each receiving a shilling for her trouble, in
consequence of an old bequest connected with some property in
that district.   About 1832 the custom was discontinued.—*Old
English Customs and Charities,* 1842, p. 100.

MIDDLESEX.

STOW, speaking of the wells near London, says that on
the north side thereof is a well called Clark's Well ; and,
in assigning the reason for this appellation, he furnishes
us with a curious fact relating to the parish clerks of London.
His words are these : " Clark's Well took its name from the
parish clerks in London, who of old times were accustomed
there yearly to assemble and to play some large history of Holy
Scripture."—Brand, *Pop. Ant.,* ii. 370, 371.

" In the year 1390, the 14th of Richard the Second, the parish
clerks in London, on July 18, plaied Enterludes at Skinner's Well,
near unto Clark's Well, which play continued three days together,

the king, queen, and nobles being present. Also in the year
1409, the tenth of Henry IV., they played a play at the Skinner's
Well which lasted eight days, and was of matter from the creation
of the world; there were to see the same most part of the nobles
and gentles of England."—*Survey of London*, 4to., 1603, p. 15.
Hawkins' *History of Music* (Novello's Ed.), p. 559, vol. 2.

MUSWELL HILL : ST. LAZARUS.

This well is situated behind the Alexandra Palace.   It formerly
belonged to the Hospital Order of St. John's, Clerkenwell—an
hospital order for lepers.   Robert Bruce had a free pass granted
to him by the King of England, in order to go and bathe in
its waters for his leprosy.   The water is slightly chalybeate and
bituminous.

ISLINGTON : SADLER'S WELL.

In a tract, 1684, it is thus described : "'The New Well at
Islington is a certain spring in the middle of a garden belonging
to the Music House, built by Mr. Sadler, on the north side of the
great cistern that receives the New River water, near Islington ;
the water whereof was before the Reformation very much famed
for several extraordinary cures performed thereby, and was, therefore, accounted sacred, and called *Holy Well.* The priests belonging to the Priory of Clerkenwell using to attend there, made the
people believe that the virtues of the water proceeded from
the efficacy of their prayers.   But upon the Reformation the well
was stopped up."—(*Antiquary*, xiii. 108.)

ISLINGTON : ISLINGTON LANDS.

" Islington lands, a famous ducking land."   The sport consisted
in hunting a duck with dogs, the duck diving when the dogs
came close to elude capture.   Another mode was to tie an owl
upon the duck's back ; the duck dives to escape the burden,
when, on rising for air, the wretched half-drowned owl shakes
itself, and, hooting, frightens the duck ; she, of course, dives
again, and replunges the owl into the water.   The frequent
repetition of this action soon deprived the owl of its sensation,
and generally ended in its death, if not that of the duck also.—
See *Strutt's Sports and Pastimes.*

SHOREDITCH : ST. JOHN'S WELL.

There was one dedicated to St. John in Shoreditch, which Stow says was spoiled by rubbish and filth laid down to heighten the plots of garden ground near it.

HAMPSTEAD : SHEPHERD WELL.

An illustration of this interesting well will be found in Hone's *Table Book*, i., 381, 382.

LONDON : ST. CLEMENT'S WELL.

A pump now represents St. Clement's Well (Strand), which in Henry II.'s reign was a favourite idling place of scholars and city youths in the summer evenings, when they walked forth to take the air.

KENSINGTON GARDENS : ST. GOVER'S.

This well is said to be still visited by the faithful who believe in the virtues of its waters.

TOTTENHAM : BISHOP'S WELL.

In a field opposite the Vicarage House, rises a spring called " Bishop's Well," of which the common people report many strange cures.—*Brand*, ii. 369.

TOTTENHAM : ST. LOY'S, OR ELOY'S WELL.

Whilst writing about a Middlesex well, may I suggest that to the list should be added that of St. Loy's, or Eloy's Well, Tottenham, if for no other reason than the uncommonness of the name in England? It is frequently to be met with in Belgium. Bedwell, whose *Brief History of Tottenham* was printed in 1631, wrote : ' *St. Loy's Well*, which nowe is nothing els but a deep pitte in the highway on the west side thereof, betweene his cell and the Crosse, almost midde way ; it is always full of water, but neuer runneth ouer ; the water thereof, as they say, doth farre excede all the waters nere vnto it ; it was within the memory of man cast, to cleanse it, because it was almost fill'd vp with muddle; and in the bottome of it there was found a very fayre great stone, which had certaine characters or letters engrau'n vpon it, but it being by the negligence of the workmen broken and sorly defaced, and no man nere that regarded such things, it is vnknown what they were, or what they might signify.'

HARRY G. GRIFFINHOOFE.

St. Stephen's Club, S.W.

LONDON : ST. PANCRAS' WELLS.

There was on the north side of St. Pancras Church a mineral spring known as St. Pancras' Wells.

ST. CHAD'S WELL.

Close to Battle Bridge was a mineral spring of great antiquity, called St. Chad's Well ; it has been swept away by the Metropolitan Railway station of King's Cross.

BAGNIGGE WELLS.

Two springs discovered 1767 ; one chalybeate, the other aperient.

BLACK MARY'S WELL.

Black Mary's Well, so called from one Mary. Some say a black woman named Wollaston leased here a conduit, to which the citizens resorted to drink the waters, and who kept a black cow, whose milk gentlemen and ladies drank with the waters.

Mary dying, the place degenerated into licentious uses about 1687. Walter Baynes, Esq., of the Inner Temple, inclosed the conduit in the manner it now is, which looks like a great oven (1813). He is supposed to have left a fund to keep it in repair. The stone with inscription was carried away during the night about ten years ago (1882).

ENFIELD : KING RING OR TIM RINGER'S WELL.

Here is a deep well named as above, whose waters never freeze nor dry up, and are considered curative for affections of the eyes.

MONMOUTHSHIRE.

CHEPSTOW : PIN WELL.

T HE Pin Well is still in some repute for its healing powers. In "good old times" those who would test the virtues of its waters said an *ave* and dropped a pin into its depth.

LLANOVER : ST. GOVER'S WELLS.

In the grounds of Llanover House are still to be seen the celebrated St. Gover Wells.

NORFOLK.

WALSINGHAM : WISHING-WELLS.

A MONGST the slender remains of this once celebrated seat of mediæval devotion are two small circular basins of stone, a little to the north-east of the site of the Conventional Church (exactly in the place described by Erasmus in his *Peregrinatio Religionis Ergo*), and connected with the Chapel of the Virgin, which was on the north side of the choir. The waters of these wells had at that time a miraculous efficacy in curing disorders of the head and stomach; but the waters have no such quality now. There has been substituted, however, another of far more comprehensive virtue. This is nothing less than the power of accomplishing all human wishes, which miraculous property the water is still believed to possess. In order to attain this desirable end, the votary, with a due qualification of faith and pious awe, must apply the right knee, bare, to a stone placed for that purpose between the wells. He must then plunge to the wrist each hand, bare also, into the water of the wells, which are near enough to admit of this immersion. A wish must then be formed, but not uttered with the lips, either at the time or afterwards, even in confidential communication to the dearest friend. The hands are then to be withdrawn, and as much of the water as can be contained in the hollow of each is to be swallowed. This done, his wishes would infallibly be fulfilled within the year, provided he never mentioned them to anyone or uttered them aloud to himself. Formerly the object of desire was probably expressed in a prayer to the Virgin. It is now only a silent wish, which will certainly be accomplished within twelve months, if the efficacy of the solemn rite be not frustrated by the incredulity or some other fault of the votary.— Brand, *Pop. Ant.*, ii. 370-371.

OUR LADY OF WALSINGHAM.

This was the object of by far the greatest number of pilgrimages. Eight crowned heads we know came here specially—Henry VIII. among them, who walked the last two miles barefoot—some few years before the Reformation, when the same image was burnt at Chelsea, only a few years before he, on his death-bed, in his agony commended his soul to the protection of that same Lady of Walsingham whose image he had destroyed. The king's banner, at least, was hung up before it in gratitude for a victory, and its shrine literally blazed with silver, gold, and jewels, brought as offerings to what was thought the Virgin's favourite English home. There were relics, of course, such as the coagulated blood of the Virgin, and an unnaturally large joint of the Apostle Peter's forefinger ; while another attraction was the "Wishing-Well." Evidences of miracles were ever at hand, such as a house not built by hands, which was placed by Divine power over the wells ; and a wicket-gate, less than an ell square, through which a knight on horseback, pursued by his enemies, was safely conveyed by the Virgin Mary, to whom he called in his due need.

The milky way in the heavens is said to have got its name from its showing the way to where the Virgin's blood was exhibited ; and the road to the shrine, *via* Newmarket, Brandon, and Fakenham, was long known as the "Walsingham Way," or the "Palmer's Way," as was also that to it from Norwich *via* Attlebridge.—*History of Norfolk*, W. Rye, 172, 173.

EAST DEREHAM : ST. WITHBURGA'S WELL.

Dedication.—St. Withburga, virgin, dau. of Annas, King of the East Angles ; sister of St. Etheldreda, foundress of Ely ; born at

Holkham, Norfolk, *cir.* 630, founded a convent at East Dereham, destroyed by the Danes 974.

Emblem.—Church in hand, and two does at her feet. (Burlingham, St. Andrew, and Barnham Broom, both in Norfolk.)

She founded the first church in Dercham ; in her representation at Burlingham on screen, the base of the church in her hand bears the words "*Ecclia de est Dærhm.*" She, and her convent, were sustained by the milk of two does, which came to the bridge over the stream, about a furlong distant, daily. At her death, she was buried in the churchyard at the west end of the church. *cir.* 742, and her tomb became reputed for the cure of disease, mental

ST. WITHBURGA'S WELL.

and bodily. Dereham was then subject to Ely, and the abbot was desirous of moving the body of the saint to the side of St. Etheldreda ; he, therefore, rifled the tomb, and conveyed the body by road and river (pursued by the men of Dereham when the theft was discovered) to Ely, on July 8, 974 (? 947). To compensate Dereham for the loss of its saint, a miraculous spring rose from the spot where the body had lain in the churchyard—"a spring of the purest water, gifted with many healing virtues"— (*Gesta Abbatum et Episcoporum Eliensis, etc., etc.*). The ruins of a chapel still remain around the spring (which still runs), the walls rising to the height of five to six feet. Upon these foundations the enormity was perpetrated in 1793 of building a "bath-house," under which a square basin was formed of brick, to enable the townspeople to use it as a bath. It was a hideous structure, containing two dressing-rooms, from which the bathers descended to the pool by steps. This building was destroyed some twenty-five years ago, and the foundations of the chapel again laid bare. The square basin still remains, full of water, which can be let off at pleasure ; and when empty one sees the pure water trickling into the basin from three or four sources. It has never ceased to run in the remembrance of the parishioners ; and however sharp a winter may be, the pool when full and stationary has never been known to contain a particle of ice. The ground enclosed by the chapel walls is laid out as a garden, and is kept as bright as possible with roses, forget-me-nots, and old English flowers ; while the following inscription is inserted over the pool in the chapel wall :

> " The Ruins of a Tomb which contained the
> Remains of Withburga,
> Youngest Daughter of
> Annas,
> King of the East Angles,
> Who died A.D. 674.
>
> The Abbot and Monks of Ely stole this precious Relique, and translated it to Ely Cathedral, where it was interred near her three Royal Sisters, A.D. 947."

SOUTHWOOD : CALLOW PIT.

On the boundary of the parishes of Southwood and Moulton, Norfolk, is a pit called, in the Act of Parliament for enclosing the parishes, " Callow Pit "; but, by the inhabitants, Caller Pit. Its antiquity is evidenced by the fact that a hollow tree, evidently of some centuries' growth, is still growing in it Formerly it was constantly full of water ; but, since the extension of drainage, in dry summers its waters frequently fail. The village tradition states that an iron chest, filled with gold, is engulfed in Callow Pit. Many years ago two adventurous men, availing themselves of an unusually low state of the water, determined to obtain the treasure. Having formed a platform of ladders across the pit, they were so far successful that they inserted a staff through the " ringle " (in plain English, the ring) in the lid of the chest, and

bore it up from the waters; and placed the staff on their
shoulders, preparatory to bearing off their prize on their temporary
bridge. Unluckily, however, one of them triumphantly exclaimed:
" We've got it safe, and the devil himself can't get it from us."
Instantly the pit was enveloped in a "roke" (reek, or cloud of
steam), of a strong sulphurous smell; and a black hand and arm
—no doubt belonging to the personage thus gratuitously
challenged—emerged from the water, and grasped the chest.
A terrific struggle ensued: one party tugging to secure, the other
to recover the prize. At last the contest ended by its subject
parting, being unable to bear the enormous strain on it. The
chest, with the treasure, sank beneath the water, never again to
be seen by mortal eye; while the bold adventurers—who had
not, indeed, met with the reward due to their daring—carried off
nothing but the "ringle," which they placed on Southwood
Church door, which it still serves to close; and where the incredulous may convince himself of the truth of the legend by
beholding it. A "headless horseman" still rides at midnight from
Callow Pit to a place called Cantley Spong, distant about a mile.
—*Notes and Queries*, 1 S. xii. 487.

SHOULDHAM : SILVER WELL.

A similar story to the above is told of the "Silver Well" at
Shouldham in West Norfolk.

TUNSTALL : HELL HOLE.

There is a Norfolk legend which brings out the connection
between pools, bells, and the under-world very clearly. Tunstall
church in that county having been destroyed by a fire, which yet
left the bells uninjured, the parson and churchwardens quarrelled
for the possession of them, and meantime the Old Gentleman
watched his opportunity and walked off with them. He was,
however, found out and pursued by the parson, who began to
exorcise him in Latin. So in his hurry he made his way through
the earth to his own abode, taking his booty with him. The
spot where he disappeared is now a boggy pool of water, called
Hell Hole, on the surface of which, in summer-time, bubbles are
constantly appearing. These, the folks say, are caused by the

continual sinking of the bells through the water on their endless journey to the bottomless pit.—*Shropshire Folk-lore*, p. 75.

Tunstall Church, situate about eight miles from Yarmouth, had been destroyed by fire, which, consuming the timbers of the ringing chamber, caused the bells to fall, happily uninjured. One would have thought that the parish priest would have been glad at their preservation, and taken steps at once to reinstate them in their old position, but instead, that worthy designed them for his own covetous purposes. In this, however, he was not alone, for the churchwardens had also laid their heads together, agreeing to sell the bells and share the spoil between them. Their plans being discovered, an angry altercation ensued when the parties met next time in the church. Each strove to get possession of the bells, and the quarrel grew fiercer, and words waxed high, when lo, a gigantic black form, the identity of which there was no disputing, appeared on the scene, and instantly seized the bells and made off. Priest and wardens, forgetting their dispute, started in pursuit, and seemed to gain on the infernal thief, when he vanished from their sight, diving straight through the earth and taking the bells with him. Where he disappeared they saw but a dark pool of water, while the bubbles rapidly rising to its surface, not only on that day, but for many days and years after, showed that whatever became of the devil, the bells at least were descending the bottomless pit. The pool obtained the name of Hell Hole, and the clump of alders above it was long known as Hell Car.—*East Anglian Handbook*, 1885, p. 71.

WEREHAM : ST. MARGARET'S WELL.

To the west of Wereham Church is a well called St. Margaret's, much frequented before the Reformation. Here, on St. Margaret's Day, the people regaled themselves with ale and cakes, music and dancing. Alms were given, and offerings and vows made, as at other sainted or holy wells.—*Excursions in the County of Norfolk*, 1829, ii. 145.

NORWICH : ST. LAURENCE'S WELL.

From a very early period there was an open common well for the use of the citizens a short distance from the public street;

7

the Court of Mayoralty, in 1547, granted the parishioners of St. Laurence a lane from the High Street to the well, together with the said well, on condition that they erected a door at the south end of the lane, to be kept open in the daytime and shut securely at night. Evidently, there had been some serious if not fatal accident, or these conditions would not have been enjoined. Of Robert Gibson, a beer brewer, is recorded under April 26, 19 Eliz. (1577): "This day it is also agreed by consent of this assembly that Robert Gybson shall have the little entry that goeth out of the street to St. Laurence Well, etc., with this proviso, that the same Robert shall, at his proper costs and charges, in a conduit or cock of lead, bring the water from the said well up into the street for the use of the common people, and for the maintenance of the same conduit or cock wherein the water shall be conveyed," etc. He erected an elaborately-adorned affair on which he caused to be inscribed the following doggerel lines recording the service he had done to his neighbours, though, at the same time, he gained some personal advantage:

" This water here caught
In sorte as yowe se,
From a *Spring* is broughte
Threskore Foot and thre.

" Gybson hath it soughte
From Saynt Laurens Wel,
And his charg this wrowght
Who now here doe dwell.

" Thy ease was his coste, not smal,
Vouchsafed wel of those
Which thankful be his Work to se,
And thereto be no Foes."

Gibson died in 1606, and was buried in the chancel of St. Laurence's Church. There is an indenture, dated August 30, 1594, in which allusion is made to this well, "commonly called St. Laurence's Well for 300 years."— *Norfolk and Norwich Arch. Journal,* x. 185. There is a sketch of this well in *Norfolk Architectural Etchings,* Plate XI.

THIS spring is in Boughton Field, near Brampton Bridge, near the Kingsthorpe Road; it is of great note with the common people. It never runs but in mighty gluts of wet, and whenever it does so, it is thought ominous by the country people, who consider these breakings out of the spring to foretell dearth, the death of some great person, or very trouble- some times.—Morton, 230.

Near the village are seven wells, in which during the ages of superstition it was usual to dip weakly infants, called berns. From whatever cause this custom was originally adopted, in the course of time some presiding angel was supposed to communicate hidden virtues to the water ; and mystical and puerile rites were performed at these springs denominated *fontes puerorum.* A dark devotion was then paid to wells, which became a continual resort of persons, productive of great disorder, so that such pilgrimages were strictly prohibited by the clergy. An inhibition of this kind appears among other injunctions of Oliver Sutton, Bishop of Lincoln, about the year 1290.—Britton's *H. of Northants,* p. 209.

Baxter, in his *World of Spirits,* p. 157, says : "When I was a schoolboy at Oundle, in Northamptonshire, about the Scots' coming into England, I heard a well, in one Dob's yard, drum like any drum beating a march. I heard it at a distance : then I went and put my head into the mouth of the well, and heard it distinctly, and nobody in the well. It lasted several days and nights, so as all the country people came to hear it. And so it drummed on several changes of times. When King Charles II. died I went to the Oundle carrier at the Ram Inn, in Smithfield, who told me their well had drummed, and many people came to hear it. And I heard it drummed once since.' — Brand's *Pop. Ant.,* ii. 369.

The well dedicated in honour of St. Laurence, was in days gone by much reverenced; vows were here made, and alms offered.

NORTHUMBERLAND.

NEWCASTLE : RAG WELL.

THERE is a well here known by the above name, formerly much frequented. The bushes around it were at one time literally covered with rags and tattered pieces of cloth.

BENTON : RAG WELL.

Brand states : "I have frequently observed *shreds* or *bits of rag* upon the bushes that overhang a well in the road to Benton, a village in the vicinity of Newcastle-on-Tyne, which from that circumstance is now, or was very lately, called the *rag well.* This name is undoubtedly of long standing. Probably it has been visited for some disease or other, and these rag offerings are the reliques of the then prevailing popular superstition. It is not far from another holy spring at Jesmond."—*H. of Newcastle-on-Tyne,* i. 339.

JESMOND : ST. MARY'S WELL.

There is a holy well here, said to have as many steps to it as there are articles in the creed. It was recently enclosed for a bathing place, which was no sooner done than the water left it. The well was always esteemed of more sanctity than common wells, and therefore the failing of the water could be looked upon as nothing less than a just revenge for so great a profanation. But, alas ! the miracle's at an end, for the water returned a while ago in as great abundance as ever. Pilgrimages to this well and chapel at Jesmond were so frequent, that one of the principal streets of the great commercial town aforesaid is supposed to have had its name partly from having an inn in it, to which the pilgrims that flocked thither for the benefit of the supposed holy water used to resort.—*Ibid.* ; Brand, *Pop. Ant.,* ii. 380, n.

St. Mark's Day is observed at Alnwick by a ridiculous custom in connection with the admission of freemen of the common, alleged to have reference to a visit paid by King John to Alnwick. It is said that this monarch, when attempting to ride across Alnwick Moor, then called the Forest of Aidon, fell with his horse into a bog or morass, where he stuck so fast that he was with great difficulty pulled out by some of his attendants. Incensed against the inhabitants of that town for not keeping the roads over the moor in better repair, or at least for not placing some post or mark pointing out the particular spots which were impassable, he inserted in their charter, both by way of memento and punishment, that for the future all new created freemen should on St. Mark's Day pass on foot through that morass, called the Freemen's Well. In obedience to this clause of their charter, when any new freemen are to be made, a small rill of water which passes through the morass is kept dammed up for a day or two previous to that on which this ceremonial is to be exhibited, by which means the bog becomes so thoroughly liquefied that a middlesized man is chin deep in mud and water in passing over it. Besides which, not unfrequently, holes and trenches are dug ; in these, filled up and rendered invisible by the liquid mud, several free men have fallen down and been in great danger of suffocation. In later times, in proportion as the new-made freemen are more or less popular, the passage is rendered more or less difficult.

Early in the morning of St. Mark's Day the houses of the new freemen are distinguished by a holly-tree planted before each door, as the signal for their friends to assemble and make merry with them. About eight o'clock the candidates for the franchise, being mounted on horseback and armed with swords, assemble in the market place, where they are joined by the chamberlain and bailiff of the Duke of Northumberland, attended by two men armed with halberds. The young freemen arranged in order, with music playing before them and accompanied by a numerous cavalcade, march to the west end of the town, where they deliver their swords. They then proceed under the guidance of the moorgrieves through a part of their extensive domain, till they reach the ceremonial well. The sons of the oldest freemen have the honour of taking the first leap. On the signal being given they pass through the bog, each being allowed to use the method and pace which to him shall seem best, some running, some going slow, and some attempting to jump over suspected places, but all in their turns tumbling and wallowing like porpoises at sea, to the great amusement of the populace, who usually assemble in vast numbers. After this aquatic excursion, they remount their horses and proceed to perambulate the remainder of their large common, of which they are to become free by their achievement.   In passing the open part of the common the young freemen are obliged to alight at intervals, and place a stone on a cairn as a mark of their boundary, till they come near a high hill called the Twinlaw or Tounlaw Cairns, when they set off at full speed, and contest the honour of arriving first on the hill, where the names of the freemen of Alnwick are called over.   When arrived about two miles from the town they generally arrange themselves in order, and, to prove their equestrian abilities, set off with great speed and spirit over bogs, ditches, rocks, and rugged declivities till they arrive at Rottenrow Tower on the confines of the town, the foremost claiming the honour of what is termed "winning the boundaries," and of being entitled to the temporary triumphs of the day.   Having completed the circuits the young freemen, with sword in hand, enter the town in triumph, preceded by music, accompanied by a large concourse of people in carriages, etc. Having paraded the streets, the new freemen and the other equestrians enter the Castle, where they are liberally regaled, and drink the health of the lord and lady of the manor.   The newly-created burgesses then proceed in a body to their respective houses, and around the holly tree drink a friendly glass with each other.   After this they proceed to the market-place, where they close the ceremony over an enlivening bowl of punch.—Hone's *Every-Day Book*, ii., 249. *H. of Alnwick*, 1882, 304-309. Dyer's *Brit. Pop. Customs*, 201, Bohn's Ed.

ALNWICK : SENNA WELL.

There is a medicinal spring about five miles from Alnwick, known as Senna Well.

FENTON : ST. NINIAN'S OR PIN WELL.

About a mile and a half north of Wooler, in Northumberland, on the flanks of the Cheviots, near to an ancient British hill fort, called the Cup and Saucer, is a copious spring of water locally known as Pin Well, or the "Wishing Well." The country maids in passing this spring dropped a crooked pin, button, or money in the water. There is a belief that the well is under the charge of a fairy, and that it is necessary to propitiate her by an offering of some sort.

THE TWEED.

Somewhere on the Tweed there exists still a belief amongst the superstitious in the power of fairies, who are supposed to affect the produce of the fisheries ; it is the custom of these persons not only to impregnate the nets with salt, but also to throw some of that commodity into the water for the purpose of blinding the mischievous elves, who are said to prevent the fish from falling victims to the snares laid for them. This practice was observed near Coldstream as late as 1879, and strange to say the net, when drawn to land, instead of being empty, as usual, contained three fine salmon.

THE TWEED.

Sir Walter Scott, in the *Lay of the Last Minstrel*, relates a story of the Spirit of the Tweed compelling the lady of the Baron of Drummelziel to submit to his embraces ; so that on the return of her lawful lord from the Holy Land, he found his fair lady nursing a healthy boy, whose age did not correspond to the date of his departure. The lady, however, was believed, and the child, to whom the name of Tweedie was given, afterwards became Baron of Drummelziel, and the chief of a powerful clan.—*Denham Tracts*, 1851, p. 18.

THE RIVER WANSBECK.

The author of *Rambles in Northumberland* gives a tradition concerning the river Wansbeck : "The river discharges itself into the sea at a place called Cambois, about nine miles to the eastward ; and the tide flows to within five miles of Morpeth. Tradition reports that Michael Scott, whose fame as a wizard is not confined to Scotland, would have brought the tide to the town, had not the courage of the person failed upon whom the execution of this project depended. This agent of Michael, after his principal had performed certain spells, was to run from the neighbourhood of Cambois to Morpeth, without looking back, and the tide would follow him. After having advanced a certain distance, he became alarmed at the roaring of the waves behind him, and forgetting the injunction, gave a look over his shoulder to see if the danger was imminent, when the advancing tide immediately stopped, and the burgesses of Morpeth thus lost the chance of having the Wansbeck navigable between their town and the sea. It is also said that Michael intended to confer a similar favour on the inhabitants of Durham, by making the Wear navigable to their city; but his good intentions were frustrated by the cowardice of the person who had to guide the tide."

SIMONBURN: ST. MARY'S WELL.

This well used for many centuries to be one of the sources of supply of water for the village.—*Arch. Æliana, New Series*, viii., · p. 63.

BELLINGHAM: ST. CUTHBERT'S WELL.

The well is just outside the churchyard wall, and no doubt supplied the baptismal element to the first converts to Christianity, as the fonts of the early Saxon times were usually open-air fountains, to which pilgrimages were often made. The church is also dedicated in honour of St. Cuthbert.

Reginald of Durham, who flourished about the year 1150 A.D., relates a miraculous cure at this well, by the usual North-Country abbreviation called " Cuddy's Well." About the period of the Norman Conquest, a man named Sproich, by the Almoner of Durham, set over the repairs of the bridges of the North Tyne, lived at " Bainlingham," whose only daughter Eda had a great love of fine garments, and was foolishly indulged therein by her parents, though themselves poor. On the morn of a certain St. Lawrence's feast, she was still working at the finishing of a rich dress—" quoddam de fusticatincto indumentum"—instead of preparing to go to church, notwithstanding her mother's rebuke. When she obstinately determined to finish it, as she was declaring her intention of working to what hour she liked, " her left hand,' which held the stuff, contracted thereupon so that she could not move the fingers to open the hand, nor could they, by force, draw away the cloth they grasped." The story adds that, in this extremity, human help being in vain, the parents first caused the

girl to *drink of the well of St. Cuthbert* by the way, and then pros-
trated themselves in the little adjoining church of St. Cuthbert all
that night, in prayer to the "Glorious Confessor," whose figure,
towards the dawning of the day, arose at the altar, descended into
the aisle, and touched the contracted hands of the maiden. The
cloth now dropped from her fingers, but the miracle was incom-
plete; for, through terror of the saintly apparition, the mother had
meanwhile also seized her daughter's hand, which she was unable
to open fully until special prayers had been offered for her recovery
at morning Mass by the priest Samuel. Then she was able joyfully
to hold up her hand in church in presence of all the congregation,
who thenceforth, with the priest, the parents, and every villager of
Bellingham, vouch for the reality of the miracle.

The interest of this relation rests in the preliminary draught at
St. Cuthbert's Well, as necessary to any hope of the maiden's cure.
—*Reg. Dunelm*, Surtees Soc., cviii. pp. 243-5.—*Ibid.*, 63, 64, 65.

GUNNARTON : LADY'S WELL.

Another remarkable well, closely adjoining the site of an ancient
church and churchyard, of which no trace, however, now remains,
exists here, called *The Lady's Well*, or simply Margaret's Well. It
springs forth in a picturesque fern-clad and moss-mantled hollow
near the Gunnarton Burn, beneath the hill on which the castle
formerly stood, and its copious flow still furnishes the chief supply
of this romantic hamlet. Indeed, it occupies, relatively to the
former pre-Reformation chapel of the village (one of the four
ancient *capellæ* of the great parish of Chollerton), a position very
similar to that of St. Cuthbert's Well at Bellingham ; and it is not
improbable that its present name denotes the special dedication
of the sacred building itself.—*Ibid.*, 65.

GUNNARTON FELL : HALLIBURN.

About a mile further up the beautiful Lady's Wood, beyond the
remarkable British earthwork called "Money Hill," from the local
tradition of a dragon-guarded hoard of treasure, the lonely ravine
and parcel of land to the south take the name of Dungill and
Dungillfield respectively from this singular fortress of pre-historic
times. At the extremity of these extensive woods we come to the
Halliwell Burn and the *Halliwell* itself, a chalybeate spring, close

by the margin of the stream in an open and undulating portion of Gunnarton Fell. Whether this sacred well partakes of the same tutelary patronage as that first described lower down the burn, that of "Our Lady," by analogy the " Blessed Virgin," I could not ascertain. But it has for a long time drawn numerous votaries to its healing waters, who frequently superadd to the normal veneration of the well a marked worship of Bacchus, bringing the "strong drink " for their libations with them in their pilgrimage to the *al-fresco* shrine.—*Ibid.*, 65, 66.

COLWELL.

This village, in the same parish of Chollerton, derives its present appellation from a well-known spring, not far from the now almost forgotten site of another early *capella*. With this an interesting relic of primitive worship used to be associated in a popular pilgrimage, and the bringing of flowers, to dress the well on or about Midsummer Sunday.—*Ibid.*, 66.

WARK : OLD KIRK WELL (1).

Three wells supply the wants of the inhabitants of the ancient village of *Wark*. One, the Old Kirk Well, issues on the roadside, beyond the present modern church, near the Kirk-field, the site of the pre-Reformation church of "St. Michael of Were " (2). The

UPPER OR HIGH WELL.

at the entrance to the village from the west by the road leading from the Wastes—the " vastæ " of Camden, (3) the

LOWER OR RIVERSIDE WELL.

On New Year's morning, within memory, each of these wells was visited by the villagers in the hope of their being the first to take what was called the " Flower of the Well," that is, the first draught drunk by anyone in the New Year. Whoever first drank of the spring would obtain, it was believed, marvellous powers throughout the next year, even to the extent of being able to pass through keyholes and take nocturnal flights in the air. And the fortunate recipient of such extraordinary powers notified his or her acquisition thereof by casting into the well an offering of flowers or grass, hay or straw, from seeing which the next earliest devotees would know that their labour was in vain, when they, too late, came to the spring in the hope of possessing the flower of the well.— *Ibid.*, 66, 67.

BIRTLEY OR BIRKLEY : CROFT-FOOT WELL.

The same custom was followed here in the last generation. The Croft-foot Well, corrupted into the Crow-foot Well, as if from the ranunculus that grows near it, derives it name from its position at the lower end of the field called the Prior's Croft, a portion of land assigned by the Umfrevilles, Lords of Prudhoe, to the Prior of Hexham Abbey, on condition of services performed in the ancient chapel, now the parish church of Birtley. There the villagers of a generation ago frequented the well in the early hours of the New Year, like their neighbours at Wark ; but they held that the fortunate first visitant of the well on New Year's morning, who should fill his flask or bottle with the water, would find that it retained its freshness and purity throughout the whole year, and also brought good luck to the house in which it remained.— *Ibid.*, 67.

RAMSHAW'S MILL, NEAR WARK.

The strong sulphur and chalybeate springs at Ramshaw's Mill, near Wark, seem until recently to have been the sites of pilgrimages on New Year's morning.—*Ibid.*, 68.

BINGFIELD : BORE-WELL.

The chief well for the pilgrimage of our dalesfolk in this district, especially in the last generation, seems to have been the *Bore-well on Erringburn*, near Bingfield. In the centre of the curious peninsula formed by the winding stream, a copious spring of water, strongly impregnated with sulphur, issues to this day. On the Sunday following the fourth day of July, that is about Midsummer Day, according to the Old Style, great crowds of people used to assemble here from all the surrounding hamlets and villages. The scene has been described as resembling a fair, stalls for the sale of various refreshments being brought from a distance, year by year, at the summer solstice. The neighbouring slopes had been terraced, and seats formed for the convenience of pilgrims and visitors. One special object of female pilgrims was to pray at the well, or express a silent wish as they stood over it,

for the cure of barrenness, like Hannah, the wife of Elkanah, at
Shiloh, or like the Roman votaries of Juno Lucina at the great
festival of the Matronalia, when women honoured their protectress,
and in particular, besought aid, her great office, to make them
fruitful. If the pilgrim's faith were sufficient, her wish at the
Bore-well would be certain to be fulfilled within the twelve
months.

This locally celebrated spring, which seems to have obtained
its present name from having been enlarged in *boring* for coal,
still retains much of its former veneration. Its day is far from
being gone by, for a very considerable number of visitors, with
tents and purchasable commodities, assembled, strange to say,
even this last year (1878), to celebrate the Old Midsummmer
Sunday at the Bore-well.—*Ibid.*, 69.

BINGFIELD : TODRIDGE FARM, HALLIWELL.

This spring was a boundary mark as far back as the year
1479.

LONG WITTON : THRUSTON WELLS.

By the banks of the Hart, near Long Witton, in a wood are
three wells which rise beneath a thick stratum of sandstone rock,
which Wallis calls *Thruston Wells*, probably from their coming
through the stone; but the people of the neighbourhood call
them Our Lady's Wells and the Holy Wells. They are all chalybeate, contain sulphur and alumine, and were formerly in high
reputation through the neighbourhood for their very virtuous
qualities. That furthest to the east is called the Eye Well, on
account of its beneficial effects in cases of inflammation of the
eyes, and flux of the lachrymal humour. It has a very ancient
inscription of four lines in the rock immediately above it, but
many of the letters have been purposely defaced. Great con-
courses of people from all parts used to assemble here, in the
memory of old people, on Midsummer Sunday and the Sunday
following, and amuse themselves with leaping, eating gingerbread
brought for sale to the spot, and drinking the waters of the well.
A tremendous dragon, too, that could make itself visible, formerly
guarded these fountains, till the famous knight, Guy, Earl of
Warwick, wandering in quest of chivalrous employment, came
this way, and waged battle with the monster. With words that

could not be disobeyed, the winged serpent was commanded from his den, and to keep his natural and visible form ; but as often as the knight wounded him, and his strength from loss of blood began to fail, he glided back, dipped his tail into the well, and returned healed and with new vigour to the combat, till the Earl, perceiving the cause of his long resistance, leapt between him and the well, and in one furious onset stabbed him to the heart. (See Richardson's *Table Book* i. pp. 145, 146, and Wallis, i. p. 17.)— *Ibid.*, 71.

MONKTON : ST. BEDE'S WELL.

At Monkton, near Jarrow, the reputed birthplace of Bede, there is a famous well which bears his name. Its waters have long been in great repute for their health-giving properties. As late as the year 1740, says Brand, it was a prevailing custom to bring children troubled with any disease or infirmity to it. A crooked pin was put in between each dipping—a curious instance of the association of ideas, for here, as at the Pool of Bethesda, beside the sheep-market in Jerusalem, only one patient could receive benefit, it seems, after each troubling of the waters. Brand's informant had seen twenty children brought together on a Sunday to be dipped in Bede's Well, at which also on Midsummer Eve there was a great concourse of neighbouring people, with bonfires, music, dancing, and other rural sports. This and other merry customs have long been discontinued. But still, when the well is occasionally cleared out, a number of crooked pins (a few years ago a pint) are always found among the mud. These have been thrown into the sacred fount for some purpose or other, either in the general way as charms for luck, or to promote and secure true love, or for the benefit of sick babies. In days when the ague was common in this country, the usual offering at this and other holy wells, by the shivering and shaking Gaffer Grays and Goody Blakes of the period, was a bit of rag tied to the branch of an overhanging tree or bush.—*Sunderland Times*, 17, vii., 1877.

About nine years ago, a friend happened to be staying a few days with an acquaintance at Monkton. On the Monday morning, it being particularly fine, he rose before six o'clock, and strolled down from the village to Bede's Well. Here he seated himself on a rail to enjoy the singing of the birds. Before long an

Irishman came up, who had been walking very fast, and was panting for breath. He took a bottle out of his pocket, stooped down and filled it from the well, put it to his mouth, and took a copious draught. "A fine morning, sir," said our friend. "Sure and it is," replied the man; "and what a holy man St. Bede must have been! You see, when I left Jarrow, I was as blind as a bat with the headache, but as soon as I had taken a drink just now, I was as well as ever I was in my life." So he filled his bottle once more with the precious liquid, and walked away, bidding our informant good-morning.—*Ibid.*, 15, ii., 1878.

HOUGHTON-LE-SPRING HOLY WELL, OR BEDE'S WELL.

The particularly fine springs of Houghton, from which the town receives its distinctive appellation of *le-Spring*, are all chalybeate. One of them, situated in Newbottle Lane, is still called the Holy Well. This name is said to have been imposed upon it in the year 700, when the Venerable Bede and his attendants passed through Houghton, and regaled themselves with "the fine beverage of nature" at this particular fountain.—*Ibid.*

Of the Holy Wells at Brancepeth, Butterby, Hartlepool, etc., little can be said, but that they all have more or less powerful medicinal properties, though without any local traditions attaching to them.—*Ibid.*, 17, vii., 1877.

SHOTLEY: HOLY WELL.

Many people journeyed up the Derwent Valley to Shotley Spa, where is to be seen one of the holy wells which the Saxons so much venerated. These sacred fountains were thought to have healing virtues, and, for aught that is known to the contrary, the saintly Ebba and her virgins may have tripped up the valley daily and paid their devotions to the limpid stream. While the Saxon remained the mother tongue, the place was denominated the Hally Well, hally being the adjective form of the Saxon word "hal," meaning sound in bodily health. Many people suppose that "hally well" is a corruption or provincialism, but as a matter of fact the name correctly describes the ancient fountain, and the fact of its still being applied to the place by the old residents in the Derwent Valley shows that the common people preserve the original of names longer than the learned. The water at Shotley

is thought to be remedial in scrofulous complaints, the universal
opinion thereabouts being expressed in a couplet :

" No scurvy in your skin can dwell
If you only drink the Hally Well."

The Holy Well is situated in the middle of the spa grounds,
and is surrounded by some romantic scenery. After passing
through the lodge gates, a broad walk or carriage road, winding
under a lofty canopy of trees, leads towards the fountain, on
reaching which the visitor observes that he has entered a natural
park, and treads on the arena, or rather the meadow floor of a
vast amphitheatre, formed by the graceful circumlocution of the
banks towering around ; the trees, of rich and varied foliage, and
rising above each other on the valley sides, appear as innumerable
spectators.—R. S. Blair, F.S.A.

ERARD'S WELL.

Hodgson, in his *Northumberland* [ii., pt. ii., p. 176], speaks of
Ulpham Feast and Erard's Well being mentioned in Ranulph de
Merlay's "Charter to the Abbot and Convent of Newminster," in
1138, though it is no longer known as "the Well of Erard."—
Ibid., 73.

HOLYSTONE : ST. NINIAN'S, OR OUR LADY'S WELL.

This well is near Alwinton, not far from the junction of two
Roman ways. That noble Welshman, the evangelist of the
Southern Picts, who died in A.D. 432, and may possibly have
visited Coventina's sacred spring at Carrawburgh, and her temple,
ere its glory had quite departed, had no doubt used it for baptismal
purposes. It is connected not only with the first introduction of
Christianity by a missionary of the British Church, but it was also
a place of note during the short-lived success of Paulinus, the
apostle of the Latin Church in Northern England. Here, under
King Ecgbert, his patron, he is said to have baptized three
thousand souls. And no wonder that it should have been so
highly honoured both by primitive pagans, as it would certainly
be with them an object of veneration, and also consecrated as a
" laver of regeneration " by the early Christian teachers. St.
Ninian's Well is still worthy of the description Wallis gave of it in
1769, as a "beautiful basin of water, rising at the east end in

bubbles perpendicular to the horizon, with fine, green sand. The bottom is variegated with it and white sand. It is walled round with freestone, hewn work, two or three courses still standing, shaded with trees and shrubs." This most copious spring is said to discharge 560 gallons of water each minute. Pins are often found in it.—*Ibid.*, 75, 76.

PALLINSBURN : WELL OF VENERING.

Paulinus is reputed to have baptized large number of persons at this famous well, where his name may still be traced.— *Ibid.*, 75.

WALLTOWN WELL.

At the Walltown Well, near the Roman station of Carvorran Magna, Paulinus is also said to have baptized many.—*Ibid.*, 75.

ST. BOSWELL'S HOLY WELL.

From which of the copious springs, and whether from one of these forming the beautiful petrifactions, the much desired supply of healing water was obtained, was not known ; but a pilgrim of this present year of grace (1878) had duly paid his votive offering to the sacred spring, in the form of the very smallest current coin of the realm—*one farthing*—and returned home in full faith, apparently, that the cure of a near relative suffering from cancer would be effected by the application of the simple and certainly harmless lotion.—*Ibid.*, 77.

CARRAWBROUGH : THE WELL OF COVENTINA'S.

This most interesting Roman well was discovered in October, 1876, on the line of the Roman wall, not far from Chollerford, containing an enormous quantity of Roman copper coins, twenty-four Roman altars, a massive votive tablet, with vases, rings, beads, brooches, and other objects. It has been fully described with illustrations of a large number of the objects found therein in vol. viii., New Series of *Archæologia Æliana*, from whence these notes are taken.

Whether the goddess Coventina was a British goddess or a goddess imported by the Roman soldier, is a question not easily decided, nor can any satisfactory derivation be found for her name. She was probably a local deity, to whose name a Roman

CARRAWBROUGH : COVENTINA'S WELL.

3

termination has been given. The founding of the temple of Coventina, writes Mr. John Clayton, must be ascribed to the Roman officers of the Batavian cohort, who had left a country where "the sun shines every day," and where, in pagan times, springs and running waters were objects of adoration.

The well was fed by three springs running south and flowing into the Tyne, and was enclosed in a temple which stood, and its

CARRAWBROOGH : COVENTINA'S WELL.

priests flourished, during the reigns of Antoninus Pius, and succeeding emperors, including that of Gratian, a period embracing more than two and a half centuries. The edicts of the Emperor Theodosius for the extermination of pagan superstition in the year 386, was probably the cause of the depositing in the well of the votive tablet, altars, and other objects of the temple, when also the priests would have been glad to flee and thus save their lives from the danger of the Theodosian persecution.

Very many oblations were presented in Coventina's Temple, or cast into the sacred well, as gifts of votaries, from time to time throughout the Roman occupation ; this is now conceded on all hands.

The votive tablet, p. 114, on which the goddess is represented as floating on the leaf of a water-lily, and holding a branch, has the following inscription :

Deae
COVVENTINAE
T. D. COSCONIA
NUS. PR. COII
I. BAT. L. M.

CARRAWBROUGH : COVENTINA'S WELL.

Expanded reading : Deæ Coventinæ Titus Domitius cosconianus Prefectus cohortis primæ Batavorum libens merito.

The lettering is perfect. The use of the double "V" in Coventina is a peculiarity, and may be accidental, or an example of the doubling of the consonant in order to give greater emphasis to the syllable.—*Ibid.*, p. 9.

Her three attendants are shown in the illustration given on p. 113. Each of the three naiads is raising in one hand a goblet, and in the other a flagon, from which is poured a stream of water.

These two illustrations have been kindly lent by the Society of Antiquaries of Newcastle-upon-Tyne.

NOTTINGHAMSHIRE.

NOTTINGHAM: ST. ANNE'S WELL.

B Y a custom, time beyond memory, the mayor and aldermen of Nottingham, with their wives, have been accustomed on Monday in Easter week, morning prayer ended, to march from the town to St. Anne's Well, anciently called Robin Hood's Well, having the town waits to play before them, and attended by all the clothing, *i.e.*, such as have been sheriffs, and ever after wear scarlet gowns, together with the officers of the town and many other burgesses and gentlemen, such as wish well to the woodward —this meeting being instituted, and since continued for his benefit. —Deering's *H. of Nottingham*, p. 125.

NEWARK: ST. CATHARINE'S WELL.

There is near Newark a well known as St. Catharine's, which was formerly very celebrated. It is situate near the earthwork called the Queen's Sconce, and the legend is, shortly, that a certain Sir Guy Saucimer, having in a fit of jealousy slain his rival, Sir Everard Bevercotes, a spring of water flowed from the spot where the murdered knight's head fell, in which Sir Guy was subsequently healed from the leprosy which befell him as a punishment for his crime. A chapel was built over the well, and dedicated to St. Catharine. This has since disappeared.

This well was formerly in the possession of my great-grandfather, who bought the site, on account of the extraordinary purity of the water, and established a linen manufactory there. The well still yields a copious supply of the purest water, and my father remembers that when he was a boy people from the town would send for the water on account of its quality.—W. J. SCALES in *Antiquary*.

THERE was a farmer who had an only daughter. She was very handsome, but proud. One day, when the servants were all afield, her mother sent her to the well for a pitcher of water. When she had let down the bucket, it was so heavy that she could hardly draw it up again ; and she was going to let loose of it, when a voice in the well said : " Hold tight and pull hard ; and good luck will come of it at last." So she held tight and pulled hard ; and when the bucket came up there was nothing in it but a frog, and the frog said : " Thank you, my dear : I've been a long while in the well, and I'll make a lady of you for getting me out." So when she saw it was only a frog, she took no notice, but filled her pitcher and went home.

Now, when they were at supper, a knock was heard at the door, and somebody outside said :

> " Open the door, my dearest one,
> And think of the well in the wood ;
> Where you and I were together, love a-keeping,
> And think of the well in the wood."

She looked out of the window, and there was the frog in boots and spurs. To it she said : " I shan't open the door for a frog." But her father said : " Open the door to the gentleman. Who knows what it may come to at last ?" So she opened the door, and the frog came in. Then said the frog :

> " Set me a chair, my dearest sweetest one,
> And think," etc.

" I'm sure I shan't set a chair ; the floor's good enough for a frog." The frog made many requests, to all of which the lady returned uncivil answers. He asked for beer, and was told " water is good enough for a frog " ; to be put to bed, but " the cistern is good enough for a frog to sleep in." The father, however, insisted on her compliance ; and even when the frog said : " Cuddle my back, my dearest sweet one," ordered her to do so, "for who knows what it may come to at last?" And in the morning when she awoke, she saw by her side the handsomest man that ever was seen, in a scarlet coat and top boots, with a sword by his side, and a gold chain round his neck, and gold rings on his fingers, who married her and made her a lady, and they lived very happy together.—*N. and Q.*, 1 S., v., 460. There is another version in Halliwell's *Nursery Rhymes.*

OXFORD.

ARISTOTLE'S WELL.

ARISTOTLE'S Well is not far from Elmer's (and Wolward's) Well in the north suburbs, "neare or in the fields of Walnercote or Ulgars—or Algar's Cote." It was anciently (as by some now) called Brumman's Well, together with that at Walton, because Brumman le Rich or de Walton lived and owned lands about the said wells, most, if not all, of which he gave by the favour of Robert D'oilly, his lord and master, who came into England with the Conqueror, to St. George's College in the Castell at his first foundation, A.D. 1074.

After his time, if not, be likely, before, it was christened by the name of Aristotle's Well, because that it was then—as now 'tis—frequented in the summer season by our Peripateticks.

In the present summer (1888) it was built over by the garden wall of a house erected on the south of the road leading to the canal bridge.—*Survey of the Antiquities of the City of Oxford*, composed in 1661-66 by Anthony Wood, edited by Andrew Clark, M.A., vol. i., 1889 ; Oxford Historical Soc., pp. 353, 354.

HOLYWELL.

On the north side of the church or chapel of St. Crosse, betweene it and the manor-house is an ancient well, from whence the parish took its name, called "Halywell," though now more properly called "Holy Well." Upon what account it hath that epithite bestowed upon it, whether for the employment of the water thereof about sacred uses for the church as is before said, or els

that by the reputed holinesse therein in respect of miracles it
wrought and the like, I am in doubt.

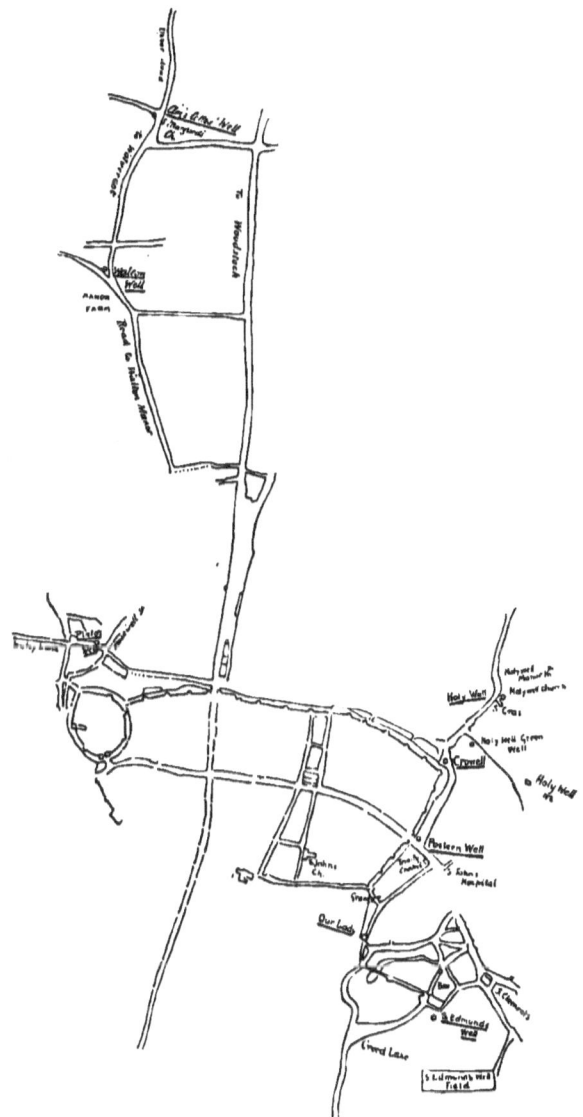

POSITIONS OF THE OXFORD WELLS.

Dr. Plot, *Natural History of Oxfordshire*, p. 49, speaks of the
use for the eyes and in some other cases.

A certain authour makes mention of a holy man called Mathew, that in old time lived here, leading the life as it should seeme of an incluse or anchorite ; and when there arose a question between the canons of Dorchester and Winchester concerning the burying-place of S. Birinus, when the Wintonians had a mind to translate his body, the said Mathew received a vision that Birinus lay "in pavimento ecclesiæ Dorcestrensis et Bertinus pone ostium," and in that manner seemed to resolve the doubt.   So that if we can say that from this man and his holy predecessors that lived here, this well should from his usuage therof for sustenance sake or his intercession to the Almighty that it might prove beneficial in curing of wounds or aches and the like, take its name, it might passe —for ought I know—as good a received truth as the legend of the vision produced by mine author.—*Ibid.*, pp. 388, 389.

The well was destroyed when drainage operations were carried out to convert Jackson's Green into a cemetery.

When it wanted a covering or shelter by the ruin of the old, if any at all, Dr. Fitzjames, Warden of Merton College, built a faire house over it of stone, with a roof to it of free stone, about the year 1488, a token of which bounty remaineth over the door therof at this time, viz., a dolphin naiant carved on a shield with another coat adjoyning sometimes quartered by the former, being the arms of the said bountiful and worthy Doctor.—*Ibid.*, pp. 389, 390.

ST. WINIFRED'S AND ST. MARGARET'S WELL.

The name Holywell is derived from another well near the church, dedicated to SS. Winifred and Margaret.   Wood says : "I find many persons yearly relieved by these wholesome waters." The water is very pure and cold, but seldom freezes, and there is a cold bath.   About 1488 the Warden of Merton erected a stone building over it to receive the prayers of the people.—*Ibid.*, p. 152.

ST. EDMUND'S WELL.

On the south side of St. Clement's Church, and neare to the ford or water called Mill Ford or Cowley Ford, which leadeth into Cowley Mede, was sometimes an ancient well called St. Edmund's Well, consecrated to such a saint that was Archbishop of Canterbury.   To which much resort of people in the raignes of Henry III. and Edward I., I find to have bin made, especially for the curing of wounds and recovery of maladyes and sicknesses, either by drinking the water therof or by bathing therin. And soe great holyness besides was it reputed to possesse by working of miracles on the vulger, that the fame thereof was spread far and neare. At length coming to the knowledge of Oliver Sutton, Bishop of Lyncoln, how strangly the people were besotted with a fond imagination of its vertues and holinesse, and that they did neglect to serve the true God by hankering after and worshipping this well, sent out his edict to the Archdeacon of Oxford, 1291, with a direful sentence therin of an anathema and excommunication to those that should anyway resort therto ; which partly speaketh to this effect :—"Ad audientiam nostram nuper certa relatione pervenit quod nonnulli, iuxta suarum mentium inconstantiam quasi vento agitate, a cultu fidei temere deviantes, locum quendam in campo iuxta ecclesiam S. Clementis extra municipium Oxon fontem Beati Edmundi vulgariter nuncupatum veluti locum sacrum vererari illumque sub simulatione sacrorum miraculorum quæ perpetrata contingunt ibidem, causa devotionis erronæ frequentare ac populum non modicum illuc attrahendo his figmentis damnatis decipere, immo pervertere, noviter praesumpserunt, errorem Gentilium iuto Christicolas introducere superstitiose conando," etc. Thus the Bishop.

" But upon what account this well should be thus frequented, whether at the said archbishop's canonization for a saint about the 29 Henry III., 1245, or upon any other event, I am in doubt. Yet for a certaine, if it was not for that particular it might arise for this : viz., that he, the said archbishop, while he was a student in Oxon, and courted by the greatest schollers of that age both for his piety and learning, did often according to his manner convers in privat with God, especially in his walkes of recreation in the fields neare Oxon. Of which Polycronicon also with a speciall remarke tells us, that he, one a time as he walked in a meede or feild neare Oxon, Jesus Christ appeared to him. And soe probably from thence a spring or well might at that place burst forth, even as St. Margaret's Well at Binsey did at the intreatyes and convers with God by St. Frideswyde, as is elsewhere expressed." The Well of St. Edmund was open till Milham Bridge fell down.—*Ibid.*, p. 288.

This well was once famous for curing distempers upon the saint's day, the people diverting themselves with cakes and ale, music and dancing ; which was innocent enough in comparison of what had been formerly practised at different places, when even the better sort of people placed a sanctity in them, brought alms and offerings, and made vows at them, as the ancient Germans and Britains did, and the Saxons and English were much inclined to.--*G. M. Lib.*, iii., 142.

Near St. Clement's, at Oxford, was a spring where St. Edmund, Archbishop of Canterbury, did sometimes meet and converse with an angel or nymph ; as Numa Pompilius did with Egeria. The well is now filled up.

CHILD'S WELL.

Child's Well, by the holyness of the chapleynes successively serving there, had vertue to make women that were barren to bring forth children.—*Ibid.*, p. 389.

STOKE OR PLATO'S WELL.

The reason why it was soe called was from a well situated therby called Stoke well, being the same which is to this day apparent to the beholders under the wall of Cornwall Close, and called beyond the memory of man by the students of this University " Platoes Well," and " Cornish Chough Well."*

It was on the north edge of the path which ran from the end of Thames (now George) Street to Hythe Bridge.—*Ibid.*, p. 365.

CROWELL.

At the east end of the street therof, and opposite to the northeast corner of the ruins of the city wall, wee had a well or spring, called Crowell, mentioned occasionally in very ancient records, and in some as a boundary to this lordship between it and the city liberties.

Dr. Rawlinson, it seems, principall of St. Edmund's Hall (1610-1632), erected a faire house covering over it of freestone, in the year 1626, and caused these two verses with his armes to be carved thereon :

> There's none will hurt this well that's wise,
> For it hurts none but helps the eyes.

To which a waggish scholler wrote this answer, with a coale under it :

* Wood, 276 B., Bod. Lib., folio xvi.

None but will hurt this well that's wise,
For it helpeth none but hurts the eyes.

But these verses with the house itself was demolished in the late warr, and the spring afterwards suffocated by the towne ditch to which it joyned.

An antient well called Crowell in Halywell parish, which is a boundary for the limits of that mannor. It was square.—*Ibid.*, pp. 385, 386.

ELMER'S WELL.

In the north suburbs there was Elmer's Well, possibly a spring in the meadows towards Wolvercote, now forgotten and unknown, having been probably destroyed by canal or railway.—*Ibid.*, p. 439.

HAROLD'S WELL.

In the west suburbs there was Harold's Well, near Osney, now quite forgotten.—*Ibid.*, p. 438.

SLAYING WELL.

There was a well in Slaying Lane, or as some call it Slaying-well Lane, called soe from the well there under Pembroke College wall. —*Ibid.*, p. 577.

JENNY NEWTON'S WELL.

Another well existed in what was Jackson's Green (now the Holywell) Cemetery, not far from Mr. Burgon's tomb, known as " Jenny Newton's Well." This was also supposed to possess great curative powers, particularly for affections of the eyes, and many a poor tailor and sempstress have I seen using it. This was destroyed together with Holy-well, when drainage operations were carried out to convert Jackson's Green into a cemetery.— *Ibid.*, p. 616.

HOLYWELL GREEN WELL.

A spring in Holywell Green or Common, found out by — Cowdrey, a precise shoemaker of St. Peter's, in the east ; made by him a well, and encompassed with stone, 1st May, 1651. A stone seat built about it by Henry Brome, gent., 1666. Holywell Green in Woods' time was the ground on which are now Holywell Vicarage and Cemetery, and the lawn-tennis courts between them and the well.—*Ibid.*, p. 386.

WALTON OR BRUMAN'S WELL.

Still remembered in the name of Walton Well Road, and having on its site a fountain, erected in 1885 by the liberality of Alderman Ward. The inscription is as follows: "1885. Drink and think of Him who is the fountain of life. With the consent of the lords of the manor, this drinking-fountain is erected by Mr. William Ward, to mark the site of a celebrated spring, known as Walton Well, adjacent to the ancient fordway into Colt Meadow, now called Walton Ford."—*Ibid.*, p. 439.

ULWARD'S WELL.

Ulward's Well called soe from John Ulward who held lands there of Dionisia Burewald, which she gave to Godstow.—*Ibid.*, p. 354.

SHOWELL OR ST. BARTHOLOMEW'S WELL.

" The Fellows of New College in Oxford have time out of mind every Holy Thursday, betwixt the houres of eight and nine, gonne to ye Hospitall called Bart'lemews, neer Oxford : where they retire to ye Chapell, and certain prayers are read and an antheme sung : from thence they goe to the upper end of ye grove adjoyning to the Chapell (the way being beforehand strewed with flowers by the poor people of ye Hospitall), they placed themselves round about the well there, where they warble forth melodiously a song of three or four or five parts ; which being performed, they refresh themselves with a morning's draught there, and retire to Oxford before sermon."—Brand's *Pop. Ant.*, ii., 378, Bohn's Ed. *Gentilisme and Judaisme*, p. 32.

RICOT PARK : HOLY WELL.

There is, or was, a holy well in Ricot Park. The water was held to be good for the eyes. The keepers formerly performed some ceremony here, before, it is presumed, it was a park.

BINSEY : ST. MARGARET'S WELL.

At the west end of this chappel, about three yards distant, is the well or spring, antiently and to this day called St. Margaret's

Well, being the very same that she by her prayers at the building
of the chapple opened. Of which heare a certaine old English
poet, who in the life of St. Frideswyde in the legend of English
saints, speaking of her various fortunes and of her passage from
Bampton to this place, saith thus :

"Ther fer with her felaisis[1] . she be laft ther
And to serve Jhesu Christ . a chapel lect arere[2]
Ther as is yit a fayr cort . and a cherche fayr and swete
Arerid in the honour . of her and Seynte Margrete
As this mayde wonyd[3] ther . in holy lyf and clene
The maydenes that were with her . gone hem ofte be mene[4]
That water was sum del to fer . hem ofte for smale dede
And cride on Seynt Friswid . that she schold hem therof rede[5]
This mayde Seynt Friswid . bad our lordis sonde
That he water thorw his gras . hem sente ner honde
So sprong ther up a welle . cler inowf[6] and clene
That fond hem water inowf . tho dorst hem nought be mene
That beside the cherche is yit[7] . in the west syde
That mony a mon hath bote do . and that men seggeth wide."*

   [1] Fellows.   [2] Raise.   [3] Lived.   [4] Bemoan.
        [5] Rid.   [6] Enough.   [7] It.

Over St. Margaret's Well was a covering of stone, and thereon
on the front the picture of St. Margaret (or perhaps St. Frideswyde), pulled down by Alderman Sayre, of Oxon, a little before
the late war, 1639.

To this well also and her image and certaine reliques in the
chapple did the people come on pilgrimage with as great devotion
to ease their burdened soules and obtaine resolutions of their
doubts, as they would to an oracle.

And here, also, when those maimed and unsound folke had bin
cured either by bathing in, or drinking of, this water, hang up
their crutches as a speciall memorandum of their cured griefs.
For which end and purpose there were severall preists that
inhabited here appointed by the Prior of St. Frideswide's purposely to confess and absolve those pilgrims.

Near to this place it was that the Lady Edyne, of Wynton, the
widdow of Sir William Lancelot, knight, had a vision. See *Twyne*,
xxi., 199.

The well wee find almost to the last frequented by superstitious
people, and especially about a hundred years before the dissolu-

* Ex Lib. MS. Bibliothecæ, Bodl. Lib., Bodl. MS. 779.

tion.   Soe much, that they were forced to enclose it—as in old time before, they had defended it—with a little house of stone over it with a lock and a dore to it.   But all decaying and going much to ruine, at the suppression of St. Frideswyde's Priory, was at last —I meane the little house—about twenty-five years agoe, pulled downe and quite taken away.   Soe that now being overgrowne with nettles and other weeds, and harbouring frogs, snails, and vermin, scarce owneth the name of a well ; noe more than the old and small building joyning to the north side of the chapple doth—as formally it did—a court.

The well is now in better condition.   When I visited it on 25th October, 1887, the churchyard was tidily fenced and very neatly kept.   At the well a descent of some five steps brought one to an arched vault, beneath which, in the centre of the flooring, was a round basin containing the water of the well, the surface of the water being about six feet below the level of the ground.   On the wall above the arch was this inscription :

"S. MARGARET'S WELL.

"S. Margaretae fontem, precibus S. Frideswidæ (ut fertur) concessum, nquinatum diu obrutumque in usum revocavit T. J. Prout, Aed. Xti alumnus, Vicarius, A. S. MDCCCLXXIV."

At the time of the restoration of this well, an Oxford wit, having regard to its proximity to the church, suggested for an inscription :

"Άριστον μεν ὕδωρ.
When you open your pew-door,
This may comfort supply
Should the sermon be dry."
Ibid., pp. 323-328, *et seq.*

The well of St. Margaret or St. Frideswide, in Binsey churchyard, scarce two miles from Oxford, is supposed to have sprung from the prayers of St. Frideswide, and many in olden times consulted it as an oracle on the state of their burdened souls ; maimed and sick persons drank and bathed in the waters, and were cured by them.   The stone edifice was in the last century destroyed, but has been restored.—*Denham Tracts*, p. 151.

The well probably takes its name from the church, which was dedicated in honour of St. Margaret.

There was a well dedicated in honour of St. Mary outside Smith Gate.

POSTERN WELL.

This well was situated on the north side of East Gate.

RUTLAND.

RYHALL: ST. TIBBA'S WELL.

THERE was here a well and a shrine in honour of St. Tibba. "'Tis now above 700 years since St. Tibba, the celebrated saint of Ryhall was taken out of her grave there and carryed to Peterborough Church by Abbot Elfin. The inhabitants there have still an obscure memorial of her, but have lost her name. They call her Queen, and say she used to walk up to Tibbal's hill, and wash her in a spring there. This is all they know of her. The truth is, on Tibbal's hill is the spring which gave name to the hill Tibb's-well-hill. 'Tis upon the hill going from Tolethorp to Belmsford bridg. On the brow of the hill, near the spring, is Hale-green, as it is still called, taking its name from the anniversary meetings held here in former times, in memory of St. Tibba, whose day is December 16. Hale is the name our Saxon ancestors gave to the solemnities they practised in the fields to the honour of saints. St. Tibba's well is now corrupted into Stibbal's-hill-well."—*Stukeley's Diaries and Letters*, iii. 167, 168 ; *Surtees Soc.*, vol. lxxx.

RYHALL: ST. EABBA'S OR JACOB'S WELL.

"Just above Ryhall is Stableford bridg, which being an odd name upon the river Guash, this opinion is proposed about it. When we read of St. Tibba, we find St. Eabba, her cozen, along with her, another devout, retired person, who commonly lived with her. Hence I conjecture that the spring just above this bridg, northward on the brow of the hill as it were, opposite to St. Tibba's well, was consecrated by our pious ancestors to St. Eabba. Then this ford over the river, before the bridg was built, would be called St. Eabba's-well-ford, corrupted into Stablesford. This same spring now is called by the shepherds Jacob's Well, and that probably is but a corruption of St. Eabba's well.

"Sts. Tibba and Eabba were of royal Mercian blood, and owned Ryhall. They were at first wild hunting girls, at last saints."—*Ibid.*, pp. 169, 170.

SHROPSHIRE.

CHETTON : HOLY WELL.

"IN the parish of Chetton there was formerly a holy well or spring. It is not known whether it had any special dedication, but the church is dedicated to St. Giles, and the waters of the spring were supposed to possess a healing virtue for cripples or weakly persons. The last person who was dipped in the well was Mary Anne Jones, about the year 1817 ; she subsequently died about 1830, aged twenty-four years, and was the eldest sister of my informant, one of the oldest inhabitants of the parish. Though considerably covered up with undergrowth, the spring is not yet entirely lost."—Miss E. Lythall-Neale.

WEST FELTON : HOLY WELL.

There is a small holy well in this parish (West Felton), in a hamlet called Woolston. The water of this well is still used by the country people for complaints of the eyes. It is a beautiful clear stream, running under a small black and white chapel into two paved square baths environed with stone walls, one of which is lower than the other. The higher one has steps down to the water, and, strange to say, there is more water in summer than in winter. Under the chapel, which overhangs the stream, is a long-shaped niche which has evidently contained the statue of the saint. At this side is a small cell, or covered place, where probably the priest or monk stood to dispense the water. The chapel is now unfortunately used as a cottage, and the beams of the roof inside are covered with whitewash. At one end there is the tracery of Tudor roses and acanthus leaves, upon what is evidently the framework of a window.—See *Shropshire Arch. Soc. Trans.*, ix. 238.

CROSMERE LAKE.

At Crosmere, near Ellesmere, is one of the number of pretty lakes scattered throughout that district. There is a tradition of a chapel having formerly stood on the banks of the lake, and it is said that the belief once was, that whenever the waters were ruffled by the wind, the chapel bells might be heard ringing beneath the surface.

LONGNOR.

The White Lady of Longnor is in the habit of coming out of the Black Pool beside the road to Leebotwood. This pool is bottomless. "Old Nancy," a well-known Longnor worthy, was shocked and scandalized to hear that the Parson's children had been so foolhardy as to skate on it in the recent hard winters. The White Lady issues out of it at night, and wanders about the roads. Hughes, the " Parson's man " at Longnor, met her once as he was going over the narrow foot-bridge beside the ford over Longnor Brook. "I sid 'er a-cummin'," he said (June, 1881), "an' I thinks, 'ere's a nice young wench. Well, thinks I, who she be, I'll gi'e 'er a fright. I was a young fellow then, yo' known—an' I waited till 'er come close up to me, right i' the middle o' the bridge, an' I stretched out my arms, so—an' I clasped 'er in 'em tight—so. An' theer was nothin'!

"She came down here to the Villa wunst," he continued, after a dramatic pause. "It was when there was a public kep' here. Joe Wigley, he told me. There was a great party held in the garden, and he was playing the fiddle. And they were all *daincin'*, and she come an' dainced, all in white. And everyone was saying : 'What a nice young 'ooman—Here's the one for me—I'll 'ave a daince ööth 'er'—and so on, like that. And she dainced and dainced ööth 'em, round i' the ring, but they could's niver ketch 'out on 'er 'and. And at last she disappeart of a sudden, and then they found out who it 'ad bin, as 'ad bin daincin' along ööth 'em. And they all went off in a despert hurry, and there was niver no daincing there no more."

Old Nancy declared that this shadowy fair one was the ghost of a lady "as 'ad bin disapp'inted," and had drowned herself in the Black Pool. But "White Ladies" has been a name for the fairies from the days of the romance of Hereward, and the

9

dancing "round in the ring" points out very clearly the class of beings among which the lady of the Black Pool should be placed. —*Shropshire Folk-lore*, p. 76.

BOMERE POOL.

"Some two centuries ago, or less, a party of gentlemen, including the Squire [of Condover], were fishing in the pool, when an enormous fish was captured and hauled into the boat. Some discussion arose as to the girth of the fish, and a bet was made that he was bigger round than the squire, and that the sword-belt of the latter would not reach his waist. To decide the bet the squire unbuckled his belt, which was there and then with some difficulty fastened round the body of the fish. The scaly knight (for so he no doubt felt himself to be) being girt with the sword, began to feel impatient at being kept so long out of his native element, and after divers struggles he succeeded in eluding his captors, and regaining at the same time his freedom and his watery home, carrying the squire's sword with him."—*Ibid.*, p. 81.

The Monster Fish of Bomere Pool is thus described: He of course lives *in* the mere, not *beneath* it, like the water-witches. He is bigger than any fish that ever swam, he wears a sword by his side, and no man can catch him. It was tried once. A great net was brought, and he was entangled in it and brought nearly to the side, but he drew his sword and cut the net and escaped. Then the fishermen made a net of iron links and caught him in that. This time he was fairly brought to land, but again he freed himself with his wonderful sword, and slid back into the water and got away. The people were so terrified at the strange sight that they have never tried to take him again, though he has often been seen since, basking in the shallow parts of the pool with the sword still girded round him. One day, however, he will give it up, but not until the right heir of Condover Hall shall come and take it from him. He will yield it easily then, but no one else can take it. For it is no other than Wild Edric's sword, which was committed to the fish's keeping when he vanished, and will never be restored except to his lawful heir. Wild Edric, they say, was born at Condover Hall, and it ought to belong to his family now; but his children were defrauded of their inheritance, and that is why there is no luck about the Hall to this day. This curse has been on it ever since then. Every time the property changes hands the new landlord will never receive the rents twice ; and those who have studied history will tell you that this has always come to pass.—*Ibid.*, p. 80.

"Many years ago, a village stood in the hollow which is now filled up by the mere. But the inhabitants were a wicked race, who mocked at God and His priest. They turned back to the idolatrous practices of their fathers, and worshipped Thor and Woden ; they scorned to bend the knee, save in mockery, to the White Christ who had died to save their souls. The old priest earnestly warned them that God would punish such wickedness as theirs by some sudden judgment, but they laughed him to scorn. They fastened fish-bones to the skirt of his cassock, and set the children to pelt him with mud and stones. The holy man was not dismayed at this ; nay, he renewed his entreaties and warnings, so that some few turned from their evil ways and worshipped with him in the little chapel which stood on the bank of a rivulet that flowed down from the mere on the hillside.

"The rains fell that December in immense quantities. The mere was swollen beyond its usual limits, and all the hollows in the hills were filled to overflowing. One day when the old priest was on the hillside gathering fuel, he noticed that the barrier of peat, earth, and stones, which prevented the mere from flowing into the valley, was apparently giving way before the mass of water above. He hurried down to the village and besought the men to come up and cut a channel for the discharge of the super-fluous waters of the mere. They only greeted his proposal with shouts of derision, and told him to go and mind his prayers, and not spoil their feast with his croaking and his kill-joy presence.

"These heathens were then keeping their winter festival with great revelry. It fell on Christmas Eve. The same night the aged priest summoned his few faithful ones to attend at the mid-night mass, which ushered in the feast of our Saviour's Nativity. The night was stormy, and the rain fell in torrents, yet this did not prevent the little flock from coming to the chapel. The old servant of God had already begun the holy sacrifice, when a roar was heard in the upper part of the valley. The server was just ringing the Sanctus bell which hung in the bell-cot, when a flood of water dashed into the church, and rapidly rose till it put out the altar-lights. In a few moments more, the whole

building was washed away, and the mere, which had burst its
mountain barrier, occupied the hollow in which the village had
stood. Men say that if you sail over the mere on Christmas
Eve, just after midnight, you may hear the Sanctus bell tolling."
—*Ibid.*, pp. 64, 65.

Here is another legend. Many have tried to fathom Bomere,
but in vain. Though waggon-ropes were tied together and let
down into it, no bottom could be found—and how should there
be? when everyone knows that it *has* none! Nor can it be
drained. The attempt was once made, and found useless ; for
whatever the workmen did in the day, was undone by some
mysterious power in the night.

In the days of the Roman Empire, when Uriconium was standing,
a very wicked city stood where we now see Bomere Pool. The
inhabitants had turned back from Christianity to heathenism, and
though God sent one of the Roman soldiers to be a prophet to
them, like Jonah to Nineveh, they would not repent. Far from
that, they ill-used and persecuted the preacher. Only the daughter
of the governor remained constant to the faith. She listened
gladly to the Christian's teaching, and he on his part loved her,
and would have had her to be his wife. But no such happy lot
was in store for the faithful pair. On the following Easter Even,
sudden destruction came upon the city. The distant Caradoc—
the highest and most picturesque of the Stutton Hills, crowned
by a British encampment, which some have supposed to be the
scene of Caractacus's last stand—sent forth flames of fire, and at
the same time the city was overwhelmed by a tremendous flood,
while the " sun in the heavens danced for joy, and the cattle in
the stalls knelt in thanksgiving that God had not permitted such
wickedness to go unpunished."* But the Christian warrior was
saved from the flood, and he took a boat and rowed over the
waters, seeking for his betrothed, but all in vain. His boat was
overturned, and he, too, was drowned in the depths of the mere.
Yet whenever Easter Even falls on the same day as it did that
year, the form of the Roman warrior may be seen again, rowing
across Bomere in search of his lost love, while the church bells
are heard ringing far in the depths below.—*Ibid.*, pp. 65, 66.

* These words were repeated as a sort of formula, necessary to the proper
telling of the story. Their connection with the two dates, Christmas and
Easter, assigned for the destruction is striking.

At Colemere the bells may be heard, according to one authority, on windy nights when the moon is full. According to another, at midnight on the anniversary of the patron saint of the chapel, whom yet another informant declares to have been St. Helen. Another story is that a monastery once stood on the ground occupied by the pool, but a spring burst forth close to it, and swelled to such a height that the waters quickly covered the monastery, and formed Colemere, beneath which the chapel bells may yet be yearly heard ringing.

Another variant runs as follows :

"They say that the old church at Colemere was pulled down by Oliver Cromwell, and the bells thrown into the mere. Once an attempt was made to get them up. Chains had been fastened to them, and twenty oxen had succeeded in drawing them to the side, when a man who had been helping said to someone who had doubted their being able to raise them : 'In spite of God and the devil we have done it.' At these words the chains snapped. The bells rolled back into the water. They heard the sound, and saw by the bubbles where they had settled, but they could not see anything more, nor has anything ever been seen or heard of them since."—*Ibid.*, p. 67.

The Eas Well, at Baschurch, in a field beside the River Perry, a mile west of the church, was frequented till twenty years ago by young people, who went there on Palm Sunday to drink sugar and water and eat cakes. A clergyman who was present in 1830 speaks of seeing little boys scrambling for the lumps of sugar which escaped from the glasses and floated down the brook which flows from the spring into the river.—*Ibid.*, p. 432.

The Berth Pool near Baschurch lies at the foot of the Berth Hill, a very curious entrenched camp on an eminence in the midst of a morass, where it was once intended to build the parish church. But the same mysterious "something" which interfered with the building on the height also threw the bells intended for it into the Berth Pool. Horses were brought and fastened to

them, but were quite powerless to draw them out. Then oxen
were tried with better success; but just as the bells were coming
to the surface of the water, one of the men employed in the work
let slip an oath, on which they fell back, crying, "No! never!"
And they lie at the bottom of the pool to this day. "Three
cart-ropes" will not reach the bottom of the Berth Pool.—*Ibid.*,
p. 68.

Between Oswestry and Llanymynech, close beside the railway,
lies a pretty little pool called Llynclys, or Llyn-y-clys, which is
variously interpreted to mean "the swallowed hall," or "the lake
of the enclosure." Early in this century there were many who
believed that "when the water was clear enough" the towers of a
palace might be discerned at the bottom; only, as the author of
the *Gossiping Guide to Wales* observes, "unfortunately there never
appears to have been a day when the water *was* clear enough."
The legend which tells of the destruction of this palace—though
now, it seems, forgotten—is recorded in an old MS. history of
Oswestry, preserved in the British Museum, and communicated
to the present writer by Mr. Askew Roberts of Croeswylan,
Oswestry, the author of the *Guide* aforesaid. It is as follows:

"About twoe miles of Oswestry w*i*thin the parishe there is a
poole called llynclis of w*h*ich poole Humffrey Lloyd reporteth
thus: German Altisiodorensis pr*e*ached sometime there against
the Pelagian heresie. The King whereof, as is there read, because
hee refused to heare that good man by the secrett and terrible
judgment of God w*i*th his pallace and all his houschould was
swallowed up into the bowelles of the earth. Suo in loco non
procul ab oswaldia est Stagnu*m* incognite p*r*ofunditatis llynclis id
est vorago palatij in hunc dictu*m*. In that place whereas not far
from Oswestry is nowe a standing water of an unknown depth
called llynclis that is the devouring of the pallace." Llynclys
Pool is one which has "never a bottom to it."—*Ibid.*, p. 68.

The great mere at Ellesmere is the subject of many legends, or
rather variants of one legend, all bearing on the same notion
of wickedness punished by a flood. Where Ellesmere stands
was once as fine a stretch of meadow-land as any in the county.

In a large field in the midst of it there was a well of beautiful water, from which everyone in the neighbourhood used to fetch as much as they pleased. At last there was a change of tenants in the farm to which the field belonged ; and the new-comer was a churlish man, who said the comers and goers trampled down his grass. So he stopped the poor people coming to the well with their cans and buckets as they had been used to do for years and years, and allowed no one to draw water there besides his own family. But no good came of such hard dealings. One morning, very soon after the people had been forbidden to come, the farmer's wife went out to the well for water, but instead of the well she found that the whole field was one great pool, and so it has remained ever since. But the farmer and all of his family who held the field after him were obliged to pay the same rent as before, as a punishment for such unneighbourly conduct.

A correspondent of *Shreds and Patches*, in 1881, picked up another version. Both are evidently genuine *folk*-tales.

" A many many years ago, clean water was very scarce in this neighbourhood." All that could be got, was what was fetched from a beautiful well in the very middle of what is now the mere at Ellesmere. But the people to whom the land belonged were so grasping that they charged a halfpenny for every bucketful that was drawn, which fell very heavy on the poor, and they prayed to Heaven to take some notice of their wrongs. So the Almighty, to punish those who so oppressed the poor, caused the well to burst forth in such volumes that it flooded all the land about, and so formed the mere. And so thenceforward there was plenty of water free to all comers.—*Ibid.*, p. 69.

A third variant has been versified by the Rev. Oswald M. Feilden, vicar of Frankton, near Ellesmere :

> I've heard it said, where now so clear
> The water of that silver mere,
>   It once was all dry ground ;
> And on a gentle eminence,
> A cottage with a garden fence,
>   Which hedged it all around.
>
> And there resided all alone,
> So runs the tale, an aged crone,
>   A witch, as some folks thought.
> And to her home a well was near,
> Whose waters were so bright and clear,
>   By many it was sought.

But greatly it displeased the dame
To see how all her neighbours came
  Her clear cool spring to use,
And often was she heard to say,
That if they came another day,
  She would the well refuse.

" Upon this little hill," said she,
" My house I built for privacy,
  Which now I seek in vain :
For day by day your people come
Thronging in crowds around my home,
  This water to obtain."

But when folks laughed at what she said,
Her countenance with passion red,
  She uttered this dread curse :
" Ye neighbours one and all beware !
If here to come again you dare
  For you 'twill be the worse !"

Of these her words they took no heed,
And when of water they had need
  Next day, they came again.
The dame, they found, was not at home,
The well was locked : so they had come
  Their journey all in vain.

The well was safely locked. But though
You might with bolts and bars, you know,
  Prevent the water going,
One thing, forsooth, could not be done,
I mean forbid the spring to run,
  And stop it overflowing.

And all that day, as none could draw,
The water rose full two feet more
  Than ever had been known.
And when the evening shadows fell,
Beneath the cover of the well
  A stream was running down.

It flowed on gently all next day,
And soon around the well there lay
  A pond of water clear ;
And as it ever gathered strength,
It deeper grew, until at length
  The pond became a mere.

To some, alas ! the flood brought death ;
Full many a cottage lies beneath
  The waters of the lake ;

And those who dwelt on either side
Were driven by the running tide
Their homesteads to forsake.

And as they fled, that parting word
Which they so heedlessly had heard,
They now recalled, I ween !
The dame was gone ; but where once stood
Her cottage, still above the flood
An island may be seen.

The connection of the island in Ellesmere with the legend is an addition of the verse-maker's.

Another version : An old woman named Mrs. Ellis had a pump in her yard. She would not sell or give any water to her neighbours. One night the well overflowed, and the next morning nothing was to be seen of her or the pump. Only the large mere covered the country, which is called after her " Elles-mere."— *Ibid.*, p. 72.

Miss Jackson has thus recorded a droll story current in the neighbourhood of Ellesmere. Kettlemere and Blackmere, two small meres of the Ellesmere group, lie close to one another. " A gentleman riding down the lane which skirts them, said to a boy whom he met : ' My lad, can you tell me the name of this water ?' pointing towards Kettlemere. ' Oh, aye, sir, it's Kettle-*mar.*' ' How deep is it ?' ' Oh, it's no bottom to it, and the tother's deeper till that, sir !' "—*Ibid.*, p. 73.

The Ladies' (or Lady's) Walk at Ellesmere is a paved causeway running far into the mere, with which, more than forty years ago, old swimmers were well acquainted. It could be traced by bathers until they got out of their depth. How much farther it might run they of course knew not. Its existence seems to have been almost forgotten, until in 1879 some divers, searching for the body of a drowned man, came upon it at the bottom of the mere, and this led to old inhabitants mentioning their knowledge of it.—*Ibid.*, p. 77.

WLFRESIMERE.

There is in England a lake which is commonly called Wlfresi-mere, that is, the mere of King Wlfer, which abounds with fish when all are allowed to fish in it, but when men are prevented from fishing in it, few or no fish are found in it.—*Ibid.*, p. 72.

In the same region is Haveringe-mere. If a person in sailing over it calls out : " Prout Haveringe-mere, or allethope cunthefere," a storm arises at once and swamps his boat. These words convey an insult, as if it were said to the lake : " 'Thou art called Haueringe-mere," *i.e.*, Hauering's mere. Both (lakes) are on the borders of Wales. The above puzzling extract is from Gervase of Tilbury, which was communicated to the Rev. H. B. Taylor, in the belief that the meres mentioned in them were probably to be identified with Ellesmere and its neighbour Newton Mere.—*Ibid.*

The White Lady of Kilsall haunts the dark walk beside the pool in the grounds of that old-fashioned mansion. She is said to be the ghost of one of the Whiston family, who were owners of Kilsall, near Albrighton, in the time of Elizabeth, and whose name is still preserved in that of " Whiston's Cross," in the same neighbourhood.—*Ibid.*, p. 77.

Two versions are here given, one in the vernacular, the other in vulgar English :

" Naw, Ah nivir 'cerd tell as anny think 'ad bin sin o' leate 'eers, but thur *was* a marmed seed thur *wonst*. It was a good bit agoo, afore moy toime. Ah darsee as it 'ud be a 'undred 'ears back. Theer wuz two chaps a-gooin' to woork won mornin' early, an' they'd 'n raught as fur as the pit soide in Mr. ——'s faild, an' they seed summat a-squattin' atop o' the waëter as did skear 'em above a bit ! Eh, they thought as 'ow it were gooin' to tek 'em roight streat off to th' Owd Lad is sen ! Well, Ah conna jŏŏst seä ezackly what it were loike—Ah wunna theer, yo' known—but it were a marmed, saëm as yo' readen on i' the paëpers. The chaps 'ad loike to 'a runned awea at the first, they wun that skeared, but as soon's iver the marmed spoken to 'em, they niver thoughten no moor o' that. 'Er v'ice was se swate an' se pleasant, they fell in lŏŏve wi' 'er theer an then, the both on 'em. Well, an' 'er towd 'em as 'ow theer wuz a treasure 'id at the bottom o' the pit, lŏŏmps o' gowd, an' dear knows what. An 'er'd give 'em all as iver they loiked if se be as they'd'n cŏŏm to 'er i' the waëter an' tek it out of 'er 'ands. So they wenten in—welly up to their chins it were —an' 'er dowked down i' the waëter an' brought ŏŏp a lŏŏmp o' gowd, as big as a mon's yed, very near. An' the chaps wun jŏŏst agoin' to tek it off 'er, an' the won on 'em sez : ' Eh,' sez 'e (an' swore, yo known), ' if this inna a bit o' luck !' An' moy word ! if the marmed didna tek it off 'em agin, an' give a koind of shroike, an' dowked down agen into the pit, an' they niver seed no more on 'er, not a'ter ; nor got none o' the gowd ; nor nobody's niver seed nothink on 'er sence."

The following is a translation :

" No, I never heard anything had been seen of late years, but there *was* a mermaid seen there *once*. It was a good while ago, before my time. I dare say it might be a hundred years ago. There were two men going to work early one morning, and they had got as far as the side of the pond in Mr. ——'s field, and they saw something on the top of the water which scared them not a little. They thought it was going to take them straight off to the *Old Lad* himself ! I can't say exactly what it was like, I wasn't there, you know ; but it was a mermaid, the same as you read of in the papers. The fellows had almost run away at first, they were so frightened, but as soon as the mermaid had spoken to them, they thought no more of that. Her voice was so sweet and pleasant, that they fell in love with her there and then, both of them. Well, she told them there was a treasure hidden at the bottom of the pond—lumps of gold, and no one knows what. And she would give them as much as ever they liked if they would come to her in the water and take it out of her hands. So they went in, though it was almost up to their chins, and she dived into the water and brought up a lump of gold almost as big as a man's head. And the men were just going to take it, when one of them said : ' Eh !' he said (and swore, you know), ' if this isn't a bit of luck !' And, my word ! if the mermaid didn't take it away from them again, and gave a scream, and dived down into the pond, and they saw no more of her, and got none of her gold. And nobody has ever seen her since then."

No doubt the story once ran that the oath which scared the uncanny creature involved the mention of the Holy Name.—*Ibid.*, p. 78.

The only ancient dedication (in Shropshire) to a Welsh saint is that of St. Owen's Well, at Much Wenlock, the existence of which in the sixteenth century is known to us from the Register of Sir Thomas Boteler, vicar of the parish.—*Ibid.*, p. 621.

St. Milburga's Well is still to be seen near the entrance to the beautiful and interesting ruins of the priory. A conduit from it, it is said, supplied a beautiful carved fountain which has lately been brought to light within the abbey precincts.—*Ibid.*, p. 417.

It is an unfailing spring, a little above the church, and at the foot of the steep bank leading up the Brown Clee Hill. It was reputed to be good for sore eyes, and was also much used for "bucking" clothes, which were rinsed in the well water and beaten on a flat stone at the well's mouth; but some ten years ago it was covered in, and altered, and I am told is now in a ruinous and unsightly condition. The legend still current in the village relates that St. Milburga was a very holy and beautiful woman, who, nevertheless, had so many enemies that she was obliged to live in hiding. Her retreat, however, became known, and she took to flight, mounted on a white horse (most authorities say a *white ass*), and pursued by her foes with a pack of bloodhounds, and a gang of rough men on horseback. After two days and two nights' hard riding she reached the spot where the well now is, and fell fainting from her horse, striking her head upon a stone. Blood flowed from the wound, and the stain it caused upon the stone remained there partly visible, and has been seen by many persons now living.

On the opposite side of the road some men were sowing barley in a field called the Plock (by others the Vineyard), and they ran to help the saint. Water was wanted, but none was at hand. The horse, at St. Milburga's bidding, struck his hoof into the rock, and at once a spring of water gushed out. " Holy water, hence-forth and for ever, flow freely," said the saint. Then, stretching

out her hands, she commanded the barley the men had just
sown to spring up, and instantly the green blades appeared.
Turning to the men, she told them that her pursuers were close
at hand, and would presently ask them, " When did the lady on
the white horse pass this way?" to which they were to answer,
" When we were sowing this barley." She then remounted her
horse, and bidding them prepare their sickles, for in the evening
they should cut their barley, she went on her way.   And it came
to pass as the saint had foretold.   In the evening the barley was
ready for the sickle, and while the men were busy reaping, St.
Milburga's enemies came up, and asked for news of her.   The
men replied that she had stayed there at the time of the sowing
of that barley, and they went away baffled.   But when they came
to hear that the barley which was sown in the morning ripened
at mid-day, and was reaped in the evening, they owned that it
was in vain to fight against God.

Mediæval hagiologists relate the flight of St. Milburga from
the too violent suit of a neighbouring prince, whose pursuit was
checked by the river Corve, which, as soon as she had passed it,
swelled from an insignificant brook to a mighty flood which
effectually barred his progress.—*Ibid.,* p. 417.

SHREWSBURY : SS. PETER AND PAUL'S WELL.

SS. Peter and Paul were obvious dedications for two wells in
a field near "Burnt Mill Bridge" in the parish attached to the
Abbey of SS. Peter and Paul at Shrewsbury.   They were "good
for sore eyes," and were much resorted to till they were destroyed
by the drainage of the field, about 1820.—*Salopian Shreds and
Patches,* July 27, 1881.

THE WREKIN : ST. HAWTHORN'S WELL.

St. Hawthorn's Well existed on the Wrekin in recent years, and
was supposed to be effectual in cases of skin diseases.   We are
told of a man who suffered from a scorbutic affection, who was
wont to walk from his home, six miles distant, before 2.30 a.m.,
that he might drink the water and bathe his face in the well
before sunrise, which was needful to the cure.   But unfortunately
his trouble was in vain.—*Ibid.,* August 17, 1881.

RHOSGOCH : WISHING WELL.

At Rhosgoch, on the Long Mountain in the *Montgomeryshire* portion of the *Shropshire* parish of Worthen, is a famous wishing-well, which is "good for the eyes" besides. "One of my cottagers," writes Sir Offley Wakeman, "who lived close to the well for two years, tells me that the bottom was bright with pins—straight ones he thinks—and that you could get whatever you wished for the moment the pin you threw in touched the bottom." "It was mostly used for wishing about sweethearts."—*Shropshire Folk-lore*, p. 422.

WELLINGTON : ST. MARGARET'S WELL.

This is renowned for its eye-healing virtues, and was yearly visited by Black Country folk and others, who *douked*, or dipped, their heads in it on Good Friday.—*Ibid.*, p. 433.

LUDLOW : BOILING WELL.

The pretty legend of the Boiling Well—so called from its continual bubbling as it rises—in a meadow beside the River Corve at Ludlow, was related to me on the spot in the year 1881, as follows. Three centuries ago the principal figure would have been described as a holy saint in disguise instead of a simple palmer.

"Years ago, you know, there was what was called the Palmers' Guild at Ludlow. You may see the palmers' window in the church now : it is the east window in the north chancel, which was the chantry chapel of the guild. The old stained glass gives the story of the Ludlow palmers; how King Edward the Confessor gave a ring to a poor pilgrim, and how years afterwards two palmers from Ludlow, journeying homewards from the Holy Land, met with the blessed St. John the Evangelist, who gave them the same ring, and bade them carry it to their king, and tell him that he to whom he had given it was no other than the saint himself, and that after receiving it again the king should not live many days, which came to pass as he said. The Palmers' Guild founded many charities in Ludlow, and among them the Barnaby House, which was a hospice for poor travellers. Many used to pass through the town in those days, especially pilgrims going to

St. Winifred's Well in Wales. And once upon a time an old palmer journeying thither was stayed some days at Barnaby House by sickness, and the little maid of the house waited on him. Now, this little maid had very sore eyes. And when he was got well and was about to go on his way, he asked of her what he should do for her. 'Oh, master,' said she, 'that my sight might be healed!' Then he bade her come with him, and led her outside the town, till they stood beside the Boiling Well. And the old man blessed the well, and bade it have power to heal all manner of wounds and sores, *to be a boon and a blessing to Ludlow as long as the sun shines and water runs.* Then he went his way, and the little maid saw him no more, but she washed her eyes with the water, and they were healed, and she went home joyfully. And even to this day the well is sought by sufferers from diseases of the eyes."

Our old informant had known a man come with a horse and cart all the way from Bromyard, in Herefordshire, to fetch a barrel of the water for his wife's use, and when the barrel was empty he came again.—*Ibid.*, p. 421.

LUDLOW: ST. JULIAN'S WELL.

St. Julian's Well, within the precincts of the Austin Friars at Ludlow, is, I imagine, like St. Julian's Church, Shrewsbury, dedicated in honour of St. Juliana, the virgin martyr of Nicomedia, who bound and scourged her demon-tempter, quenched the fire prepared to burn her with her tears, and arose unhurt and refreshed from a boiling caldron, and thus may have been considered a patroness of healing waters.—*Ibid.*, p. 420.

LUDLOW: WISHING WELL.

In a valley called "Sunny Gutter," near Ludlow, is a wishing-well, into which you must drop a stone, and the wish you form at the moment will be fulfilled.—*Ibid.*, p. 422.

OSWESTRY: ST. OSWALD'S WELL.

The famous well of St. Oswald makes no figure in the authentic history of the saint. In all probability it was a pagan sacred spring frequented long before his time, to whom it was afterwards dedi-

cated. An undated deed of the thirteenth century describes
certain land as being situated near the Fount of St. Oswald. In
the fifteenth century the chronicler Capgrave writes that *in the
plain called in English Maserfeld*, "the church which is called the
White Church is founded in honour of St. Oswald, and not far
from it rises an unfailing spring, which is named by the inhabitants St. Oswald's Well." Leland, in the sixteenth century, adds

OSWESTRY : ST. OSWALD'S WELL.

that in his day it was said that "an eagle snatched away an arm
of Oswald from the stake, but let it fall in that place where now
the spring is," which gushed forth where the incorruptible arm of
the saint rested. A chapel, he says, has been erected over it, the
ruins of which were still to be seen in Pennant's time (1773), but
have now disappeared. But the waters of Oswald's Well still
flow freely at the foot of a woody bank in a field on the outskirts

of Oswestry, next to that now used as the Grammar School playground. A little stream runs from the well to a pool below. Above and behind it is secured from falling soil or leaves by walled masonry, probably about a hundred years old, opening in front in a rounded archway, beneath which the stream flows away. In 1842 a local antiquary, the late Mr. J. F. M. Dovaston, wrote that "the feeble and the infirm still believe and bathe in the well, and did more so until it was enclosed in the noisy playground. Bottles of its waters are carried to wash the eyes of those who are dim or short-sighted, or the tardy or erring legs of such as are of weak understandings." Nowadays it seems chiefly used as a wishing-well, and many are the ceremonies prescribed for attaining the heart's desire thereby. One rite is, to go to the well at midnight, and take some of the water up in the hand, and drink part of it, at the same time forming the wish in the mind. The rest of the water must then be thrown upon a particular stone at the back of the well, where the schoolboys think that King Oswald's head was buried, and where formerly a carved head wearing a crown projected from the wall. In Mr. Dovaston's boyhood this was in good preservation, but in 1842 he says wanton tenants have battered it to a perfect mummy. If the votary can succeed in throwing all the water left in his hand upon this stone, without touching any other spot, his wish will be fulfilled.

A young girl at Oswestry, about three years ago, obtained the wish which she had breathed into a small hole in the keystone of the arch over the well.

Another approved plan is to bathe the face in the water, and wish while doing so ; or, more elaborately, to throw a stone upon a certain green spot at the bottom of the well, which will cause a jet of water to spout up in the air. Under this, the votary must put his head and wish, and the wish will be fulfilled in the course of one or two days.

Another plan savours of divination : it is to search among the beech trees near the well for an empty beechnut-husk, which can be imagined to bear some sort of likeness to a human face, and to throw this into the water with the face uppermost. If it swims while the diviner counts twenty, the wish will be fulfilled, but not otherwise.—*Ibid.*, pp. 427, 428.

ACTON BURNELL : THE FROG WELL.

By the side of the Roman road between Ruckley and Acton
Burnell, yclept the Devil's Causeway, and half-way down the
Causeway Bank, there rises out of a ferny, flowery bank a most
beautiful spring, which drips into a deep rocky basin, partly
natural, of great gray slabs of stone, placed there by the hand of
man.   Behind it rises the ancient Causeway Wood, with its yews
and hollies, its ash and mountain-ash trees.   The spring is never
known to fail, even in the dryest seasons.   Its waters, say the folk,
are always cold in summer and warm in winter, and, needless to
add, they are good for sore eyes.   Will it be believed that this
beautiful fountain, fit only for the fairest of water-nymphs, is the
scene of what seems like a fragment of the " husk-myth " of the
Frog-Prince (see p. 115) ?   Here the Devil and his imps appear
in the form of frogs.   *Three frogs* are always seen together ;
these are the imps ; the largest frog, being Satan himself, remains
at the bottom and shows himself but seldom.—*Ibid.*, pp. 415, 416.

WORFIELD : ST. PETER'S WELL.

This well is dedicated in honour of the patron saint of the
church, and is situated in the churchyard to the west of the
church.

WEM : ST. JOHN'S WELL.

St. John's Well shared the dedication of a neighbouring chantry
chapel, which was probably built on account of the celebrity of
the well.   The legend of St. John causing a serpent to show itself
in the poisoned chalice of which he then drank unharmed, sufficiently accounts for the dedication.—*Ibid.*, p. 420.

MINSTERLEY : LADY WELL.

The name of the Lady Well Mine at Minsterley preserves the
memory of another ancient holy well ; but I believe the present
church at Minsterley is dedicated to (in honour of) the Holy
Trinity.—*Ibid.*

DONINGTON : ST. CUTHBERT'S WELL.

This well, still resorted to for bathing weak eyes, is just below
Dorrington Church (near Allbrighton), which is believed to have
the same dedication, and which it doubtless preceded in sanctity.
—*Ibid.*

RORRINGTON : HOLY WELL.

Of the "Halliwell Wakes" at Rorrington (a township in the parish of Chirbury), I am able, thanks to the kindness of Sir Offley Wakeman, to give a full account, gleaned from the old folk of Rorrington and its neighbourhood, who attended the wake in their youth.

It was celebrated on Ascension Day at the Halliwell or Holy Well, on the hillside at Rorrington Green. "Are you going to the Halliwells on Thursday?" one neighbour would say to the other as the time drew near. The well was adorned with a bower of green boughs, rushes, and ·flowers, and a Maypole was set up. The people "used to walk round the hill with fife, drum, and fiddle, dancing and frolicking as they went," and then fell to feasting at the well-side, finishing the evening by dancing to the music of fiddles. They threw pins into the well, an offering which one old man, a blacksmith at Hope, says was supposed to bring good luck to those who made it, and to preserve them from being bewitched ; and they also drank some of the water. But the pure spring water was not the only, or chief, material of the feast! Soon after Chirbury Wakes (St. Michael's) a barrel of ale was always brewed on Rorrington Green, which on the following Ascension Day was taken to the side of the Holy Well and there tapped. Cakes of course were eaten with the ale ; they were round, flat buns, from three to four inches across, sweetened, spiced, and *marked with a cross.* They were supposed to bring good luck if kept.

The wake is said to have been discontinued about the year 1832 or 1834, at the death of one Thomas Cleeton, who used to brew the drink.—*Ibid.*, pp. 433, 434.

HAUGHMOND ABBEY.

There is a well at Haughmond Abbey, still covered by its fifteenth-century well-house.

PITCHFORD : PITCH WELL.

This well gives the name to the village of Pitchford, near Shrewsbury.

CORFHAM : FAIR ROSAMOND'S WELL.

A highly interesting fragment of English history is preserved here in the name of the well—Fair Rosamond's.

URICONIUM.

Mr. Wright records a tradition, picked up at our famous "buried city" of Uriconium, to the effect that on the northern side of Watling Street, not far from the place where it crosses the Bell Brook, there is near the brook-side a *buried well*, at the bottom of which vast treasures lie hidden. As a local rhyme expresses it :

> "Near the brook of Bell
> There is a well,
> Which is richer than any man can tell."
> Miss C. S. Burne, *Shropshire Folk-lore*, p. 84.

BETCHCOT : WELL-DRESSING.

The roadside well at Betchcot, near Smethcote, in the Pulver-batch country, was dressed with flowers on the 14th of May up to the year 1810, or thereabouts.

NEWPORT : MERMAID.

Newport owed its existence as a chartered borough to its Vivary, a pool or mere dammed up at the upper end of the level marsh, known as the Wildmoors, which here are contracted to a narrow neck. From this Vivary the burgesses were bound to supply fish for the king's table, a service of which the three fishes in the borough arms are a reminiscence.

The pool seems, however, to have gradually dried up, perhaps through neglect ; its site was "waste" in 1749, when the lord of the manor, with the steward and burgesses, made a grant of it to trustees, who were to keep the bridge or Cool Dam in repair. We cannot be wrong in thinking this was the original home of the Mermaid of Newport, as she is invariably called, though she now lives in Aqualate Mere, in Staffordshire, a remarkable sheet of water about two miles higher up the Wildmoors. Many can tell how they have "seen summat" on the wooded banks of the great mere.—*Ibid.*, p. 640.

BRISTLINGTON : WELL OF ST. ANNE-IN-THE-WOOD.

THIS well is in St. Anne's Wood; near it was a building, probably used as a guest-house, and also a chapel, which was formerly attached to Keynsham Abbey, a monk of this abbey generally residing on the spot.

Pilgrimages were made to it, and on the well being cleared, in 1878, many coins and tokens, offerings of the pilgrims, were found. July 26 was the day on which the pilgrimages were usually made.

The water of this well was formerly considered good for affections of the eye.

The chapel was dismantled, and the pilgrimages, against which Latimer once preached a sermon in Bristol, were suppressed in 1536.

ASHILL : ST. NIPPERHAM'S.

At Ashill, near Ilminster, is a well which on the first Sunday in May is agitated by bubbles, and the sick and lame used to be brought to bathe there. St. Nipperham is believed to be a corruption of St. Cyprian.

DOULTING : ST. ALDHELM'S WELL.

Near Doulting is still shown St. Aldhelm's Well of wonder-working water.—*Denham Tracts.*

GLASTONBURY : ST. MARY'S WELL.

St. Mary's Well is situated in the crypt of the Chapel of our Lady, in a recess, and vaulted over; it runs northward under the priory. It is said to have been used for washing purposes.

ISLE OF THORNS.

When St. Peter consecrated the church of the monastery of the Isle of Thorns, after having been ferried over by Eldric, the fisherman, he evoked with his staff the two springs of the island. —Dean Stanley's *Hist. Remains of Westminster Abbey*, 2nd ed., p. 21.

ALFORD : ALFORD WELL.

There is a chalybeate spring, known as Alford Well, about three-quarters of a mile from the church ; it is now disused.

CHEW MAGNA : BULLY WELL.

Of Bully Well no legend is forthcoming. Its waters are said to be efficacious for diseases of the eye.

THE RIVER : SEVERN.

The fourteen daughters of Brecan were turned into as many rivers, which, in all their maiden purity, fall into the Severn.

BATH.

The city of Bath has a curious and somewhat comic tradition (which is noticed in its local guide-books), that the old British King Bladud, d. 844 B.C. (father of King Lear or Leal, d. 799 B.C.), being reduced by leprosy to the condition of a swine-herd, discovered the medicinal virtues of the hot springs of Bath, while noticing that his pigs which bathed therein were cured of sundry diseases prevailing among them. Warner, one chief writer on the history of Bath, quotes this tradition at large from Wood, a local topographer of the preceding century, who gives it without authority. Warner states that, although the legend may appear absurd, it is noticed and credited by most British antiquaries of antiquity.—*N. and Q.*, 2 S., ix. 45.

The following epigram on the " Bristol Hogs " is by a clergyman of the name of Groves, of Claverton :

> When Bladud once espied some Hogs
> Lie wallowing in the steaming bogs,
> Where issue forth those sulphurous springs,
> Since honor'd by more potent Kings,
> Vex'd at the brutes alone possessing
> What ought t' have been a common blessing,
> He drove them thence in mighty wrath,
> And built the mighty Town of Bath.
> The hogs thus banished by their Prince,
> Have liv'd in Bristol ever since.

There was, in 1464, a well in this parish called St. John's Well, to which an immense concourse of people resorted, and many who had for years laboured under various bodily diseases, and had found no benefit from physic and physicians, were, by the use of these waters, after paying their due offerings, restored to their pristine health.—Collinson's *H. of S.*, iii. 104.

It was customary on Holy Thursday to carry persons here afflicted with disease.

STAFFORDSHIRE.

THIS beautiful spring was a favourite resort of the Lady Wulfruna, the foundress of the old Collegiate Church at Wolverhampton ; and from this association with her sanctity, it acquired the reputation of possessing some miraculous virtues, which were much in request by the devotees of subsequent times, who named it " Wulfruna's Well." This was also a Druidical appropriation : for with that order of men all running streams which took a direction from west to east were accounted sacred. It supplies the water to Dunstall Hall, near which it is situated, the home of the Hill family.

Mr. Lawley, however, in the *Midland Weekly News*, has assigned a somewhat different site to this ancient well. He considers that it was situated at Spring Vale, near Bilston. In an old document belonging to Bilston occurs the following reference to it :

" To ye South of Wolferhamtune is a famous springe, called Ladie Wulfrune's Sprynge, where shee usyd to come and washe. Y^e legende tells us y^t ye ladie Wulfrune prayede for y^t God woude endue ye well wyth powers of noe ordinarie vyrtue, inasmoche as yᵗ hath curyd manie, as it were myraculouslie healynge yᵉ lame, yᵉ weake and impotent, and dyvers sufferyng fro mortall diseases, as manie there bee yᵗ cann testifie."

It would be interesting to know the site of a well possessing such valuable powers; but though tradition has not left anything on record by which we can sufficiently localize it, its former exist- ence is still preserved in the name of Spring Vale, by which the district is still known. Further, a street in Cann Lane, lying in the direction of Spring Vale, at its northern end, is known by the name of Holywell Street.

The custom of well-dressing is or was observed here.

BILSTON : CRUDELY OR CRUDDLEY WELL.

The town was anciently the possessor of a famous well dedi- cated to some old Saxon saint. The well in question was known in colloquial phrase as "Crudeley" or "Cruddley" Well, and was situate just off Lichfield Street, near to the entrance to Proud's Lane. In mediæval times this well was largely resorted to not only by the townspeople, but by others from the surrounding neighbourhood, on account of its being a "holy" well. It gradually lost its sanctity as the people grew more enlightened (!), and subsequently came under the control of the parish authorities, who kept its winding apparatus in proper repair, as is very clear from the parochial accounts. To show this more clearly, I sub- join the following items taken from the constables' accounts for the several years mentioned therein :

1809.

	£	s.	d.
For repairing Cruddeley Well ..	0	4	2
„ locking up the well	0	15	0

1811.

For locking up the well	1	0	0

1815.

For chain and ironwork for			
Cruddeley Well	3	3	4

This latter item, it is most amusing to state, became the subject of an appeal to the Stafford Quarter Sessions, when Edward Wooley (the famous screw manufacturer and hero of the old story of "How Wooley lost his Watch"), John Bowen (the well-known landlord of the Angel Inn, Hall Fold), J. B. Whitehead (the blank tray manufacturer), and William Taylor (a former overseer), appealed against the legality of certain items in the accounts of the overseers, of which the repairs of Crudelcy Well was one. This well continued to supply the townsfolk of the locality with water until towards 1830, when the supply ceased through the working of the mines, and the shaft was filled up. In the Saxon calendar we have a St. Creadda or Credda, and it was to his memory the well was in all probability dedicated. This well is said, on the authority of an old manuscript found among the town documents many years ago—which were, unfortunately, sold as waste paper!—on the building of the present Town Hall, to have borne a Latin inscription, running thus :

> Qui non dat quod habet
> Dæmon infra ridet.

Which has been Englished thus :

> Who does not here his alms bestow
> At him the demon laughs below.

—Contributed by G. T. Lawley.

WOMBOURNE : OUR LADY'S WELL.

Another famous local well, which has fortunately escaped the destructive hand of time, is that near Wombourne, known by the name of "Our Lady's Well," or "Lady Well." It is cut out of the solid rock, which crops out at the top of a lofty hill, situate between Wombourne and Lower Fenn. The well is of considerable antiquity, and several species of cryptogamic plants give to the surface of the stone a venerable appearance. It is supposed to have been sacred to the virgin in mediæval times, and its waters to have possessed curative properties. Here, ages ago, a holy hermit is said to have dwelt, and to have been visited by many persons in search of consolation and instruction.

The well is still a favourite resort of local pleasure-seekers, who go to drink of the cooling and delicious beverage, and ruralize in the adjacent wood.—*Ibid.*

TIXALL.

Dr. Plott gives us some particulars of a famous well, known as Tixall Well, near the church at that place, which, having survived the superstitious veneration formerly attaching to it, was afterwards used to supply, by some method of forcing, the district around.—*Ibid.*

MILTON : NEW WELL.

The New Well, as it is called, is annually decorated with flowers and boughs, the festivities extending over two days. At noon, each day, a procession is formed at the well, and marched through the village, headed by a band, and followed by the May Queen riding on a gaily-decorated pony, attended by her maids of honour, Jack-o'-the-Green, Robin Hood, and the Morris-dancers. This motley cavalcade, accompanied by the inevitable crowd of hangers-on and sightseers, pause at vantage points along the line of route and go through some antics preliminary to the more serious performances that follow on the return to the fields adjoining the well. Here the customary maypole-dancing, old English sports, and amusements, such as wrestling, sack-racing, etc., are indulged in, and prizes distributed by the well-dressing committee to the various successful competitors.—*Ibid.*

ENDON : WELL-DRESSING.

At the village of Endon similar festivities attend the annual well-dressing—usually on May 29 or 30. The principal well in the village is most elaborately and even artistically adorned, and the smaller well—for there are two in this case—comes in for its share of floral decorations. Here the festival is under the patronage of the vicar of the parish, who opens the first day's proceedings by a service in the church and the delivery of an appropriate sermon. On the conclusion of this solemn preliminary, a procession is formed near the church of the maypole-dancers and other participators in the festival, and then they proceed to the enlivening strains of a brass band to the wells, where hymns are sung, and a few suitable words addressed to the audience by the vicar. At the conclusion of this semi-religious introduction to the two days' amusements, the most important feature of crowning the May Queen is performed. The girl selected for this honour is gaily decorated with flowers, and is conducted with much ceremony to a floral throne provided for her, where, being seated she is crowned with a wreath of flowers. Being thus invested with royal powers, she straightway signifies her pleasure that the maypole-dancers should go through their evolutions to the sounds of enlivening music. This over, the usual sports and amusements are indulged in.

Carried out as above, it is pleasant to contemplate the keeping up of such an old-fashioned custom ; and it is only to be regretted that so few of our village communities retain it among their annual social relaxations. It is somewhat remarkable that in the south of the county well-dressing has become as extinct as the dodo.—*Ibid.*

BIBROOKE : WELL-DRESSING.

The custom of well-dressing obtains, or did obtain here.

CROXTON : PENNYQUART WELL.

There is a well in a field at Croxton, in the parish of Eccleshall, called Pennyquart Well, because, it is said, the water from it, being especially pure, used to be sold at a penny a quart.—*Shropshire Folk-lore,* p. 70 *n.*

ANDRESSY : HOLY WELL.

In a rental of the Earl of Uxbridge, written in the reign of Edward VI., it was specified that Andrew's Isle, *alias* Mudwin's Chapel, was let to John Hewitt at will at the annual rent or sum of three shillings and threepence. There is every reason to believe that this well and chapel were situate on the flat meadow opposite the churchyard, as this spot is still known as Annesley or Andressy, and the part of the river dividing the island from the adjacent shores is called the Modwens or Mudwens.—*Ibid.*

UTTOXETER : PENNY CROFT ON THE FLATTS.

This well was once scrupulously kept, and flowers yearly adorned it, because it was believed to possess great curative properties. According to the *Reliquary* it was called " Penny Croft," from the pence the afflicted offered for the use of its healing virtues. It has lately been turned into a common drinking-place for cattle. —*Midland Weekly News,* contributed by G. T. Lawley.

UTTOXETER : MARIAN'S WELL.

The ancient name Marian or Mary's Well has in more modern times been changed to " Maiden's " or " Marden's Wall " (Well)

—wall here having the same meaning as well. It was situated on the rise of a hill called the "High Wood." Its waters were once very famous for their healing powers, and many people from the parts adjacent frequently fetched some of its water to administer to persons suffering from various diseases, when the medicine of the professional man had failed to effect a cure or give relief.

It had also a strange legend attached to it, which may account for its modern name. It was believed to be haunted by the ghost of a young woman, and on this account people were so much afraid that few of them could be found hardy enough to go near it after dark. This superstition would appear to be a survival of the time when wells were believed to be inhabited by spirits, whose aid was invoked by means of divination. Fortune-tellers frequently took advantage of this superstition to extort money from the ignorant and foolish, pretending to call up the spirits to the surface of the water, in order that the person desiring knowledge of the future might question them. Females in particular were guilty of this superstition, arising out of a weakness and anxiety to know who would be their future spouse.—*Ibid.*

RUSHTON SPENCER : ST. HELEN'S WELL.

There was a famous well here known as St. Helen's, which was endowed by the superstitious with several very singular quali-ties. It sometimes became suddenly dry after a constant over-flow for eight or ten years. This occurred in wet as well as in dry seasons, and always at the beginning of May, when springs are generally believed to be at their highest, and the dry season lasted till Martinmas. It was locally believed that this occurrence fore-told some great calamity, as war, famine, pestilence, or other national disaster. It is said to have become dry before the out-break of the Civil War, before the execution of Charles I., before the great scarcity of corn in 1670, and in 1679 when the miscalled Popish plot was discovered. So says Dr. Plott.—*Ibid.*

CHECKLEY : WELL IN THE WALL.

Between Upper and Lower Tean, in the parish of Checkley, is a spring of a remarkable character, denominated the "Well in the Wall," as it rises from under a rock. An old tradition says

that this unaccountable spring throws out all the year round—
except in July and August—small bones of different sorts, like
those of sparrows and chickens.—*Ibid.*

BLYMHILL : ELDER WELL.

Here is a noted well, known as "Elder Well," said to be
blessed with valuable medicinal properties, and to be a sovereign
remedy for the eyes, on which account it used to be annually
"dressed" with flowers and branches of trees, and rustic games
and amusements indulged in by those attending.—*Ibid.*

SHENSTONE : ST. JOHN'S WELL.

At Shenstone, near Lichfield, a little distance from the church,
was a well called "St. John's Well," after the saint in whose honour
the parish church is dedicated. It was looked upon as sacred
from the miracles or cures wrought by its waters on St. John the
Baptist's day, June 24. For this reason was a sanctity placed
upon it by the faithful, who brought alms and offerings, and made
their vows at it.—*Ibid.*

BURTON-ON-TRENT : ST. MODWEN'S WELL.

This well was at one period famous for the cure of the king's
evil and other unaccountable cures, in grateful memory of which
the people still adorn it with flowers and boughs.—*Ibid.* (Shaw's
Staffs.)

CANWELL.

A custom similar to the above obtains here.—*Ibid.*

BREWOOD : LEPER'S WELL.

There was a famous sulphureous well here accounted a sovereign
remedy for leprosy. England's *Gazetteer* (1751) informs us it is
used at "present" by both man and beast against cutaneous
diseases, so that many of the inhabitants boil their meat in and
brew with it. Nightingale (*Beauties of England and Wales*) tells
us that "processioning was prevalent at Brewood at the annual
celebration of well-dressing there."—*Ibid.*

INGESTRE : ST. ERASMUS' WELL.

Here is another well famous for the cure of the king's evil,
known as "St. Erasmus's Well," of sulphureous quality. In the

reign of Henry VII. a chapel was built near this spring. The Chetwynd MS., in the Salt Library, at Stafford, records that "an aged man, formerly clerk there, told Walter Chetwynd that the adjoining wells were much frequented by lame and diseased people, many whereof found there a cure for their infirmity, inasmuch that at the dissolution thereof, the walls were hung about with crutches, the relics of those who had benefited thereby. Nor was the advantage small to the priest, the oblations of the chapel being valued in the king's books at £6 13s. 4d."—*Ibid.*

WILLENHALL : ST. SUNDAY.

In Dr. Wilkes' MS. is a reference to this famous well. He tells us that a holy well existed in that town, which was curiously dedicated to St. Sunday, and that it was celebrated for the cure of several diseases. It bore the following inscription : "Fons occulis morbisque cutaneis diu celebris. A.D. 1728." Where this well was is now a matter of impenetrable mystery, a fact which may be accounted for in the almost complete covering of the original surface of the land by the refuse of the mines.—*Ibid.*

WEST BROMWICH : ST. AUGUSTINE'S WELL.

A holy well formerly existed here, which it was the custom every year to adorn with garlands, to the accompaniment of music and dancing, in honour of its patron, St. Augustine, who

> As early bards do telle,
> Gave to Bromwych this holy welle.

The well derived its name from the monks of Sandwell, who no doubt derived considerable revenues from its medicinal virtues.
—*Ibid.*

WILLOWBRIDGE.

At Willowbridge, in the north of the county, was a medicinal spring, originally discovered, it is said, by Lady Bromley. A rare and curious pamphlet of the seventeenth century was written in praise of its virtues by a celebrated physician, named Samuel Gilbert.

The water, according to Dr. Plott, carried with it the most rectified sulphur of any mineral spring in the county.—*Ibid.*

Half a century ago or more, there was a famous well here known by the prosaic name of "The Alum Well." Tradition has not left anything on record respecting its virtues, nor do I know where it is located.—*Ibid.*

"Leland, in his Itinerary, says: 'Stowe Church, in the easte end of the towne, where is St. Chadd's Well, a spring of pure water, where is seen a stone in the bottom of it, on the whiche, some say, St. Chadd was wont, naked, to stand in the water and praye. At this stone St. Chadd had his oratory in the tyme of Wulphar, King of the Merches.' The superstitious custom of adorning this well with boughs, and of reading the Gospel for the day, at this and at other wells and pumps, is yet observed in this city on Ascension Day."—Harwood's *History of Lichfield,* p. 509 (published 1806).

This custom is still continued in Lichfield (see *Shropshire Folklore,* s.v. "Ascension-tide," pp. 348, 349, on "Traces of Well Worship"), but the procession only goes round the boundaries of the Close as there described, and does not go out to Stowe and St. Chad's Well. I can hear of no current superstition, custom, or tradition about the well.—*C. S. B.* See Dyer's *Brit. Pop. Customs,* p. 215.

It is popularly believed that it is dangerous to drink of the water of St. Chad's Well, as it is sure to give a fit of the "shakes." Yet, in spite of the attendant's remonstrances, I took a good draught, and, instead of ague, experienced only great refreshment in a fatiguing walk on a sultry day.—*Rev. C. F. R. Palmer.*

Great and Little Chatwell are two tiny hamlets in the (civil) parish of Gnosall, Staffordshire. At Little Chatwell is a well called St. Chad's, approached by old stone steps, the water of which is of very good quality and highly thought of for tea-making. At Great Chatwell is a bit of old sandstone wall with a fragment of a window, the remains of a chapel.

The lady who lives at St. Chatwell House, and whose father lived there before her (whether previous generations owned it I don't know) says that "*according to tradition* the well was consecrated by St. Chad," but how she got this tradition I don't know, or whether it is more than the *supposition* of her own family. The late owner of Little Chatwell (Mr. J. H. Adams, who had a great love of antiquities) called his house *Chadwell Court.* The name Chatwell (pronounced *Chattle*) is said to have formerly been Chadwell, but I don't know of anyone who has seen any old deed in which it was so spelt. Not that I doubt the etymology.—*C. S. Burne.*

TAMWORTH : ST. RUFINUS.

There was a well of St. Rufinus at Tamworth, on the Warwickshire side of the town, mentioned in the Hundred Rolls, *temp.* Edward I. It was almost entirely destroyed by fire, June 15, 1559, and the restoration was very slow, occupying more than forty years. It is possible, the well having fallen into discredit, it was at this period finally destroyed and the road to it blocked up. Certain it is that the well is never mentioned after this period, and there has not been any public well in existence for 300 years, as far as any deed records.

ELLERTON : THE KING'S WELL.

"'This well is situated at the furthest extremity of our parish (Adbaston). There are two cottages one mile from Ellerton ; the well is in the garden of one of them. It is in first-rate condition, the water clear as crystal, surrounded by large stones, with steps down to the water. The cottages are built in Elizabethan style, though the stone has been replaced by bricks in a recent reparation. It is said that King Charles I., when staying at Chetwynd Park on the way to Market Drayton, one day drank of this well ; also that King Charles II. changed his clothes in one of these very cottages for a countryman's smock and clogs."*—*Eldon Butler.*

Adbaston Vicarage, *August* 19, 1890.

* Charles II. did not come so far north in the flight from Worcester: the story probably refers to some other fugitive from the battle. The Duke of Buckingham, Earl of Derby, and others fled in this direction, and several of them were concealed in the neighbourhood for some time.—*C. S. B.*

" Black Mere " or " Blake Mere " is a small pond of irregular shape, lying in a little hollow on the summit of the high hill of Morridge, about three and a half miles east-north-east from Leek.

Great was the horror in which Black Mere was held by our ancestors, and strange beliefs were connected with it. Camden, quoting Richman, says it is :

> A lake that with prophetic noise doth roar ;
> Where beasts can ne'er be made to venture o'er—
> By hounds, or men, or fleeter death pursued,
> They'll not plunge in, but shun the hated flood.

Dr. Plott, however, in his *History of Staffordshire*, says : " The water of the Black Mere is not as bad as some have fancied, and I take it to be nothing more than such as that in the peat-pits, though it is confidently reported that no cattle will drink of it, no bird light on it or fly over it ; all of which are as false as that it is bottomless, it being found upon measurement scarce 4 yards in the deepest place ; my horse also drinking when I was there as freely of it as ever I saw him in any other place ; and the fowls are so far from declining to fly over it, that I spoke with several that had seen geese upon it ; so that I take this to be as good as the rest, notwithstanding the vulgar disrepute it lies under."

" Amongst the unusual incidents that have attended the female sex in the course of their lives, I think I may also reckon the narrow escapes that have been made from death ; whereof I met with one mentioned with admiration by everybody at Leek, that happened not far off at the Black Mere at Morridge, which, though famous for nothing for which it is commonly reputed, as that it is bottomless ; no cattle will drink of it, or birds fly over or settle upon it (all of which I found to be false), yet it is so for the signal deliverance of a poor woman, enticed hither in a dismal stormy night by a bloody ruffian, who had first gotten her with child, and intended in this remote, inhospitable place to have despatched her by drowning.

" The same night (Providence so ordering it) there were several persons of inferior rank drinking in an alehouse, the ' Cock,' corner of the market-place and Stockwell Street at Leek, whereof one having been out and observing the darkness, and other ill circumstances of the weather, coming in again, said to the rest of his companions that he were a stout man indeed that would venture to goe to the Black Mere of Morridg in such a night as that; to which one of them replying that for a crown, or some such summe, he would undertake it; the rest joining their purses said he should have his demand. The bargain being struck, away he went on his journey with a stick in his hand, which he was to leave there as a testimony of his performance. At length coming near the Mere, he heard the lamentable cries of this distressed woman begging for mercy; which at first put him to a stand, but being a man of great resolution and some policy, he went boldly on, however, counterfeiting the presence of divers other persons, calling 'Jack, Dick, and Thom,' and crying, 'Here are the rogues we look'd for,' which being heard by the murderer, he left the woman and fled, whom the other man found by the Mere side, almost stript of her clothes, and brought her with him to Leek, as an ample testimony of his having been at the Mere, and of God's Providence too."

This mere is also termed the " Mermaid Love," from an old tradition that one of those fabulous creatures dwells in it ; in fact, some of the peasants thereabouts are ready to swear that, when some years ago the "love" was partially "let off," one appeared predicting that if the water were allowed to escape "it would *drown* all Leek and Leekfrith." This vain idea has given origin to the sign of a neighbouring roadside inn, "The Mermaid," a place frequently visited by sportsmen when shooting in the vicinity. —*Reliquary*, O.S., iii. 182.

AQUALATE MERE : MERMAID.

The mermaid herself appears at one particular spot on the approach of any great calamity. On one occasion, when long ago some dredging or "rundeling out" operations were going on in the mere, she put her head out of the water, and, mistaking the intention of the workmen, and warned no doubt by the destruction of her first home, she uttered the thoroughly Salopian prophesy :

" If this mere you do let dry,
Newport and Meretown I will destr'y."
Miss C. S. Burne, *Shropshire Folk-lore*, p. 640.

SUFFOLK.

IPSWICH : HOLY SPRING.

N EAR St. Clement's Church, Ipswich, is or was a holy spring.

SUDBURY : HOLY WELL.

About half a mile from the town is a spring of exceedingly pure water, which is supposed to possess the power of healing many painful diseases; in consequence the water is called holy water.

LOWESTOFT : BASKET WELLS.

The parvise over the porch of St. Margaret's Church is known as the " Maids' Chamber," in consequence of two maiden sisters, named respectively Elizabeth and Catharine, who lived a recluse life, inhabiting it; they left a sum of money for the sinking of two wells, between the church and the infirmary, called the Basket Wells, Basket being said to be a corruption of Bess and Kate, the names of the donors.

WOOLPIT : OUR LADY'S WELL.

Near the church is the famous well of " Our Lady," to which pilgrimages were wont to be made in days of yore.

ACTON : WIMBELL POND.

Near the haunted " corner," known as the " nursery corner," is a pool called Wimbell Pond, in which tradition says an iron chest of money is concealed; if any daring person ventures to approach the pond, and throw a stone in the water, it will ring against the chest, and a small white figure has been heard to cry in accents of distress, " That's mine !"—W. Sparrow Simpson, D. D.

SURREY.

WARLINGHAM : PROPHETIC SPRING.

" IN a grove of ewtrees within the Manour of Westhall, in the parish of Warlingham, as I have frequently heard, rises a spring upon the approach of some remarkable alteration in church or state, which runs in a direct course between Lille Hills to a place call'd Foxley-Hatch, and there disappears, and is no more visible till it rises again at the end of Croydon town, near Haling pound, where with great rapidity it rushes into the river near that church. . . . It began to run a little before Christmas, and ceas'd about the end of May, at that most glorious æra of English liberty the year 1660.   In 1665 it preceded the plague in London, and the Revolution in 1668."—*Nat. Hist. and Antiq. of Surrey*, iii. 47, 48.

CARSHALTON : ANNE BOLEYN'S WELL.

Anne Boleyn's Well, close to the churchyard, according to tradition, burst forth from the stroke of her horse's hoof.

FARNHAM : ST. MARY.

There was a holy well here dedicated to the Virgin Mary, in a curious cavern known as "Mother Ludlam's Cave."

SUSSEX.

RUSPER : NUN'S WELL.

ON the south-western side of the parish was situated the small establishment of Benedictine nuns who for three hundred years were the rectors and patrons of Horsham Church.   When this priory was founded, and by whom, appears to be a matter of great obscurity.   At a short distance from the house, surrounded by copse-wood and overhanging trees, is a small well of a circular form, and surrounded by cut stone, overgrown with moss. A flight of winding steps leading to it from an adjoining eminence adds a peculiar romantic and pleasing effect to this venerable work of antiquity, which is known by the name of "Nun's Well."

No account is to be found of its history, though it may perhaps have belonged to the neighbouring castle—Sidgwick. The tradition among the inhabitants affirms that a subterraneous passage connects this castle with the nunnery at Rusper, which is eight miles distant, but no attempt has been undertaken to ascertain the truth of this conjecture.

A tradition also states that the old convent bell was sunk in a pond in front of the house, and has disappeared in the mud.

In the appendix to the *History and Antiquities of Horsham*, Dudley Howard, 1836, from which work the above is quoted, it is asserted that near the building is a very deep well, said to have been used as a place of destruction for those members of the convent who had dared to break the vow of chastity.

SIDGWICK CASTLE: ST. MARY'S OR NUN'S WELL.

Sidgwick Castle is in the parish of Broadwater, between Nuthurst and Horsham, about two miles and a half eastward from the latter.

About thirty yards from the outer moat is a well beautifully constructed of large blocks of hewn stone. It is called "The Nun's Well." Why, it is difficult to say, as this castle never was a religious house; it is also sometimes called "St. Mary's Well."

HORSHAM: NORMANDY WELL.

This well obtains its name from the part of the town in which it stands, and which is supposed to have been used by the Norman Brotherhood, who lived in the first house, next the churchyard, of the row east of the church called "The Normandy." This house still retains the name of the "Priests' House." The "Normandy Well" is open, and runs partly under one of the houses; it is only about four feet in depth, and yet in the longest drought the water always stands up (*sic*) sufficiently high to allow a pail to be dipped into it. It has been the custom to use the water from this well for the baptisms in the church.—*Horsham: its History and Antiquities*, Miss D. Hurst, 1868, pp. 32, 33.

MAYFIELD PALACE : ST. DUNSTAN'S WELL.

Adjoining the kitchen apartments at the lower end of the hall is a well of considerable depth—Black's *Guide to Sussex*, 1884, says it is reputed to be 300 feet deep—and supplied with the purest water. It is called " St. Dunstan's Well," and was probably dedicated in his honour, and consequently the resort of pilgrims and the reputed scene of miracles. It is guarded by four walls, having one entrance.—*Suss. Arch. Coll.*, ii. 244.

LEWES : PIN WELL.

On the opposite side to the Friends' Meeting House, enclosed by brick walls, is a perennial spring that bursts out from the adjoining chalk-ridge, and rushes into the neighbouring brooks. This spring bears the ancient name of " Pin Well," and in former times enjoyed some celebrity. It was within the limits of the grounds belonging to the Grey Friary ; it was approached by steps. The road from Pin Well to the bottom of School Hill was commonly called " The Friars' Walk." It is near the station. Pins were formerly dropped into it. The well is now —1890— filled in ; but its site, a small irregularly shaped piece of ground, is still distinguishable, being surrounded by a low brick and flint wall, having on the side fronting Friars' Walk a stone tablet with " Pin Well " cut on it.

A writer of the last century makes the following remarks anent the well : " Pynwell Street, so called from Pynwell, a very pure spring, which rises near the west end of ' Friars' Wall,' and was so called from Pinn or Pynn, a pine-tree, which formerly shadowed it, leads from School Hill, down by All Saints' churchyard, on the west, but formerly had its direction on the other side, nearly opposite ' Pynwell.' "—*History of Lewes and Brighthelmstone*, by Paul Duncan, Lewes, 1795, p. 366.

(The accounts of these five wells have been kindly supplied by C. T. Phillips, Lewes.)

EASTBOURNE : HOLY WELL.

" The chalybeate springs at Holywell, a short distance west of the Sea Houses, are highly worthy the attention of the visitor. The quality of the water is said intimately to resemble the far-famed springs of Clifton, and it has been found highly beneficial in many of the diseases for which the mineral waters of Bristol are almost deemed a specific."

The analysis, however, proves them to consist of simple, but very fine, surface water.

"Not far distant there was a chapel dedicated to St. Gregory. Tradition states that the French, in one of their marauding expeditions, landed here, burnt the chapel, and carried off its bell to some church in Normandy. The chroniclers are silent as to this event."—*History of Sussex*, Horsfield, 1831, vol. i., 291. *Sussex*, by Lower, 1870, vol. i., 151. *Suss. Arch. Coll.*, xiv. 125.

BUXTED : WISHING-WELL.

It is situated in the parish of Buxted, two miles from Uckfield, and at the back of the house exists an old hermitage hewn out of the solid rock, formerly consisting of three chambers, with fireplace and chimney. The well is in an orchard in front (and north) of this anchorite's cell, the rocks cropping out on the west side, sheltering the ground, and enabling former owners to train vines over them, and obtaining for it in past years the name of the "Vineyard." About half-way down the orchard is, as the gardener informed me, the so-called "Wishing-well," about 10 feet in diameter, and some 5 feet deep (I did not measure it), containing some 2 feet of water, the steining of rough stone, with a few blocks apparently worked, and a gap or opening on the east side, probably the former approach, or "dipping-place." The water was much fouled by ducks, but the man told me that before they were kept, and the well was clean, the water was very clear and good, the supplying spring welling up in the centre of the well, and maintaining a fairly uniform depth. I know very little about the subject of wells, and the information given perhaps should be received with caution ; but from its situation so near a hermitage of very ancient date, and its apparent age and care in construction, I think it probably *may* have been excavated and built by the recluse. The gardener could not inform me why it was called the "wishing-well," and knew of no tradition respecting it.—C. T. Phillips.

HORSTEAD KEYNES : HOLY WELL.

"The village is situated in a delightfully undulated sylvan country, about five miles from Hayward's Heath Station. It has

many surroundings of antiquity in old houses, etc.   It has also
a holy well, a chalybeate spring; but, so far as I know, there is no
legend attached to it."—From Nibbs and Lower's *Churches of
Sussex.*

STEYNING: HOLY WELL.

"A subsidiary chapel to the parish church, dedicated to St.
Mary, was situated on the south side of the High Street, and near
it a holy well, now covered over."—*Ibid.*

WARWICKSHIRE.

ALLESLEY: DUDLEY'S SPRING.

THIS spring, in the parish of Allesley, has been long held
in estimation among the lower orders for foretelling, as
they believe, the dearness of corn; and many old people
have been in the habit of watching its operations, and placing
much faith in them.—Rev. W. T. Bree, in Loudon's *Mag. of Nat.
Hist.*, 1829, ii. 297.

ATHERSTONE: CORN SPRING.

There is a spring here of a similar kind to the one at Allesley,
and with the like virtues attached to it.—*Ibid.*

SUTTON COLDFIELD: ROWTON WELL.

There is a spring in Sutton Coldfield, long known as Rowton
Well.   It was at one time in much repute as a medicinal well, but
the virtues of its water have long since disappeared.—*Hist. War-
wicks.*, T. Tom Burgess.

SKETCHLEY WELL.

This well was supposed to have the power of sharpening the
wits of those who tasted its waters.   Hence it was a common
remark to make to a witty person that "he had been to Sketchley."
—*Ibid.*

WHITMARSH: HOLY WELL.

Formerly there was a well by the side of the Whitmarsh brook,
to the south of the footway from Whitmarsh to Radford.   "The

ancient inhabitants, when removing their bell from the old church to its present site, brought it to this holy well to be freshly conse- crated. In doing this it fell into the water and gradually dis- appeared. The country people who wish to know coming events cast stones into the well at night, and in the morning their ques- tions are answered by the sounding of the bell." The site is now drained, but the little stream of water which flows into the Whit- marsh brook is still believed to be possessed of healing powers, and people come from great distances to procure its waters.— *Ibid.*

BERKSWELL.

There is a remarkable well near Berkswell churchyard.—*Ibid.*

BURTON DASSETT.

There is a well here which appears to have been used for the purposes of baptism and immersion.—*Ibid.*

WESTMORELAND.

KIRKBY STEPHEN: LADY WELL.

A T Kirkby Stephen is a wonderfully copious spring, on the brink of the Eden, known by the name of Lady Well, which has within these few late years been appropriated to private uses. This semi-sacrilegious act was committed by Francis Birkbeck, of Kirkby Stephen, who diverted the current of its waters down to his brewery to convert into ale, and that, too, without the slightest opposition on the part of the inhabitants of that wonderfully improving little country town. The well had ever been looked upon as public property. Let justice be done.— *Denham Tracts.*

PATTERDALE: ST. PATRICK'S WELL.

As Saint Patrick passed down this beautiful valley he is said to have founded the church and blessed the well. Thus we have St. Patrick's church and St. Patrick's well to this day, the ancient name of the valley being Patrickdale.

For many centuries the Holy Well was used for the purposes of baptism.—*Rev. J. Wilson.*

WILTSHIRE.

HINDON : PROPHETIC STREAM.

A T Funthill Episcopi, higher towards Hindon, water riseth and makes a streame before a dearth of corne, that is to say, without raine, and is commonly lookt upon by the neighbourhood as a certain presage of a dearth ; for example, the dearness of corne in 1678.—*Nat. Hist. Wilts.*, p. 32.

MORECOMBE BOTTOM.

At Morecombe Bottome, in the parish of Broad Chalke, on the north side of the river, it has been observed time out of mind that when the water breaketh out there, that it foreshewes a deare yeare of corne, and I remember it did so in the yeare 1648.—*Ibid.*, p. 33.

BANERSTOCK : MERRY WELL.

The water of this well is considered very efficacious in cases of diseases of the eye.

WORCESTERSHIRE.

DROITWICH : ST. RICHARD'S WELL.

T HIS custome is yearly observed at Droit-Wich in Worcester-shire, where on the day of St. Richard the [Tutelar Patron Saint] of ye well (*i.e.*) salt-well, they keepe Holy day, dresse the well with green Boughes and flowers. One yeare, *sc.* A° 64, in the Presbyterian times it was discontinued in the Civil-warres ; and after that the spring [stopt, dried, shranke up] or dried up for some time. So afterwards they [revived, kept] their annuall custome (notwithstanding the power of ye Parliament and soldiers) and the salt water returned again, and still continues.

This St. Richard was a person of great estate in these parts, and a briske young fellow that would ride over hedge and ditch, and at length became a very devout man, and after his decease was canonized for a saint."—*Aubrey's Remains of Gentilisme and Juda-isme*, p. 33. Folk-lore Soc. Pub.

CLENT : ST. KENYLM'S WELL.

On the Clent hills stands a little chapel of ancient date dedicated to St. Kenylm, a Saxon prince who was murdered by desire of his step-sister and buried near. On the body being taken up, a spring with healing powers of a miraculous kind rose, and received the name of St. Kenylm's Well, the chapel was built, and a little town sprang up.

MALVERN : HOLY WELL.

This well is situated on the eastern side of the hills, two miles southward of Malvern. There is a pump-room for the fashionable and other invalids.

ST. ANNE'S WELL.

This well is situated behind the Crown Hotel.

YORKSHIRE.

DONCASTER : ROBIN HOOD'S WELL

OVER a spring called Robin Hood's Well, three or four miles on this side, north of Doncaster, and but a quarter of a mile only from two towns called Skelborough and Bourwallis, is a very handsome stone arch, erected by the Lord Carlisle, where passengers from the coach frequently drink of the fair water, and give their charity to two people who attend there.

Epigram on Robin Hood's Well, a fine spring on the road ornamented by Sir John Vanbrugh, the architect, by Roger Gale, Esq. :

Nympha fui quondem latronibus hospita sylvæ
Heu nimium sociis nota, Robine tuis,
Me pudet innocuos laticis fudisse scelestis,
Iamque viatori pocula tuta fero,
En pietatis honos ! Comes hanc mihi Carlislensis
Ædem sacravit quâ bibis, hospes, aqua.

—*Stukeley's Diaries and Letters*, iii. 273 ; *Surtees Soc.*, vol. lxxx.

THIRSK : LADY WELL.

An old historian of the town says : "In the marsh near the
church flows a spring of pure and excellent water, commonly
called Lady Well, doubtless a name of no modern description."—
Yorks. Folk-lore, p. 199.

STAINLAND : ST. HELEN'S WELL.

The part of the village in which the well is situated has always
been known as Helliwell, and from this, or one of the several
Helliwells of Halifax, an old family takes its name. The well is
known as St. Helen's, and near it, now formed into cottages,

STAINLAND, YORKSHIRE.

was a building formerly used, according to tradition, as a chapel.
A large stone on one of the walls is called the Cross, and Watson
states that strangers sometimes make pilgrimages to this cross and
well.— *Yorkshire Notes and Queries*, pp. 158, 159.

BRETTON.

This well, an illustration of which is given from a photograph by Messrs. Hall, bears the following inscription :

"This well was built by ye
Right Honbl. Grace Countess of
Eglintown in 1685 relict of Sir
Thomas Wentworth kt
Baronet after married
to Alexander Cook of
Eglintown."

BRETTON.

Nothing further can be gathered about it.

YORK : THE OUSE.

There is an old tradition, possibly credited by some at the present time, that if anyone casts five white stones into a particular part of the river Ouse, near the city, as the clock in the Minster tower strikes one on May morning, he will see on the surface of the water, as if looking into a mirror, whatever is desired of the past, present, and future.

YORK MINSTER.

There is a draw well with a stone cistern in the eastern part of the crypt of York Minster where King Edwin is said to have been baptized in 627. A wooden oratory was erected over it before the stone building was thought of; the crypt is about 40 feet by 35 feet.

ST. PETER'S WELL.

This well of excellent water is now covered by a decorated pump, and is situated eastward in the south-west window in the Zouch chapel in the Minster.

HEATH.

Nothing appears to be known respecting this well; however, an

HEATH.

illustration of it, from a photograph by Messrs. Hall, of Wakefield, may bring to light something of interest not forthcoming.

This well in the village street is named in honour of St. Chad, founder of Lichfield Cathedral, who died March 2, 672.

Wulfhere, King of Mercia, had two sons, Wulfade and Rufine, who were put to death by their father on his finding them at worship in the cell of St. Chad. Remorse followed, and, at the instance of his queen, Ermenilda, he sought the counsel of the hermit, and fully adopted the faith of his murdered children.

Canon Raine, of York, states that previous to A.D. 1603 there were nine windows in the west cloister of Peterborough Cathedral,

LASTINGHAM : ST. CHAD'S WELL.

in which the following story of the conversion of King Wulfhere was related, and to which were subjoined these mottoes :

The hart brought Wulfade to a well,
That was besyde Seynt Chaddy's cell.

Wulfade askyd of Seynt Chad,
" Where is the hart that me hath lad ?"

" The hart that hither thee hath brought,
Is sent by Christ that thee hath bought."

Wulfade prayed Chad, that ghostly leech,
The faith of Christ him for to teach.

Seynt Chad teacheth Wulfade the feyth,
And words of baptism over him seyth.

Seynt Chad devoutly to mass him dight,
And hoseled Wulfade Christ his Knight.
Wulfhere contrite hyed him to Chad,
As Ermenyld him counselled had.
Chad bade Wulfhere, for his sin,
Abbeys to build his realm within.
Wulfhere endued, with high devotion,
The Abbey of Brough with great possession.

Leg. and Trad. of Yorks., ii. 114, 115.

The following occurs on one side of the building erected over the well :

C.EDD
ABBIE LÆSTINGÆ FUNDATOR
A.D. 648
OBIIT A.D. 664 ET SEPULTUS EST
IN ECCLESIA A DEXTRA ALTARIS.

On the front of the well are the words " Cedd's Well " placed over the mouth whence the water flows.

WINSTY : GREENWELL SPRING.

The builder of Swinsty Hall was a man named Robinson, a weaver, residing at first in a lowly cottage where the hall now stands.

Whence he came no one knew, and whither he went, when he departed to seek a fortune in London, no one cared. But to London he went, and while there the black plague came upon that city, and swept away a large portion of the inhabitants. Houses were left tenantless and deserted. Often no relatives remained to bury the dead, or claim the money and valuables left behind. Our enterprising adventurer from Swinsty made good use of his opportunities, and from the bodies of the dead, and the houses deserted and desolate, he soon gathered together a large treasure of gold and silver. When he determined to depart with his spoils, he found that it required a large waggon and a team of horses to deport it down into Yorkshire.

In due time he arrived at his former abode ; but the story and dread of the plague had preceded him. No dwelling was open to him, no hand would come near to assist him with his treasures, or even to obtain food and lodgings. He was constrained to deposit his wealth in a barn, and himself to take up his abode there also. This barn, at some little distance from the hall, yet exists. He next, to remove all fear of contagion, proceeded to wash all his gold and silver, piece by piece, in a spring of pure water near, and yet known as the Greenwell Spring.

In course of time he purchased the site of his former dwelling, and the estate around it, and by means of his large ill-gotten wealth he caused the hall to be erected. The Greenwell Spring still flows on, but the tradition respecting the builder is exploded by the prosaic title-deeds. — *Leg. and Trad. of Yorks.*, ii. 184, *et seq.*

BARDEN : HART-LEAP WELL.

This well, celebrated both by tradition and by the poet Words-· worth, is situated about two miles from Barden, near the road leading from Richmond to Leyburn. The tradition is that on one occasion there was a chase of extraordinary duration and speed in this locality, in which both horses and hounds dropped off one after another, until at length a single horseman remained. Worn out at last, the exhausted hart — an animal of unusual strength and beauty — gave three tremendous leaps down the declivity, and dropped dead beside this well.

Until lately "three several pillars, each a rough hewn stone," marked the site of the three astonishing leaps, but these stones have either been removed, or they are concealed by a recent wall. The well or spring is nearly choked up.

BRADFORD : CLIFFE WOOD, BOAR'S WELL.

This well is still known as the Boar's Well. In *Legends and Traditions of Yorkshire* the following story of it is given : "Cliffe Wood, near the town, was, in the days of John of Gaunt, the home of an immense wild boar. This brute was so destructive, and so great a terror to the inhabitants, that they ultimately petitioned the king to offer a reward for its destruction. To this well it resorted to quench its thirst. A valiant youth of the neighbourhood, watching his opportunity when it was drinking, thrust it through with a hunting-spear. He at once cut out its tongue, and started with it in his possession, as an evidence of his triumph, to the royal court to claim the reward. Meanwhile another man came to the well, and finding the boar lying dead, he cut off the head, and also repaired with his trophy to the king, thinking to claim the royal reward. As chance would have

it, he arrived before the true hero.   While, however, the award
was in suspense, the latter also arrived.   An investigation took
place.   The head was examined, and, being found minus the
tongue, the claim of the bearer of it was disallowed, and the
royal bounty bestowed upon the rightful claimant.   The reward
consisted of certain lands in the vicinity, to be held upon the
condition that the holder and his heirs should give one blast
upon a hunting-horn on St. Martin's Day ; and whenever John
of Gaunt should be passing through Bradford, in attendance on
his liege lord, into Lancashire, the man, or his heirs, should attend
upon him with a hunting-spear and a dog.

BRADFORD : SPINK WELL.

Spink Well is near Bradford ; it was nigh this well that the
famous wild-boar is said to have been killed.   Being near Cliffe
Wood, the name may have been derived from the song-birds
there formerly, such as the bull spink, the gold spink, etc.—
Yorks. Folk-lore, p. 196.

BRADFORD : HOLY WELL.

This holy well, not far from Manningham Lane, probably
derived its name from having at some time been dedicated to some
saint.   The inhabitants of Bradford were wont in ancient times
to resort on Sundays to these wells as a common place of meeting,
to drink of the waters and partake of their preternatural virtues.
—*Ibid.*

DUDLEY HILL : THE LADY'S WELL.

The Lady's Well, in the " Roughs," on the west side of Dudley
Hill, within late years, was in great repute for its waters.—*Ibid.,*
p. 197.

EVERINGHAM : ST. EVERILDA'S WELL.

In the garden here, belonging to Lord Herries, is a well dedicated in honour of St. Everilda.   It is square, and was formerly
resorted to by the villagers, but is now closed.

GARGRAVE: ST. HELEN'S.

The water of this well was a certain cure for sore and weak
eyes.   Whitaker states that in his time votive offerings, such as

ribbons and other decorative articles, were commonly to be seen tied to the bushes near these wells.

GRINTON : CRACK POT, OR THE FAIRY'S HOLE.

A curious cavern near the mouth of a small rivulet, at the bottom of which is a deep pool of water, formed by water running from the rock ; it is known as "The Fairy's Hole" now, but in more ancient times it bore the appellation "Crack Pot."

BOLTON-IN-CRAVEN : KING HENRY VI.'S WELL.

King Henry VI., while a fugitive at Bolton Hall, desiring a bathing-place during the hot summer days, and none such being available, his host endeavoured to supply the want of his august guest. He therefore proceeded within the walled-in garden with a hazel divining-rod in his hand, which soon indicated the presence of water below. Ordering the spot to be dug up immediately, water issued therefrom in abundance, and the well in the form of a bath was thus made for the convenience of the king. It is said to be still in existence and known as King Henry VI.'s Well. The king in his gratitude prayed that the well might ever flow on, and that the family of his host might be never extinct.

> "O, may it flow eternally,
>   And while the spring shall bubble,
> May you and yours live peaceably,
>   Free from all care and trouble.
> And while it murmurs down yon vale,
>   O, may no son or daughter
> Of Pudsay's lineage ever fail
>   To drink this crystal water.
> What though with honour and largesse
>   You ne'er may be requited,
> Your loyalty and my distress
>   Shall ever be united.
> With fair hewn stones let this be walled—
>   Stones that will perish never—
> And then the fountain shall be called
>   'King Henry's Well' for ever."
>   Littledale: *Craven Legends.*

WAKEFIELD : ROBIN HOOD'S WELL.

Robin Hood's Well is reputed to be the starting-place of a padfoot called in the neighbourhood the "Boggard of Longar Hede." It haunted a three-lane end after leaving the well. One poor fellow said he saw it walk beside him for a quarter of a mile up the lane, and that very night his aunt died. It was of the size of a calf, with horned head, with long shaggy hair, and eyes like saucers; fastened to one of its hind legs was a chain, and usually a cry heard following it as of a pack of hounds.

BARNSDALE: ROBIN HOOD'S WELL.

There is another well named after the famous outlaw, near where the Great North Road or Watling Street crosses Barnsdale, between Doncaster and Ferrybridge.

NEWTON KYME: ST. HELEN'S WELL.

This well is still venerated, as the shreds and scraps of linen hung on the surrounding bushes sufficiently attest. The St. Helen here commemorated is, of course, the Empress Helena, the mother of Constantine.

EGTON: BEGGAR'S OR LOVER'S BRIDGE.

There are two legends connected with the bridge which spans the river Esk at Egton, near Whitby. One tradition terms it "The Beggar's Bridge," in consequence of a beggar named Thomas Furees, who in early life was nearly drowned while endeavouring to cross the swollen stream by the stepping-stones—the usual method of crossing—off which he fell into the water. He then made a vow that should he ever be able to do so, he would build a bridge at the place for the safety of his fellow-creatures. He proceeded to Hull, and in course of time amassed a large fortune, and, not forgetting his vow, he built the bridge, on which his initials and the date, 1621, were placed. There is a monument to him and his wife in Holy Trinity Church, Hull; he died in 1631. In the other legend of "The Lover's Bridge," the subject is that of a lover trying to cross the river at this point on his way to seek his sweetheart in Glaisdale, before leaving her to seek his fortune abroad. Having repeatedly tried to cross the current, he at length gave up the attempt and

> Exhausted he climbed the steep side of the brae,
> And looked up the dale ere he turned him away;
> Ah! from her far window a light flickered dim;
> And he knew she was faithfully watching for him.

The Lover's Vow.

I go to seek my fortune, love,
   In a far, far distant land ;
And without thy parting blessing, love,
   I am forced to quit the strand.

But over Arncliffe's brow, my love,
   I see thy twinkling light ;
And when deeper waters part us, love,
   'Twill be my beacon bright.

If fortune ever favour me, —
   Saint Hilda ! hear my vow !—
No lover again, in my native plain,
   Shall be thwarted as I am now.

One day I'll come to claim my bride,
   As a worthy and wealthy man !
And my well-earned gold shall raise a bridge,
   Across the torrent's span.

The rover came back from a far distant land,
   And he claimed of the maiden her long promised hand ;
But built; ere he won her, the bridge of his vow,
   And the lovers of Egton pass over it now.

Ingledew : *Ballads of Yorkshire.*

RAYDALE : SEMERWATER.

Where the lake now is was once a town of some size. The legend is that many years ago a poor old man (some variants say " Christ ") wandered into Raydale, and besought food from house to house. Every door was closed to him except that of a very poor couple living in a small white cottage on the hill, who bade him welcome, and placed their humble food before him. In the morning, after pronouncing a blessing on the house and its inmates, he departed ; and as he left the house, he turned towards the city, and pronounced these awful words :

" Semerwater rise, Semerwater sink,
   And swallow all the town,
Save this little house on the hill
   Where they gave me meat and drink."

Whereupon the water rose and covered all the houses, save the little one above mentioned.—Whitaker's *Richmondshire* ; Barker's *Three Days in Wensleydale.*

The following is a rhymed version of the old legend of the origin of Semerwater :

In ancient times, as story tells,
The saints would often leave their cells,
And stroll about, but hide their quality,
To try good people's hospitality.
It happened on a summer's day,
As authors of the legend say,
A tired hermit—a saint by trade—
Taking his tour in masquerade
Disguised in tatter'd habits, hied
To an ancient town on Raydalside ;
Where, in the stroller's canting strain,
He begged from door to door in vain ;
Tried every tone might pity win,
But not a soul would let him in.
Our wandering saint in woeful state,

RAYDALE : SEMERWATER.

Treated at this ungodly rate,
Having through all the city pass'd,
To a small cottage came at last,
Where dwelt a good old honest pair,
Who, though they had but homely fare,
They kindly did this saint invite
To their poor hut to pass the night ;
And then the hospitable sire
Bid his good dame to mend the fire,
While he from out the chimney took
A flitch of bacon from the hook,
And freely from the fattest side
Cut out large slices to be fried;

Then stepp'd aside to fetch him drink,
Fill'd a large jug up to the brink,
And saw it fairly twice drained off,
Yet (what was wonderful—don't scoff!)
'Twas still replenish'd to the top,
As if he ne'er had touched a drop.
The good old couple were amaz'd,
And often on each other gaz'd ;
Then softly turned aside to view
Whether the lights were turning blue.
The gentle pilgrim was soon aware,
And told his mission in coming there:
"Good folks, you need not be afraid,
I'm but a saint," the hermit said.
" No hurt shall come to you or yours ;
But for this pack of churlish boors,
Not fit to live on Christian ground,
They and their cattle shall be drown'd,
While you shall prosper in the land."
At this the saint stretched forth his hand—
"Save this little house! Semerwater sink !
Where they gave me meat and drink."
The waters rose, the earth sunk down,
The seething floods submerged the town ;
The gen'rous couple there did thrive,
And near the lake aye long did live,
Until at good old age they died,
And slept in peace by Semerside.

J. B. Haines : *Yorks. Folk-lore,* p. 211.

BURNSALL : THOR'S WELL.

In pagan times, and possibly in the days of the early Christians
well-worship prevailed in the parish of Burnsall, and evidences or
it are still remaining. There is "Thorshill," and Thor's Well,
signifying the well of the God of Thunder. This was undoubtedly
dedicated by the pagans; and among their successors it was
customary for the early Church to rededicate these places in honour
of their saints. Hence the two Burnsall wells dedicated respectively in honour of St. Margaret and St. Helena. These wells are
worth seeing, and it is a fact that remnants of well-worship existed as
recently as the middle of the last century, when the young people
used to visit the wells every Sunday evening and drink the waters
with sugar added.

OSMOTHERLEY.

The village of Osmotherley is seven miles from Northallerton in the Cleveland hillside. Tradition has it that Osmund, King of Northumbria, and his wife, had an only son Oswy, heir to his kingdom. The " wise " being consulted at his birth, foretold the child would on a certain day be drowned. The mother in every way endeavoured to stave off the catastrophe, and as the time for the fatal event neared, she fled with the boy to the top of Osnaberg, or Roseberry Topping, as it is now called, safe as she surmised from any watery depths. Here she awaited the passing away of the fatal day. Having fallen asleep through fatigue, the young prince wandered away from her, and came across a small well. Seeing his face reflected in the water, he endeavoured to grasp it, fell in, and was drowned. The mother on awaking traced his footsteps to the spot, where she found the dead body of her child. The body was buried in the churchyard close by ; the mother died shortly after, and was buried beside him. The heads of both are said to be still seen at the east end of the church.

A similar account is that some years ago there lived in a secluded part of Yorkshire a lady, who had an only son named Os or Oscar. Strolling out one day with her child, they met a party of gipsies, who were anxious to tell her the child's fortune. After being much importuned, she assented to their request. To the mother's astonishment and grief they prognosticated that the child would be drowned. In order to avert so dreadful a calamity, the infatuated mother purchased some land, and built a house on the summit of a high hill, where she lived with her son a long time in peace and seclusion. Happening one fine summer's day, in the course of a perambulation, to have fatigued themselves, they sat down on the grass to rest, and soon fell asleep. While enjoying this repose, a spring rose up from the ground, which caused such an inundation as to overwhelm them, and side by side they found a watery grave. After this had occurred, the people in the neighbourhood named it Os-by-his-mother-lay, which has since been corrupted into Osmotherley.

COTTINGHAM : KELDGATE.

Keld is the old Saxon name for a spring or a well. In Cottingham are some intermittent springs bearing this name, which are supposed by many to be regulated in their very irregular periods of activity and repose by the flowing of the Derwent, although that river is twenty miles distant.

> " When Derwent flows
> Then Keldgate goes."

MOXLEY NUNNERY : ST. JOHN'S WELL.

About a mile from the nunnery, at the corner of the wood called St. John's Wood, was formerly an ancient building, consisting of a small dome of stone and brick over a spring, well known in the neighbourhood as "St. John's Well." There is still discernible the remains of a causeway leading from the nunnery in the direction of this well. The water is reported to possess medicinal properties, and there is a large and convenient store cistern built on the east side, into which the water is admitted for the purpose of bathing.

It was much resorted to in the days of superstition, and there are still the remains of stone steps for the more easy descent thereto. Near the mouth which admits the water into the bath is a large stone, called "the wishing stone," and many a faithful kiss has this stone received from those who were supposed never to fail in experiencing the completion of their desires, provided the wish was delivered with full devotion and confidence.

THORPARCH : ST. HELEN'S WELL.

It was usual for those who consulted the oracle at this well to make an offering there of a scrap of cloth. This was fastened to an adjoining thorn, which, being literally covered with pieces of rag, presented a peculiar appearance.

LEEDS : REVOLUTION WELL.

On the near side of the hill in Moortown Lane is a drinking well known as " Revolution Well," erected in memory of William of Orange ; and close by a field containing a small clump of trees, and supposed to contain the remains of men killed in battle of Stainbeck. There is an upright stone post a few yards from the supposed burial-ground bearing a Latin inscrip-tion, alluding to the above-named revolution, and put there in memory of it by a Mr. Oates, who dwelt at the house in Stain-beckdale.

At the foot of the Ridge is a well known as "Cuddy Well," the water being good for tender eyes, and for anyone who is short of iron in the system, as the doctors say. That the water contains a large amount of iron is shown by the rusty incrustation on the sides of the stream. Anyhow, people come long distances for this water for the above purposes, instead of having to send to Harrogate for it.

St. Peter's Spring is intensely cold, but beneficial to such as are troubled with rheumatism, rickets, etc.—*Mag. Brit.*, 1733.

The Eyebright Well, near Monk Pits, is, or was, celebrated as a cure for sore eyes.

The following are mentioned as "Old Wells of Leeds."— 1. Jacob's Wells, near Brunswick Hotel, Camp Road. 2. A pump or well in Sunny Bank, near the Infirmary. 3. A canker well, at the bottom of Cankerwell Lane. 4. Also back of Spring-field Place, in the narrow road leading from Kendal Lane or Little Woodhouse. 5. A spa pump or well, near the Leeds Arms, West Street. 6. Hebblethwaite's Pump, where the inhabitants of St. James's Street, Woodhouse Lane, fetched a deal of water; it was in the Tenter Fields, about where the lodge is now. 7. There was also a spa pump at Holbeck Moor, near the workhouse.—*Leeds Mercury Supplement.*

The origin of Bever-lee, the town of Beverley, which was in the ancient wood Deira, is referred to in the old religious ceremony of drawing the shrine, or emblematical Beaver, out of the lake in the wood, and placing it in security on an eminence in the sight of the assembled multitude. This rite was performed near the course—Hwyl—of the stream, which was hence called " Hull," in honour of Ked (Ceres), whence the name of a street in Beverley, called Ked or Keldgate. This female divinity was also denomi-nated *Hen-wen*—old lady—whence, perhaps, Hen-gate and Lady Gate; and was the daughter of Llyr, whence Lair-gate. The Ark or Beaver was also named *Aren* or *Ern*, whence Hurn Moor, the eminence on which it was placed after being drawn out of the lake was, in common with the Ark itself, considered as a mystical Bedd or Pastos.—Oliver's *Beverley*, 12.

BEVERLEY : COBBLER'S WELL.

In a hollow on Beverley Westwood is a stone trough, into which a spring of exceedingly cold pure water once flowed abundantly. It is quite dry now, and has been for some years, but it still retains the name of "Cobbler's Well." Tradition tells how a cobbler of Beverley, jealous of his wife, drowned her in this well, while in a mad drunken state ; but he cheated the law by dying almost immediately of remorse and grief.—*Ibid.*, p. 56.

BRAYTON : OUR LADY'S WELL, OR THE FAIRY'S PIN WELL.

It was in the days of yore—a period as difficult to find in our chronologies as fairyland in our geographies—that a buxom lass lived in Selby. She was but a serving-maid in a household, but she was good-looking, and attracted the notice of the lads of the town who were looking out for wives to preside over their house-holds. She was a good girl, too, hard-working, and kept her house clean and in good trim, which was noticed by the fairies, who thought to do her a good turn. There were many young bachelors who sought her hand in wedlock, some of whom she liked for one thing, some for another ; whilst she utterly rejected several, there remained a few from whom she was unable to select one upon whom to bestow her hand.

In this state of indecision she one day strolled out for a walk, and came to Brayton Barf, a mile or two from Selby, an eminence standing solitary, and rising to a height of about 150 feet from the valley of the Ouse. Its slopes were overgrown by forest trees, and at the summit was a small pool of water, fed by a spring, which was visited by the young people of Selby on holiday occasions to drink of it, from a belief that it possessed some sort of virtue in love matters.

Joan, the young lass in question, had often been there before, and had enjoyed looking on the prospect spread around. On this occasion she felt a singular impulse to climb the hill, partly perhaps to drink of the water, hoping that it might enable her to come to a right decision in the matter of her lovers. She scrambled up the side, through the thicket and briars, and in process of time came to a soft plateau at the top, with the little pool of sparkling water in the middle. She had been thinking of her lovers as she came up, the one who came uppermost in her thoughts being Robin the Bowyer. She drank of the stream, saying:

"Oh, good fairy of the well, present to my mind in a dream the image of him who is destined to be my husband," and then she lay down and slept, and the vision appeared before her of Robin, dressed in festal array, and approaching her with a wedding-ring in his hand.

Brayton Barf was at this time the abiding-place of a tribe of fairies, who dwelt there in perfect harmony and in a constant round of pleasurable existence. They had noticed the ascent of the hill by Joan, whom they knew as a favourable specimen of her rough and somewhat savage race of mortals, and they determined to make use of her for certain purposes of their own. They understood the value of metal implements and weapons, but were not able to smelt them for their own use, and they had to depend upon the inferior race for such metal articles as they required by filching them from these mortals. Their principal food was honey, of which they could procure an exhaustless supply from the stores of the bees; but to their refined tastes this stored honey tasted somewhat stale, and they infinitely preferred shooting the bees, as they came home laden with it newly gathered, and regaling themselves on the rifled sweets taken fresh and luscious from the body of the bee. The fairies may be said to have been in what we term the Stone Age, or, as it applied to them, would more properly be the Wood Age, for they shot the bees by means of bows and arrows, the former made of vine and other tendrils, and the latter consisting of sharp thorns. These thorn-arrows were not, however, altogether satisfactory; they were seldom perfectly straight, and shot wide of the mark, and frequently, when the bee was hit, the point of the arrow, instead of penetrating, was bent or broken off.

A short time previously they had come into possession of a pin, which had been dropped near the well by some love-stricken maiden. This they at once saw was precisely what they wanted as arrows in the place of thorns, and they had matured a plan for obtaining a supply of them when Joan came opportunely in their midst, and they determined upon making her the medium. They watched her taking the draught of water, heard her invocation, and caused the vision of Robin to appear before her in her dream. Whilst she lay asleep on the hillside they anointed her eyelids with a magical unguent, which would cause her to wake up in fairyland.

When she opened her eyes it was moonlight, but such a moon as she had never before seen or conceived of, casting as it did over nature a light equal in intensity to that of the sun ; not, however, glaring, yellow, and dazzling, as is the wont of that luminary, but shedding forth a soft yet lustrous radiance of silver sheen, lighting up every object on which it lay with celestial beauty, and imparting to the spirit of the beholder a charming volatility and an almost irresistible impulse to dance and sing and rejoice in the mere happiness of existence. She looked around, and all the familiar objects in the neighbourhood had assumed monstrous proportions ; the hill of Brayton had become a mountain, and the little pool at the summit a lake ; the thicket had become a dense forest ; the cottages scattered about the plain below had expanded into dimensions capable of housing giants, and the cattle and flocks had developed into antediluvian monsters. But what surprised her the most was that she herself was not the Joan who lay down to sleep a few hours ago, but had become a huge, coarse-skinned, ill-shapen monstrosity, more like a female ogre than anything else she could compare herself to. The fact was that she looked upon the world and herself with the eye of a fairy, and saw everything under an altogether different aspect from that of her ordinary mortal outlook.

Casting her eyes around, she was still more surprised to see crowds of little people, although to her fairy eyes they appeared of the natural size and herself a giantess compared with them. They were a merry, vivacious assemblage, clustered in groups or going to and fro about the lake, their tiny voices—for her ears had not been anointed—sounding like the humming of insects. They were all gaily dressed—the gentlemen in garments of woven, or rather plaited, fine grass, with interweavings of other brilliantly-coloured fibres, and with hats adorned with the breast-feathers of the robin redbreast ; the ladies in dresses of woven spider threads or of fine floss silk, embroidered with filaments of gay colours, or studded with sparkling little gem-lets, their usual head-dress being a butterfly's wing, a charming finish to their costumes, worn as it was coquettishly on one side of the head.   They were variously occupied, but all in pleasurable pursuits, and would have reminded a modern, could he have seen it, of Hyde Park and the Serpentine on a summer's day in June.   There were cavaliers galloping about on grasshoppers, stopping occasionally to raise their hats to fair ladies riding in carriages of walnut shells, drawn by teams of two or four black beetles ; whilst pedestrians were lounging about ogling the fair passers-by, as the same class may be seen doing, leaning on the rails of Rotten Row.   On the lake might be seen many a laughing group sailing about in shell-boats of the nautilus class, and others riding about on the surface, seated astride harnessed sticklebacks.   Others there were soaring aloft into the air on the backs of butterflies and moths ; many a merry circle of dancers whirled around, combining a kind of kiss-in-the-ring game along with it—and very productive of mirth this diversion seemed to be, judging from the never-ceasing bursts of laughter and shouts of delight.   Some of them might be seen climbing up the flower-stems, seeking a period of repose and sleep among the petals of tulips and other cup-shaped flowers ; and others, after a siesta there, might be observed descending to join again in the sports for ever going on.

Joan gazed on this scene with amazement, and wondered who the merrymakers might be.   She had never seen them before, never heard of any such people, and concluded that they must either be foreigners, or that she—especially as the country she was so familiar with appeared to her under so strange an aspect —was under the spell of an enchanter.   She was endeavouring to solve the problem, when she perceived a little green gentleman coming towards her.   He bore in his hands a wand tipped with a tiny diamond, scintillating like a star, and girdled round his waist was a sash of some flimsy material, embroidered with what appeared to be small cabalistic characters.   He approached, hat in hand, and bowing with profound respect, said :

" Fair denizen of the other world—princess, it may be—who have deigned to favour us with your presence, will you permit me to approach you, and condescend to allow me to pay my respects by kissing your lovely hand ?"

" I don't know who you may be," she replied ; "but, if it is any pleasure to you, you are welcome to kiss my clumsy fist.

But you must understand that I am no princess, but just a maiden of Selby, hard by, and that my hands are not lovely, but roughened by hard household work."

"Fair maiden," continued he, impressing a kiss on what must have appeared to him her large, clumsy digits, "I swear to be your knight for ever. May I ask you to become a partaker, or at least an observer, of our sports?" and she assenting, he conducted her with infinite grace to a spot where she could better observe the animated spectacle.

"Might I be so bold as to ask you who you are?" she inquired of her cicerone.

"We are fairies," he replied, "and you are in fairyland, a spot that but few mortals are permitted to visit. We have observed you (for we often come among you, although unseen by mortal eye) to be a very favourable specimen of your race—clean, tidy, industrious, and good-tempered—and have selected you as our medium of communication with the mortals of this vicinity."

Several more of the fairies, seemingly of high and influential position, had now gathered round and joined in the conversation. In the course of it they told her that they were aware of her predilection towards matrimony, and knew that several swains were contending for her hand, amongst whom she had a difficulty of choosing. Further, they had noticed her drinking of the pool, and lying down to sleep with the hope that the draught might cause her to see in a dream her future husband; and that they had caused the vision of Rob the Bowyer to appear before her, he being the best one to make her a good and loving husband.

"There is no virtue whatever of that kind in the water at present," said they, "but your simple act has inspired us with the idea of conferring a favour on the maidens of your race. We intend imbuing the water of the pool with a quality in the nature of a charm, to be brought into operation by a very easy process. It is that any maiden desirous of seeing a vision of her future husband may (if she be chaste and pure), by the simple act of dropping a sharp, well-pointed, and straight pin into the pool, see the face of the young man destined to be her husband reflected in the water, or will dream of him the next time she sleeps. And it is our wish that you may communicate this secret to your friends and neighbours."

The fairies then left her and mingled with the various groups of pleasure-seekers, whilst Joan sat pondering on the revelation made to her and on the promise of investing the spring with such a marvellous property, until at length she felt an irresistible fit of drowsiness come over her, and she sank back in slumbers, when the fairies came and carefully removed all the magic ointment from her eyes.

Again she dreamt of Robin, as was very likely, after the con- versation respecting him which she had held with the fairies. When she awoke the sun was just appearing over the eastern horizon, and the silvery moon had disappeared. She looked around, and saw that all the natural features of the landscape had dwindled down again to their natural proportions. Brayton Barf was no longer 'a mountain, and the beautiful lake was again nothing more than a small pool or spring of water. She looked round for her little friends, but they had all vanished, not a vestige of them remaining ; grasshopper horses, walnut-shell chariots, shell- boats, sticklebacks, and butterflies had all gone, one thing only remaining to indicate that the fairies had been there—a ring dis- tinctly marked on the turf of a darker tint of grass, such as may still be seen where the little folks have been gambolling in many a field and meadow even to the present day—which marked the spot where she had witnessed the dance under the moonlight.

After a while she went down the hill and told the people of Selby of what she had seen, what she had been told, and of the gracious promise made by the fairies. Some believed her ; others did not ; but the young, marrying, thinking damsels of the town placed full credence in her narrative, and one after another went to the fairy well, dropped in their pins, and saw, or imagined they saw, the reflection of a male face in the water, or the vision of some eligible young bachelor in their dreams ; and thus the reputation of the fairy well spread far and wide, and the fairies got an ample supply of metal arrows wherewith to bring down their honey-laden bees. In after-times an abbot of Selby, jealous of the influence of the fairies over the fair sex, whose whole allegiance he considered was due to the Church, went up the hill, and with much ceremonial exorcised the fairies, and re-christened the pool the " Well of Our Lady " ; but the young damsels con- tinued their faith in the fairies, as they do even now to some extent, as pins are still frequently dropped in the water, which is eagerly scanned for the lineaments of the wished-for swain. It

remains only to add that Joan and Rob were soon after united
in the bonds of wedlock, had a numerous progeny, and lived
happily together to their lives' end.—*Leeds Mercury Supplement.*

Another Version.

Brayton Barf is a solitary hill, but little more than a mile south-
west of Selby. It is a very conspicuous object, rising to a height
of some 150 feet above the surrounding flatness of the Vale of
Ouse, and extends the view to the towers of York, to the hills of
North Lincolnshire, the Yorkshire Wolds, and the western range
up to Pomfret and Leeds. The hill is now nude, but until some
thirty years ago it was covered with timber, which was one of the
last relics of the original wood, extending to the brink of the
Ouse, into which Abbot Benedict cut when he started the Abbey
of Selby. It is a circumstance of singularity that on the crest of
this hill there is a pit or well in which water is found, but the
fluid is never of the most tempting quality; what it would be if
the well were properly cleansed I cannot say. It is variously
called "Lady Pin Well" and "Our Lady's Well"; and it has
been a custom from time immemorial for those who visited that
well to drop a pin or coin therein to propitiate Our Lady or the
fairies. The custom is a remarkable survival of extreme antiquity;
and it is not the least curious feature of its history that, notwithstanding the interposition of Our Lady, the fairies still remain
the presiding deities, as they are likely now to continue. The
origin of the complex title of our well at Brayton seems to be
found in the piety either of one of the olden vicars of Brayton,
or in one of the abbots of Selby, who were owners of the Barf.
The superstitious peasantry, while traversing the monks' wood for
windfall firewood, and occasionally, no doubt, for a bit of poaching,
would cast their pin into the well under the impulse of their
wish, and so transmit the legend to their children. The monk,
seeing beauty and piety in the simple custom, and wishful at the
same time to remove the pagan superstition in favour of his own
creed, substituted Our Lady for the fairies in the name of the
well, and so gave to the object of his own intense adoration the
blind and soulless devotion that had for so many centuries flowed
in another channel. And yet how little have his efforts succeeded,
for though he has added the name of Our Lady, he has not
destroyed the tradition of the fairies.

13

CROPTON : OLD WELL.

As the old well at Cropton, a week or two ago, made a strong complaint of its neglect and an urgent appeal for renovation at the hands of the proper authorities, again we refer to some old manuscripts which afford interesting matter respecting it and the village generally. From these we quote that : The well is seventy-seven yards deep, and the water from it is considered of the finest quality for drinking purposes that can be found far or near.   The church, which is a chapel of ease, has lately been rebuilt in the Gothic style, and in pulling down the old edifice many sculptured stones were brought to light, which are still preserved in the church or churchyard.   The church is situated high and bleak, on the edge of a stupendous hill, and in the edifice is a monument erected to the memory of Captain William Scoresby, the well-known explorer of the Arctic regions.   The churchyard contains several ancient tombstones, and the far-famed Cropton Cross, on which is the following doggerel rhyme :

> On Cropton Cross there is a cup,
> And in that cup there is a sup ;
> Take that cup and drink that sup,
> And set the cup on Cropton Cross top.
>
> *Malton Messenger.*

FLAMBOROUGH.

Near Flamborough is a circular hole, resembling a dry pond, in which a Flambro' girl committed suicide.   It is believed that anyone bold enough to run nine times round this place will see Jenny's spirit come out, dressed in white ; but no one yet has been bold enough to venture more than eight times, for then Jenny's spirit called out—

> " Ah'll tee on me bonnet,
> An' put on me shoe,
> An' if thoo's nut off,
> Ah'll secan catch thoo !"

A farmer, some years ago, galloped round it on horseback, and Jenny did come out, to the great terror of the farmer, who put spurs to his horse and galloped off as fast as he could, the spirit after him.   Just on entering the village the spirit, for some reason unknown, declined to proceed farther, but bit a piece clean out of the horse's flank, and the old mare had a white patch there to her dying day. — Nicholson's *Folk-lore of East Yorkshire*, p. 81.

SCARBOROUGH : OUR LADY'S WELL.

The well, which may still be seen on the Castle Hill, near the ruins of the old Castle Chapel dedicated to the Virgin, is partially covered with a possibly useful, though hideous-looking pump. Medicinal properties were formerly ascribed to the waters of this well by the faithful.

HINDERWELL : ST. HILDA'S WELL.

There is a holy well at this place dedicated to St. Hilda. Tradition says that the monks, in the journeys between Whitby

HINDERWELL : ST. HILDA'S WELL.

Abbey and Kirkham Abbey, always made this well one of their resting-places. On Ascension Day the children of the neighbourhood assemble here carrying bottles containing pieces of liquorice, which they fill at the well. Hence Ascension Day is frequently termed Spanish-water Day. The well is now covered by a pump.

WITTON : CAST-AWAY WELL.

Almost at the top of the fell is a beautiful spring called " Cast-away Well " and a grotto.

HAMMER : ST. DIANA'S WELL.

There is another well here known as St. Diana's, supposed to be a memorial of Roman Paganism.   The fountain is considered so pure that a very old rhyme is still current :

> " Whoever eats Hammer nuts and drinks Diana's watter
> Will never leave Witton while he's a rag or tatter."

The Hammer woods contain excellent nuts, and the Witton people are proverbial for their attachment to their native place.

THRESHFIELD NEAR LINTON, IN CRAVEN : OUR LADY'S WELL.

There is a well here honoured with the above title, which is looked upon as being a sure and certain place of safety from all supernatural visitants.

Dr. Dixon relates the story of a native on his way home, late at night, from the public-house, being a spectator of some perform-ances of Pam, the Threshfield Ghost, and his imps.   Unfortu-nately the secret spectator sneezed, and then, in homely phrase, " he had to run for it," and only escaped condign punishment at the hands of the spirits by taking refuge in the very middle of " Our Lady's Well," which they durst not approach.   They, how-ever, waited at such a distance as was permitted them, and kept their victim nearly up to his neck in the cold water, until the crowing of the cock announced that the hour for their departure had arrived, when they fled, but not without vowing how severely they would punish him if he ever came again, and was caught eavesdropping at their parties.—*Stories of Craven Dales.*

HARPHAM : ST. JOHN'S WELL.

At Harpham, in the East Riding, on a vast level common, is a well dedicated in honour of St. John of Beverley, who, it is reputed, was born in this village.   The well is by the roadside ; here he is said to have worked many miracles through the virtues of its waters.   It is believed to possess the power of subduing the wildest and fiercest animals.   William of Malmesbury relates that in his time the most rabid bull, when brought to its waters, became quiet as the gentlest lamb. The covering stones, though heavy, were lying about in 1827, having been knocked over by a passing waggon. They have since been replaced. It is an object of considerable interest from its connection with St. John of Beverley. It is illustrated in Hone's *Table Book*, part ii., p. 545.

HARPHAM: DRUMMING WELL.

At the same village there is, in a field near the church, another well called "The Drumming Well."

About the time of Edward II. or III.—when all the young men of the country were required to be practised in the use of the bow, and for that purpose public "butts" were found connected with almost every village, and occasionally "field-days" for the display of archery were held, attended by gentry and peasant alike—the Old Manor House near this well at Harpham was the residence of the family of St. Quintin. In the village lived a widow, reputed to be somewhat "uncanny," named Molly Hewson. She had an only son, Tom Hewson, who had been taken into the family at the manor, and the squire, struck with his soldierly qualities, had appointed him trainer and drummer to the village band of archers.

A grand field-day of these took place in the well-field, in front of the Manor House. A large company was assembled, and the sports were at their height, the squire and his lady looking on with the rest. But one young rustic, proving more than usually stupid in the use of his bow, the squire made a rush forward to chastise him; Tom, the drummer, happened to be standing in his way. St. Quintin accidentally ran against him, and sent him staggering backward, and, tripping, he fell head-foremost down the well. Some time elapsed before he could be extricated, and when this was effected the youth was dead. The news spread quickly, and soon his mother appeared upon the scene. At first she was frantic, casting herself upon his body, and could not realize, though she had been warned of the danger of this spot to her son, that he was dead. Suddenly she rose up and stood, with upright mien, outstretched arm, and stern composure, before the squire. She remained silent awhile, glaring upon him with dilated eyes, while the awe-stricken bystanders gazed upon her as if she were some supernatural being. At length she broke the silence, and in a sepulchral tone of voice exclaimed : "Squire St. Quintin, you were the friend of my boy, and would still have been his friend but for this calamitous mishap. You intended not his death, but from your hand his death has come. Know, then, that through all future ages, whenever a St. Quintin, Lord of Harpham, is about to pass from life, my poor boy shall beat his drum at the bottom of this fatal well!—it is I—the wise woman, the seer of the future—that say it."

The body was removed and buried, and from that time, so long as the old race of Quintin lasted, on the evening preceding the death of the head of the house the rat-tat of Tom's drum was heard in the well by those who listened for it.—*Leeds Mercury.*

HOLDERNESS : ROBIN ROUND-CAP WELL.

The Hob-Thrust, or Robin Round-Cap, is a good-natured fellow who assists servant maids by doing their work in the early morning. . . . The Rev. W. H. Jones relates a story of a Holderness farmer who had his life made so miserable by one of these impish spirits that he determined to leave his farm. All was ready, and the carts, filled with furniture, moved away from the haunted house. As they went, a friend inquired, " Is tha flitting ?" and before the farmer could reply, a voice came from the churn, " Ay, we're flitting !" And lo ! there sat Robin Round-Cap, who was also changing his residence. Seeing this, the farmer returned to his old home. By the aid of charms, Robin was enticed into a well, and there he is to this day, for the well is still called Robin Round-Cap Well.—Nicholson's *Folk-lore of East Yorkshire,* pp. 80, 81.

ATWICK : HOLY OR HALLIWELL.

Between Atwick and Skipsea there races along occasionally the headless man, mounted on a swift horse ; and between Atwick and Bewholme, at the foot of the hill on which Atwick church stands, there is a spring and pool of water, overhung by willows, haunted by the " Halliwell Boggle."—*Ibid.,* p. 78.

KEYINGHAM : ST. PHILIP'S WELL.

Near Keyingham is a spring of water called "St. Philip's Well," into which the girls, when wishing, used to drop pins and money.

MIDDLEHAM : ST. ALKELDA'S WELL.

There is a spring here, the waters of which are considered very beneficial for weak eyes, said to have been dedicated to St. Alkelda.

WATTON ABBEY.

Watton Abbey is believed to have an underground passage to Beverley Minster, or, as some say, to the " Lady Well " at Kilnwick, whose holy waters have been most powerful in working miraculous cures.

BOWES : ST. FARMIN'S WELL.

At Bowes, North Riding, is one of those ancient springs or fountains which our ancestors looked upon as sacred. This spring of beautiful water is popularly known as St. Farmin's Well. Who *St. Farmin* was I wot not ; but there was *Firman*, a bishop of Usez in *Languedoc*, and to him, no doubt, this spring was dedicated by the Norman clergy, who would be settled at Bowes as chaplains at the castle, shortly after the Conquest, in honour of their saintly countryman.—*Denham Tracts.*

MOUNT GRACE : ST. JOHN'S WELL.

It is a custom for visitants to this well to bend a pin, throw it into the water, and wish. The bottom of the well is literally covered with pins. Mr. C. W. Smithson, Northallerton, in his handbook on the Priory, says :

" In the wood, at the south-east corner of the ruins of Mount Grace, in a spot rather difficult to find, is the well whence the supply of water for the Priory was obtained. It is strongly built of squared stone, walled round and protected by a picturesque dome of hewn stone, which is apparently modern. It is known as St. John's Well, but young women call it the ' Wishing Well,' and it is a source of amusement to them to cast bent pins into the water and then utter the dearest wish of the heart, which must be done in silence or the wish will not be fulfilled."

FOUNTAINS : ROBIN HOOD'S WELL.

On the south side of the Skell, not far from the abbey ruins, is "Robin Hood's Well," near to which, according to the old ballad, the "Curtal Friar" of Fountains encountered the "Forester bold," and threw him into the river and grievously belaboured him.

KNARESBOROUGH : ST. ROBERT'S WELL.

A short distance above Grimbald's Bridge, in a field called Halykeld-Sykes, on the north side of the river Nidd, is "St. Robert's Well." There is also a chapel of St. Robert of Knaresborough, which was confirmed by charter to the Brethren of the Order of the Holy Trinity at Knaresborough by Richard, Earl of Cornwall.

KNARESBOROUGH : DROPPING WELL.

This celebrated dropping and petrifying well is situated in the Long Walk, a well wooded grove between the two bridges. The well has historic associations apart from its petrifying powers, caused

KNARESBOROUGH : DROPPING WELL.

by the lime with which the water is strongly impregnated—as at Matlock Bath—from being the birthplace of that renowned sorceress and prophetess, " Old Mother Shipton."

Near to the famous " Dropping Well "
She first drew breath, as records tell,
And had good beer and ale to sell
    As ever tongue was " tipt " on.
Her " Dropping Well " itself is seen ;
Quaint goblins hobble round their queen,
And little fairies tread the green,
    Call'd forth by Mother Shipton.

COVERDALE : ST. SIMON'S WELL.

Near to Coverham, on the banks of the Cover, is a now
neglected well, at one time used as a bath, and supposed to have
been dedicated in honour of St. Simon.

There is a local tradition prevalent that St. Simon, the
Canaanite and Apostle, was buried here ! " an evident mistake,"
remarks the historian of Wensleydale.

STAINTON : HEZZLE WELL.

The " Hezzle Well " is said to be an excellent spring of water,
enclosed, by the wayside a little to the west of the village of
Stainton, near Barnard Castle.   It is a saying that

The water of Hezzle Well
    Will make tea by itself.

GIGGLESWICK : EBBING AND FLOWING WELL.

This celebrated well is situated at the foot of Giggleswick Scar,
a limestone rock, about a mile from Settle, going towards Clapham.
The water periodically ebbs and flows at varying intervals,
depending upon the quantity running at the particular time.
Sometimes the phenomenon may be observed several times in
the course of one hour, and on other occasions once only during
several hours.

Of this well, our old friend Michael Drayton, in his famous
Polyolbion, has left us the following account :

In all my spacious tract, let them so wise survey
My Ribble's rising banks, their worst, and let them say,
At Giggleswick, where I a fountain can you show,
That eight times a day is said to ebb and flow.
Who sometime was a nymph, and in the mountains high
Of Craven, whose blue heads for caps put on the sky,
Amongst th' Oreads there, and Sylvans made abode
[It was ere human foot upon those hills had trod],

GIGGLESWICK: EBBING AND FLOWING WELLS.

THE SAME FROM AN OLD PRINT.

Of all the mountain kind, and, since she was most fair,
It was a Satyr's chance to see her silver hair
Flow loosely at her back, as up a cliffe she clame,
Her beauties noting well, her features, and her frame.
And after her he goes ; which when she did espy
Before him like the wind the nimble nymph doth fly ;
They hurry down the rocks, o'er hill and dale they drive ;
To take her he doth strain, t' outstrip him she doth strive,
As one his kind that knew, and greatly feared his rape,
And to the topick gods by praying to escape,
They turned her to a spring, which as she then did pant,
When wearied with her cause her breath grew wondrous scant.
Even as the fearful nymph, then thick and short did blow,
Now made by them a spring, so doth she ebb and flow.

An itinerant writer of the seventeenth century observed of this well :

Near the way as the traveller goes
A fresh spring both ebbs and flows ;
Neither know the learned that travel
What procures it, salt or gravel.

The legend of Gormire is like that of Semer Water, one of a submerged town ; the pool or lake is situated at the foot of White-stone Cliff, on the slope of the Hambleton hills, not far from the small town of Thirsk.

Here is said to have once stood a large and populous town, the destruction of which was caused, not by a flood, but by an awful earthquake. One day, all of a sudden, the earth was violently convulsed, the side of the hill opened, and swallowed up the whole town, with its inhabitants, and their belongings. This was followed shortly after by a volume of water which quickly covered the site where the town had stood—as was the case with Sodom and Gomorrah. The lake is said to be unfathomable, having no bottom to it. Occasionally, however, the chimneys and tops of the houses are visible to those who are venturesome enough to embark on the surface of the waters of this mysterious lake.—See *Legends and Traditions of Yorkshire*, Parkinson, ii. 95, for another version.

St. Mongah's Well is in the lower reach of Copgrove Park, four miles west-south-west of Boroughbridge, near to the gamekeeper's residence there, and in an outbuilding close to that house is an open air-bath, which is filled by water from this spring. The water contains no mineral, its chief virtue being its intense coldness. Formerly this water was in great repute, and many people visited this spring every year; indeed there was a kind of "hospitium" erected here for invalids who came to reside. The following rules, taken from Dr. Clayton's edition of Sir John Floyer's work on *Cold Baths and Cold Bathing*, published about 1697, are of interest, especially as they were written for use of those who wended their way to this well :

"That the people resort here to be recovered of fixed pains, whether with or without tumour, rheumatism, quartans, strains, bruises, rickets, all weakness of the nerves, etc.

"They are immersed at all ages from six months to eighty years. Children are dipped two or three times and immediately taken out again. Adults stay in fifteen to thirty minutes. They use no preparatory physic, nor observe any diet before nor afterwards, but a draught of warm ale or sack.

"Diseased people go from the bath to bed, but healthful people put on their clothes, *and go where they please.*"

St. Mongath, Mongo or Kentigern, was a native of Scotland, from whence, we know, he migrated to North Wales, where he founded a religious community. He acquired a great reputation on account of his sanctity and learning.

Later in life he returned to his own country, where, on the banks of the Molendinar, near Glasgow, he founded an abbey, over which he presided until his death in A.D. 560.—A. D. H. Leadman, F.S.A., *Old Yorkshire*, vol. v., p. 25.

AISLABY : ST. HILDA'S WELL.

About a mile from the village of Aislaby, near Whitby, is a fine spring of water, which runs directly into the river Esk, known as "St. Hilda's Well."

ESHTON : ST. HELEN'S WELL.

It was customary for the younger folk to assemble and drink the water of this well mixed with sugar on Sunday evenings. The ceremony appears now to have died out. It was in vogue late in the last century.

Waddow Hall at Waddington, in the parish of Mitton, is separated from Lancashire only by the river Ribble. Within the grounds of the hall, and near the banks of the river, is the well from which the water-supply of the place is obtained, and known as Peg o'Nell's Well.

Peg o'Nell was a young woman who, "once upon a time," was a servant at the hall. She had, upon a certain day, a bitter quarrel with her master and mistress, who, upon her departure for the well to obtain the domestic supply of water, wished that before she came back she might fall and break her neck. The wish was realized. The ground was covered with ice, and by some means the girl slipped and, falling, broke her neck.

In order to annoy those who had wished her this evil, her spirit continually revisited the spot, and, with shrieks and hideous noises of all kinds, allowed them no rest, especially during the dark nights of winter.

She became the evil genius of the neighbourhood. Every disagreeable noise that was heard was attributed to Peggy ; every accident that occurred was brought about by Peggy. No chicken was stolen, no cow sickened or died, no calf was bewitched, no sheep strayed, no child was ill, no youth or maiden took to bad ways, but Peggy came to be regarded as at the bottom of the mischief.—*Ibid.*, ii. 106, 108.

St. Simon's Well here was formerly held in great estimation ; what its properties were is unknown. It is supposed that the monks of Coverham had a chapel here dedicated in honour of St. Simon.

" Still Are, swift Wherfe, with Oze the most of might,
High Swale, unquiet Nidd, and troublous Skell."

" Castleford women must needs be fair,
Because they wash both in Calder and Aire."

The Holy Well, with any legends that may have been connected with it, is now a thing of the past.

There is a well here at which St. Paulinus is said to have baptized many. It is on a hill about two miles from the railway-station.

Little or nothing seems to be known about its past history, the origin of the name, or the reason of its notoriety. The waters were on Palm Sunday supposed to assume all sorts of colours. It was on Palm Sunday, too, that the annual fair was held on Howley Hills, the site of the ruins of Howley Hall, close by, called Field Kirk fair. I think it most essential to the consideration of this question that we should not lose sight of the importance of Palm Sunday in the religious calendar, the name of the fair, and the proximity of Wood Kirk ("the church in the wood"). No doubt the wood in which the well is situated, the site of Howley Hall and Wood Kirk, would all be embraced in the arms of an extensive primeval forest. The very name of Wood Kirk testifies as to its great antiquity. We are told by Leland that "at Woodchurch, in Morley wapentake, near Dewsbury, was a cell of black canons, from Nostel, valued at seventeen pounds per annum." A recent writer in the *Weekly Supplement* says : "There is every reason to suppose that here, in the recesses of the primeval forest which overspread at one time the hills and dales of this district, an ancient Saxon church stood ; and now again, in support of the idea of a church existing here for centuries, we find in Burton that William, Earl of Warrene, and Ralph de Insula (De l'Isle), and William his son, gave Woodchurch to Nostel Priory by the hands of Archbishop Thurston." Readers of history will no doubt be cognizant of the fact that Thurston was Archbishop of York during the reign of Henry II., who was on the throne during the greater part of the latter half of the twelfth century, so that it will be observed that it is now seven centuries since Woodchurch was transferred from its previous owners to the canons of Nostel ; and there is no reason to doubt, as has been before observed, that it was then an old church, and had existed from Saxon days. We are told that it was to the canons of Woodchurch that Henry I. made the grant of a charter to hold a fair (Lee Fair), which charter was confirmed by Stephen, and has continued unto the present time, more than seven centuries. It would seem obvious from this that Woodchurch had been ruled by a body of canons prior to its being conveyed to the owners of Nostel Priory, otherwise there is some error in dates. However, this religious establishment must have been of some importance and the centre of a district, even in those days, whose condition imperatively demanded a mart for the sale of its products and the purchase of its requisites; hence the decision of the King to grant a charter. What more probable than that, as tradition says, on the site of Howley Hall, or near to, stood the residence of a Celtic chief, and that that, too, would be supplanted by the abode of the Saxon thane, and the latter would be co-existent with Wood Kirk, the kirk depending to a considerable extent on the thane for its existence?

After a mature and careful consideration of all the circumstances, I have been irresistibly driven to the conclusion that the name—St. Ann's, or Lady Anne's, Well—is of a religious or saintly origin, and that the Field Kirk fair, too, is the survival of some ancient religious custom. The traditional account which received credence when I was a boy was that the name of the well had its origin in connection with the following circumstance: A fair lady of the hall, once upon a time, went into the wood along with her maid to drink at the well, sat down, and, overcome with the beauty of the surrounding scenery, fell unconsciously into the arms of Morpheus, and whilst in that oblivious state was pounced upon by some wild beast and worried to death. Her name being Anne, the well ever after was called Lady Anne's Well. Another account says it took its name from a lady of the house of Savile, named Anne. Admitting there is some foundation in fact for the foregoing story, as there is for most traditional stories, it could not apply to a Lady Savile, as it is a well-known fact that wild beasts, such as wolves, etc., were exterminated long before the Savile family became Lords of Howley. Not so in Celtic, Roman, Saxon, Danish, and even Norman times, as these animals are said to have then abounded. Hence follows the bare possibility of such an incident as the above taking place during the residence of some Saxon thane at Howley, and the victim being a pious daughter of the same, closely connected by virtuous ties with the church in the wood.

What is it, I should like to ask, that has enshrined this well in

the hearts of the inhabitants of the surrounding district, tempted
the spirit of poetry to hover over it, and cast around it a halo of
romance ? Is it some such a tragical occurrence as the foregoing,
the account of which, like the snowflake in its flight through the
air, gathered substance in its descent ; or has it been sanctified by
the frequent visits of some saintly lady resident at the manor-
house close by, and connected by the purest of ties with the old
kirk ? Perhaps these are questions which can never be satis-
factorily answered, and my endeavours to demonstrate the affinity
of this well, the Field Kirk fair, Wood Kirk, and the owners of
the ancient manor of Howley may be futile, visionary, and specu-
lative, yet I hold that no other reasonable conclusion can be
arrived at. No doubt the scenery here in days long gone by
would be enchanting in the extreme—the hall standing on an
eminence, and surrounded on two sides by a valley, through
which ran silvery streams, in one of which sported fish, and on
whose banks stood the proverbial water-mill. Not far from the
bank of the other stream, which wound its way along a wooded
valley, was situated the ancient well. As I remember the scenery
as a boy, it then wore a different aspect from what it does to-day.
Up to that time, to a certain extent, it retained its rural features.
It had not been robbed of its ennobling and tranquillizing influences. The Muses found there an abode — henceforth they
will know it not. Mills have been built, pits have been sunk,
railways have been constructed, all in the immediate neighbourhood, which have done much to destroy the scenery, and mar its
effects on the lover of Nature. The smoke emitted from the
numerous chimney-stacks long since destroyed the fine oaks that
once adorned the Batley end of Soothill Wood. The railway
passing up the wooded valley, and close to the ancient well,
seems to have added the finishing touch, and completely annihi-
lated all the remaining beauties.

Across the wood, in the direction of Soothill, stretches a footpath, which used to be a regular lovers' walk. Ascending the
hillside by this footpath may be obtained a splendid view of the
valley below. Seated on the grass that skirts the footpath, and on
naturally formed terraces, by its side, on festive and other occasions
might have been seen vast numbers of pleasure-seekers. I have
seen it literally covered ; whilst at the well, on rising ground on
the other side of the valley, might have been seen the elderly

matron dispensing the precious fluid to a numerous offspring : perhaps the bashful maiden, partaking of Nature's cooling gift, who, on the approach of the sterner sex, would have willingly beaten a hasty retreat could she have done so unobserved. I have seen many impressive, endearing scenes around this well, scenes which time will never efface. Many simple, innocent scenes have been enacted here which I doubt not will be often repeated in the future, as its quietude will be no more, and its secluded retreat a thing of the past.—*Notes and Queries*, No. 517, *Leeds Mercury Supplement.*

APPENDIX.

FORMS OF BLESSING A WELL.

BENEDICTIO PUTEI.

V. Adjutorium nostrum in nomine Domine.
R. Qui fecit cœlum in terram.
V. Dominus vobiscum.
R. Et cum spiritu tuo.

OREMUS.

Domine Deus Omnipotens qui in hujus putei altitudinem per crepidinam fistularum copiam aquarum manare jussisti, præsta, ut Te adjuvante atque bene ✠ dicente per nostræ officium functionis, pulsis hinc phantasmaticis collusionibus ac Diabolicis insidiis, purificatus atque emendatus hic puteus perseveret. Per Christum Dominum. *R.* Amen.

Mabillon gives a form of blessing a well according to a Bobbio MS. This document is very ancient ; for, writing of it in 1724, he stated : " Scriptus est codex ante mille annos."

The venerable MS. which contains the subjoined form is the *Missale Sancti Columbani.*

BENEDICTIO SUPER PUTEUM.

Domine Sancte Pater Omnipotens Æterne Deus, qui Abraham, Isaac, et Jacob, patres nostros Fœderis fodere atque ex his aquam bibere propicia divinitate docuistis. Te supplices deprecamur, ut aquam putei hujus ad communis vitæ utilitatem celeste benedictione sanctifices, ut fugato ea omni Diaboli tentationis, seu pollutionis incursu, quicunque ex ea, deinceps biberit, benedictionem Domini nostri Jesu Christi percipiat. *R.* Amen.

BLESSING OVER A WELL.

O Lord, holy Father omnipotent, Eternal God, who hast taught Abraham, Isaac, and Jacob our fathers of the Covenant, to dig for and drink water from these places, by kind providence, we humbly pray Thee that Thou wilt sanctify the waters of this well to the use of the life of all with heavenly benediction, that every temptation of the Devil being driven away, and from all other assaults of evil whatsoever, each one successively that drinks may receive the blessing of our Lord Jesus Christ.   Amen.

BENEDICTIO PUTEI (*from the Leofric Missal*).

Deprecamur Domine, clemenciam pietatis tuæ, ut aquam hujus cœlesti benedictione sanctifices, ut ad communem vitam concedas salutrem, et ita ex eo fugare digneris omnem diabolicæ temptationis incursum, ut quicunque ex eo abhinc hauserit biberitue, vel in qui(bus) libet necessariis usibus hausta aqua usus fuerit, totius virtutis ac sanitatis dulcedine perfruatur, ut tibi sanctificatori et salvatori omnium domino gratias agere mereatur. Per.—(Ed. F. E. Warren, p. 225).

From an English Pontifical, early fifteenth century.

BENEDICCIO PUTEI NOVI.

Deprecamur Domine, clemenciam pietatis tue, ut aquam putei hujus celesti bene✠diccione sancti✠fices: ut ad communem vitam concedas salutrem, et ita ex eo fugare dignaris omnem diabolice temptacionis incursum ut quicunque ex eo abhinc hauserit biberitue, vel in quolibet (*sic*) necessarios usus haustam aquam fuserit, tocius virtutis ac suauitatis dulcedine perfruatur ut tibi semper sanctificatori et salvatori omnipotente deo gracias agere mereamur.   Per Dominum.

Benediccio fabarum, et fructum quorumcunque nouerum.—Brit. Museum, Lansdowne MS., 451.

From the Pontifical arranged by Gul. Durandus, Bishop of Mende (1286-1296).

BENEDICTIO NOVI PUTEI.   7C'.

Supplices te precamur Domine tue clemenciam maiestatis, ut aquam putei huius celesti benedictione sanctifi✠ces, et ad communem uite usum concedas esse salutrem, sieque ab eo omnem uim dyabolice potestatis fugare digneris ut cuncti ex ea bibentes tibi serviendo iugis sospitatis dulcedine pociantur. Per Dominum. —MS. copy of fourteenth century, in possession of Rev. E. S. Dewick, M.A., F.S.A., F.G.S.

Sacerdotale secundem usum sancte Romane Ecclesie.

DE BENEDICTIONE NOVI PUTEI.

V. Adiutorium nostrum. Domine exaudi. Dñs vobiscum.

ORATIO.

Supplices deprecamur Dñe clemenciam pietatis tue, ut aquam putei huius celesti bene✠dictione sancti✠fices : et ad communem vite usum concedas esse salutrem : et ita ex ea fugare digneris omnem diabolice tentationis incursum : ut quicunque ex eo hauserint, vel biberint, vel in quibuscunque necessariis usibus hausta aqua usi fuerint, totiles virtutis ac sanitatis dulcedine perfruantur : ut tibi sanctificatori et saluatori omnium domino gratias agere mereamur. Per Christum Dñm nostrum.

OREMUS—ORATIO.

Domine Deus oꝑs, qui in huius putei altitudinem, per crepitudinem fistularum, copiam aquarum manare vississti : presta, ut te vibente atque benedicente, per nostre officium functionis repulsis hinc phantasmatibus, calliditabus, atque insidiis diabolices, purificatus atque emundatus semper hic puteus perseveret. Per Christum Dominum nostrum. Postea aspergat aqua benedicta.— Venetiis, 1569, fo. 217.

These four latter are variants of the form in the Gregorian Sacramentary, and were kindly supplied by the Rev. E. S. Dewick, The last one has a collect added, probably comparatively modern, and perhaps local.

SAINTS IN WHOSE HONOUR WELLS ARE DEDICATED.

INDEX.

Edwin, xxi
Egton, 180
Egyptians, viii, xx
Ellerton, 160
Ellesmere, 134
Elmore, 67
Eltisley : St. Pandiania or Pandonia, 5
Ely : St. Audrey, 5
Endon, 154
Enfield : King Ring or Tim Ringer's, 91
Eshton : St. Helen, 204
Eskdale : St. Catharine, 41
Ethnology in Folk-lore, xx
Everingham : St. Everilda, 178
Everton, 83
Exeter : Lions, 64
Exeter : St. Anne, 64
Exeter : St. Sidwell, 65
Eyeford : Milton's, 74

Farnham : St. Mary, 164
Fenton : St. Ninian's, 102
Fior Usga, xii
Flamborough : Jenny's, 194
Fontinalia, xiv, 47
Fountain's Abbey : Robin Hood's, 199
Fowey : Dozmary Pool, 28
Franks, xii
Fritham : Iron or Leper's, 77
Frodsham : Synagogue, 7

Gardner, Percy, xiv
Gargrave : St. Helen's, 178
Genesis, xi, xviii
Germany, xiii, xviii
Giant's Caves, 42
Giggleswick : Ebbing and Flowing, 201
Gilcrux : Tommy Tack, 42
Gildas, xix
Gilsland, 43
Glastonbury : St. Mary, xxi, 149
Glentham : Newell, 88
Glonhilly : Lugger of Croft Pasco Pool, 22
Gloucestershire, xv
Gomme, G. L., xx
Gormire, xii
Grade : St. Rumon, 32
Grasswood : Beggar's Gill
Great Cotes, 87
Greek account of the Deluge, x
Greeks, viii, xv
Greenteeth, Jenny, viii
Gregorian Sacramentary, 213
Greystoke : St. Kentigern, 44
Grimm's Teutonic Mythology, x, xv
Grinton : Crack Pot, 179

Gulval : Holy, 20
Gunnarton : Lady's, 105
Gunnarton : Halliburn, 105
Gwavas Lake, 23

Hailweston : Holy, 1
Halifax : Holy, 205
Hambleton Hills : Lake Gormire, 203
Hamer : St. Diana, 196
Hampstead : Shepherds, 90
Harbledown : Leper's, 80
Harpham : Drumming, 197
Harpham : St. John's, 196
Haughmond Abbey, 147
Haveringe Mere, 138
Hayfield : Mermaid's Pool, viii, 45
Heath, 174
Hebblaldstow : Julian's, 87
Heilborn, xviii
Heilbrun, xviii
Heiligenbrunn, xviii
Heilwag, xvii
Hensting : Jacob's, 77
Hesiod, xiii
Hessian custom, xviii
Hexton : St. Faith, 79
Hinckley : St. Mary or Our Lady, 87
Hinderwell : St. Hilda, 195
Hindon : Prophetic, 170
Holderness : Robin Hood, 198
Holystone, 111
Holywell : Holy, 1
Holywell-cum-Needingworth, 2
Holywell : SS. Winifred and Margaret, 120
Horace, Ode of, xiv
Horsham : Normanby, 165
Horstead Keynes : Holy, 167
Houghton-le-Spring : Bede's, 110
Howley Hall : Lady Anne, 206
Hutton : Collinson's, 44

Ibberton : St. Eustachius, 67
Ilkeston, 59
Indians, viii
Ingestre, 157
Inus, spring, xv
Ipswich : Holy, 163
Irish Homily, xix
Irthington : Holy, 38
Isle of Thorns, 149
Islington : Lands, 89
Islington : Sadler's, 89

Jarrow : Bede's, 72
Jenny Greenteeth, viii
Jesmond : St. Mary, 100
Jordan, river, vii

Elliot Stock, Paternoster Row, London.